A MATTER OF
CHARACTER

Robin Lee HATCHER

A MATTER OF CHARACTER

THE SISTERS OF BETHLEHEM SPRINGS

A NOVEL

ZONDERVAN®

ZONDERVAN.com/
AUTHORTRACKER
follow your favorite authors

ZONDERVAN

A Matter of Character
Copyright © 2010 by RobinSong, Inc.

This title is also available as a Zondervan ebook.
Visit www.zondervan.com/ebooks.

This title is also available in a Zondervan audio edition.
Visit www.zondervan.fm.

Requests for information should be addressed to:

Zondervan, *Grand Rapids, Michigan 49530*

Library of Congress Cataloging-in-Publication Data

Hatcher, Robin Lee.
    A matter of character : the sisters of Bethlehem Springs / Robin Lee Hatcher.
        p.   cm.
    Includes bibliographical references and index [if applicable].
    ISBN 978-0-310-25807-0 (pbk.)
    1. Women authors — Fiction. 2. Idaho — History — 20th century — Fiction. I. Title.
PS3558.A73574M38 2010
813'.54 — dc220   2010008986

All Scripture quotations are taken from the King James Version of the Bible.

Any Internet addresses (websites, blogs, etc.) and telephone numbers printed in this book are offered as a resource. They are not intended in any way to be or imply an endorsement by Zondervan, nor does Zondervan vouch for the content of these sites and numbers for the life of this book.

Cover design: Laura Maitner-Mason
Cover illustration: Aleta Rafton
Interior design: Christine Orejuela-Winkelman

Printed in the United States of America

Let the words of my mouth,
and the meditation of my heart,
be acceptable in thy sight,
O LORD, my strength, and my redeemer.

Psalm 19:14

A MATTER OF
CHARACTER

PROLOGUE

Propelled by a white hot fury, Joshua Crawford pushed open the door to Gregory Halifax's office so hard it hit the wall with a loud *wham*. Startled, Gregory looked up a split second before Joshua slapped the newspaper onto the desk.

"What is this garbage?" Joshua demanded.

Gregory's expression changed from one of surprise to a smirk. "So you read it."

"Of course I read it, and I'm here to demand a retraction."

"A retraction? For what?"

"For what you wrote about my grandfather."

Gregory laughed softly. "You must be joking. The article is about dime novelists. The part about Richard Terrell was the words of the author, not mine."

"But you made what Mr. Morgan wrote in his novels sound as if it was fact rather than fiction. It's not."

"How do you know it's not? Tell me. What do you know about your grandfather before he settled in St. Louis? Nothing, that's what. You've said so yourself."

"Did you contact anyone in Idaho to try to confirm that the character in Morgan's books *is* based on the real Richard Terrell?"

"I didn't need to. I interviewed the publishers for my story. And again, the focus of my article is the men who write dime novels, not on the characters found in their books."

"But in the process you've dragged my grandfather's good name through the mud. I want a retraction."

Gregory pushed back his chair and stood, the smile gone from his face. "When you prove anything I wrote is in error, then come see me again, and we'll have this discussion. Until then, get out."

For one moment, Joshua thought he might be able to control his temper. For one very brief moment—just before he caught Gregory's jaw with a right hook followed by a left jab to the gut. Gregory flew backward into the wall. The glass in the office door rattled again. Joshua readied himself for the other man to fight back. To his dissatisfaction, it didn't happen. Gregory's eyes were still unfocused when more men poured into the office and grabbed Joshua by the arms, hauling him away. One of the men was Joshua's boss, Langston Lee.

"You're fired, Crawford. Collect your things and get out. I won't have my reporters brawling. You hear me. Get out or I'll call the police."

Joshua longed to turn his rage onto his boss, to give Langston Lee a little of what he'd already given Gregory Halifax. But he had enough good sense left to resist the urge. He was already out of a job. He didn't want to spend time in a jail cell besides.

But so help him, he would get a retraction out of this newspaper. He would prove Gregory Halifax was a shoddy reporter and see that he was fired. He would hear Langston Lee apologize. And he would make certain D. B. Morgan never again maligned his grandfather in print.

This wasn't over yet.

ONE

OCTOBER 1918

Maybe it was time to kill Rawhide Rick. He'd served his purpose, the old rascal. He'd hunted buffalo and fought Indians and stolen gold from hardworking miners and sent men to the gallows. Now might be the time for him to meet his Maker. The trick was deciding how to kill him.

Daphne McKinley rose from her desk and walked into the parlor, where she pushed aside the curtains at the window.

A golden haze blanketed Bethlehem Springs. It had been a beautiful autumn. The prettiest one yet in her three years in this serene Idaho mountain town. The trees had been the brightest of golds, the most fiery of reds, the deepest of greens. Daphne had spent many a mild afternoon walking trails through the forest, enjoying the colors and the smells.

If Rawhide Rick — who by this point in the series of books had become the infamous Judge Richard Terrell — was dead, what would become of the dashing Bill McFarland, hero of The McFarland Chronicles? Without his arch enemy, his life might become rather dull. Or perhaps it was Daphne who would find life dull without Rawhide Rick. Wicked he was, but he certainly kept things interesting whenever he was around.

She rubbed her eyelids with the tips of her fingers, and when she pulled them away, she noticed ink stains on her right hand. Her fountain pen was leaking. Perhaps it was time to buy a typewriter. But would writing on a machine feel the same?

Daphne turned from the window, her gaze sweeping the parlor. She'd come to love this small house on Wallula Street. Since moving into it soon after Gwen—its previous owner—married Daphne's brother, she'd delighted in making it her home, decorating and furnishing it in ways that pleased her. Daphne's childhood homes had been large and filled with servants waiting to attend to her slightest wish. But she had often been forced to live by the timetables of others. Now she could do as she willed, when she willed. The freedom she enjoyed was intoxicating.

The best part was when she wanted to be with family, she got into her motorcar—her very own, quite wonderful McLaughlin-Buick—and drove to her brother's home to play with her young nephew and infant niece. She was completely dotty over the two of them. She loved to crawl around on the floor with Andy—he would turn two at the end of November—the both of them squealing and giggling. And there was nothing like cuddling three-month-old Ellie. Daphne thought the baby girl smelled like sunshine.

A sigh escaped her. She hadn't time for daydreaming about Morgan's and Gwen's darling children. She must decide what to do. If she was going to kill the judge, she needed to notify Elwood Shriver at once. Wavering in indecisiveness served no good purpose.

She returned to her small office. The floor around her desk was littered with wadded sheets of paper. It was always thus when words frustrated her. "So wasteful," she scolded softly.

As she sat down, she took up the five-day-old newspaper. News of the war half a world away was splashed across the front page. More than a million American men—just boys, many of them—were now fighting in Europe alongside the Allied Powers. The end was near, some said. She prayed to God they were right. Too many had died already. Others, like Woody Statham, would wear the scars from their war wounds for the remainder of their lives—if not on their bodies then in their souls.

She flipped through several more pages of the newspaper, but nothing she read captured her imagination or sparked her creativity. Besides, she'd read every article before, some of them several times.

Maybe her problem wasn't with Rawhide Rick. Maybe the problem was Bill McFarland. Maybe she was tired of him. Maybe *he* should die.

"Maybe the whole lot of them should perish," she muttered as she laid the newspaper aside.

She spun her chair toward the bookcase beneath the office window. There, on the bottom row, were copies of The McFarland Chronicles by D. B. Morgan, all ten volumes. And if she didn't decide soon what to do about Rawhide Rick, ten volumes would be all there were.

There was no question that Daphne loved writing stories of adventure and danger in the West of forty and fifty years ago. And while she would concede that her books were not great literature, they were entertaining, for readers and for herself. But there were days like today when she was tempted to contact her editor in New York City and tell him that she (D. B. McKinley, whom Elwood Shriver thought to be a man) was retiring and thus so must D. B. Morgan (the pseudonym used on her books). However, she knew she would miss the storytelling were she to give it up. After all, it didn't take much effort to clean her small house or cook the occasional meal. Without her writing pursuits, what would she do with her time?

It would be nice if she could discuss her feelings with someone, but there wasn't another person, in Bethlehem Springs or elsewhere, who knew she was the author of dime novels. She wasn't sure her brother would believe her if she told him. The only soul who might suspect anything was Dedrik Finster, the Bethlehem Springs postmaster, because of the mail she sent and received, but his English wasn't the best and he probably had no idea that Shriver & Sons was a publishing company. Why would he?

Maybe what she needed more than anything was a drive out to the Arlington ranch and a long visit with Griff Arlington, Gwen and Cleo's father. That man had given her more story ideas in the last three years than she could ever hope to put on paper. It was Griff who had told her about the escapades of the real-life Richard Terrell, every bit as much a scoundrel as her fictional character, although perhaps in different ways. Yes, a visit with Griff was just what the doctor ordered.

Her mind made up, she rose and went in search of hat, gloves, and coat.

⚜

Joshua stepped from the passenger car onto the platform and looked about him. A large family—father, mother, and six children—were being escorted into the railroad station by a young man in a blue uniform. They were on their way to a hot springs resort located north of Bethlehem Springs. He knew this because they had spoken of little else during the journey, and Joshua couldn't have helped but overhear their conversation as they'd been a rather boisterous group.

He, on the other hand, was headed into the town that appeared to be about a quarter mile or so up a dirt road that passed between two low-slung hills. Switching his valise to the opposite hand, he set off in that direction.

The first building he saw upon entering Bethlehem Springs was a church. All Saints Presbyterian, according to the sign out front. Catty-corner from All Saints was the *Daily Herald*, his destination. He crossed the street and entered the newspaper office. Familiar smells — newsprint, ink, dust — filled his nostrils.

An attractive but pale-looking woman, dressed in black, came out of the back room, hesitated when she saw him, then moved forward, stopping on the opposite side of a raised counter. "May I help you, sir?"

"Yes." He set down his valise and removed his hat. "My name is Joshua Crawford. I'm here to see Nathan Patterson."

"I'm sorry, Mr. Crawford." Her voice broke, and it took her a moment to continue. "Mr. Patterson passed away." She drew a long breath and released it. "I'm his widow. Perhaps I can assist you."

Either Nathan Patterson had been much older than his wife or he had died tragically young, for Joshua guessed the woman to be no more than in her early thirties.

"I ... I'm sorry, ma'am. I didn't know. Mr. Patterson recently offered me a job as a reporter for the *Daily Herald*. I've just arrived in Bethlehem Springs."

"Yes. I'm sorry. I'd forgotten your name. Nathan told me to expect you."

Joshua had counted on this job. Without it, he couldn't afford to stay in Idaho. He would barely have enough money for train fare back to St. Louis, as long as he didn't spend a night in the hotel, and even then he wouldn't have much left over to buy food. He would be extremely hungry before he reached Missouri. Not to mention that he wouldn't have a job waiting for him when he got there—unless he was successful here first.

"I'm glad you've come, Mr. Crawford. My husband would be heartbroken to see this newspaper fail. I assume you can do more than report?"

"Ma'am?"

"You are qualified to manage the paper, I trust."

Manage it? That was more than he'd expected. But if it worked out . . . "Yes, I am qualified," he answered—with more confidence than he felt.

"Good. Nathan's final instruction was for me to offer you the job as managing editor of the *Daily Herald*. If you're interested, that is."

He hadn't thought to be in Idaho more than a month or two. Surely he could discover the information he needed, take care of matters, and return to Missouri before Christmas. On the other hand, success as a managing editor would look good on his résumé, would give him many more opportunities than simply working as a reporter for a small paper.

"Are you interested, Mr. Crawford?"

He had few other options. None, actually. Not if he wanted to honor his grandfather's memory. Not if he wanted to restore his own good name and get back his old job. Taking the job as managing editor didn't mean he would be here forever. He could keep the newspaper running until Mrs. Patterson found his replacement. It was the least he could do for the man who had paid his train fare from Missouri to Idaho. "Yes, Mrs. Patterson. I'm interested."

"The pay will be ninety-five dollars a month to start. I know it isn't the sort of salary you must have received at a large newspaper, but you'll have a place to live for free." She pointed at the ceiling. "There's an apartment above the office with a kitchen and bath. It hasn't been used for several years, but with a bit of elbow grease, it should clean up well and prove adequate for a bachelor such as yourself."

Ninety-five a month. Not quite twelve hundred a year. Less than Langston Lee had paid him back in St. Louis, but more than the sum Nathan Patterson had offered when he'd applied for the job with the *Daily Herald*. With a place to live thrown in, the salary would allow him to put money aside for when he returned to Missouri.

"That sounds fine," he answered.

Mrs. Patterson gave him a fleeting smile. "Good. Now let me show you to your quarters. I'm sure you must be weary from your journey. We can begin work in the morning."

⸛

Daphne was invited by Griff Arlington to have supper with the family and to spend the night at the ranch as she occasionally did, but she declined. Griff's storytelling about his early days in Idaho had done just what she'd hoped. Ideas were rolling around in her head, and she was desperate to get them on paper before they disappeared like a puff of smoke in the wind.

As soon as she walked into her house, she tossed her coat over the nearest chair, dropped her hat on the table, and hurried into her office, where she lit the lamp and began scribbling as fast as she could. It seemed she barely drew a breath for the next hour. When she looked up at last, she saw that night had fallen over Bethlehem Springs. Her stomach growled, reminding her that she'd missed supper. Still, she had little desire to cook. This seemed like a good evening to pay a visit to one of the town's restaurants.

Daphne had three choices — the Gold Mountain, which served the most wonderful breakfasts; the restaurant inside the

Washington Hotel where she liked to dine before an evening at the Opera House; and the South Fork, famous for their pies and home-style fare. She decided on the latter.

As she walked briskly along Wallula Street toward Main, her way was lit by street lamps, one of many improvements made during Mayor Gwen McKinley's term of office, which had ended almost ten months earlier. Daphne thought it unfortunate for the town that her sister-in-law had retired from public service. She hoped that, when her nephew and niece were older, Gwen would run for office again.

As Daphne neared the office of the *Daily Herald*, she noticed light spilling through the windows of the apartment above it, something she'd never seen before. Was the newly widowed Christina Patterson up there, perhaps sorting through memorabilia from her marriage? Should Daphne postpone her evening meal another hour and see if she could offer the woman any comfort or assistance?

Nathan Patterson's death had been a shock to the town. A man of thirty-seven years, he'd looked in the pink of health. To have him weaken and die so suddenly had taken everyone, especially his wife, by surprise. And even while they grieved the loss of a friend, many wondered about the future of the *Daily Herald*. It had been almost a week since the last edition. What would become of the newspaper without Nathan at its helm?

A shadow fell across the nearest window, and Daphne stopped on the sidewalk, still pondering what she should do. Would Christina welcome a visit from her or had she gone up there to escape intrusion? Daphne remembered all too well how difficult the death of a loved one could be. She'd been a girl of sixteen when her beloved father died, a young woman of twenty when she'd lost her mother. Even now, all these years later, she felt a painful sting in her chest, knowing she wouldn't see either of them again this side of heaven.

She also remembered that sometimes she'd wanted to be alone with her memories, alone to cry and mourn. And so she decided not to disturb the new widow and instead moved on, rounding the corner onto Main Street and entering the South Fork Restaurant a few moments later.

Delicious scents filled the dining room, making her stomach grumble once again. It was late enough that the dinner crowd had come and gone. There were customers at only two tables—Mabel and Roscoe Finch, who worked for her brother and sister-in-law, and Ashley Thurber, the elementary school teacher. Daphne greeted each one of them before sitting at a table in the corner, her back to the wall. Whenever she dined out, she preferred similar seating. It allowed her to study others without being too obvious. She loved to watch and listen to people. She'd learned a great deal from the habit, and much of what she'd learned had made it into her stories at one time or another.

Sara Henley—a shy, plain girl of eighteen—approached Daphne, a pad in her hand and a smile on her face. "Evening, Miss McKinley."

"Good evening, Sara." Daphne returned the girl's smile. "How are you?"

"Wonderful." Sara lowered her voice. "My dad's agreed I can study art. I won't leave for school until spring, and I have to save every cent I earn to help cover my expenses. But all winter I can look forward to going."

Daphne touched the back of Sara's hand with her fingertips. "I'm glad for you. You have a wonderful talent. You must promise that you'll write and tell me all about the school and its instructors once you're there."

"'Course I will. If it wasn't for your encouragement, I never would've had the nerve to ask my dad to let me go."

Daphne had done little besides tell Sara that she shouldn't give up on her dreams, no matter how long it took, that God could open doors in surprising ways if she would simply trust Him. But she was glad Sara had found her words to be helpful and even more glad that Sara's father had consented. "I believe art school will be the making of you. Wait and see if I'm not right."

Sara blushed bright red. "I'd better take your order, Miss McKinley." She glanced over her shoulder toward the kitchen. "Mr. Boyle will wonder what's keeping me."

"Is there any meatloaf left?"

"Sure is."

"Then that's what I'll have. With gravy on the potatoes, please."

"I'll bring it right out."

As Sara disappeared into the restaurant kitchen, the front door opened, letting in the cool night air along with a man Daphne had never seen before. He was tall, at least six feet, perhaps a little more. He had brown hair that was shaggy near his collar, and unless the poor light in the restaurant deceived her, there was the shadow of a beard under the skin of his jaw and upper lip.

Who was he? Not a cowboy nor a miner. That was clear by the clothes he wore. His suit appeared of good quality, but even from where she sat she could tell it had seen its share of wear. A man of trade perhaps or a salesman. Definitely not a guest of her brother's spa, for he looked neither wealthy nor in poor health.

At that moment, the stranger turned his head and his gaze met hers. She swallowed a gasp of surprise. Good heavens! He had the most astonishing eyes. What color were they? She wished she could tell. So pale. Perhaps blue. Or maybe a silvery-gray. No, they were blue. She was sure of it. And she seemed unable to look away, even when she knew she should. Thankfully, he broke the connection and moved to a table, sitting in a chair with his right side toward her.

Daphne drew a hungry breath into her lungs. Until that moment she hadn't known she'd held it.

Could I capture his eyes with words? What a character he would make. He could be Bill's friend. Perhaps he could ride with him for the next few adventures. What name should I give him?

She pulled a small notebook and the stub of a pencil from her pocket and made a few notes to herself.

In Daphne's fourth, fifth, and sixth novels, her hero, Bill McFarland, had courted a woman in Idaho City, but she'd grown tired of waiting for him to propose and had married someone else. Perhaps this new friend with his magnetic eyes could help Bill find the right woman, one who wouldn't object to his adventurous spirit. Then again, Bill would have to watch out or his new friend might steal the right woman for himself.

The thought caused her to glance up from her notebook—only to discover he was looking in her direction. Her breath caught for a second time and a blush warmed her face as she dropped her gaze again. Oh, yes. Mr. Blue Eyes would definitely make things interesting for the readers of The McFarland Chronicles.

She hoped her dinner would arrive soon. Another late-night writing session was looming.

⁓

December 5, 1871

There comes a time in a man's life when it seems prudent that he look hard at his past, to remember from whence he came, to learn to be grateful for God's mercy, perhaps even for the purpose of becoming a cautionary tale for others. And so I have decided to write an account of my life, from beginning to the present, knowing all the while that the future will be significantly different from those years that have gone before.

In truth, I already know that my life will soon change for the better. I know this because, at the age of fifty, I am about to take a wife. No former associate of mine could be more surprised at this news than I am. I never believed I was the marrying kind. Nor would I have believed a woman as fine as my Annie would agree to be my wife, especially after she learned of my less than pristine past.

But I am getting ahead of myself. A record of my life should begin at the beginning. And so it shall.

I was born on a small farm in Missouri in the winter of 1821, the youngest of five children, all boys. My parents came to the region after the War of 1812, along with many other settlers. Like most everyone they knew, my parents were poor. They eked out a living the only way they knew how, through hard work and sweat and tears. They weren't educated, and they yearned for something quite different for their children.

It amazes me, as I look back, that my mother managed to teach her sons so much when she never attended school a day in her life. Not that I appreciated her efforts back then. All I wanted when I was a lad was to go fishing or hunting or even just to lie on my back on a hot summer day and watch the clouds drift by. Still, despite my lack of enthusiasm, I learned to read and write and do arithmetic. I even came to appreciate, albeit many years later, the wisdom and enjoyment that could be found in books.

My parents were god-fearing people, but since there was no church within easy distance of our farm, it fell to my father and mother to see that their sons came to know the Bible and to embrace the tenants of the Christian faith. In this regard,

I was even less enthusiastic. Rebellion resided in my stubborn heart, and it did not matter if my father took a strap to me or my mother sweetly entreated me. I would not yield.

Perhaps, given enough time, I might have come to know the God my parents believed in. But there wasn't enough time. They died of the fever when I was eight years old, along with two of my brothers. Moses was ten and Oliver was nine. That was in the winter of 1829. February, I believe. There was deep snow on the ground and the temperatures were frigid. My surviving two brothers could manage no more than shallow graves as the ground was frozen hard.

I have never confessed this to a living soul, but I cried myself to sleep at night more often than not in the months that followed.

My two oldest brothers, Jefferson and Lyman, took over running the farm and raising me. They did the best they were able, them being just boys themselves, Jefferson not yet eighteen, Lyman only sixteen. I wish now that I had appreciated them more.

After I stopped crying myself to sleep at night, anger took the place of tears. I was angry with everyone, and my temper got me into plenty of trouble. I was fourteen the year I hit Lyman so hard I broke his nose. Of course, he gave me back in kind. A few weeks later, I struck out on my own.

I never knew what happened to my brothers. By the time I got to an age and a place where I wanted to get in touch with them, where I would have liked to see them again, they were gone. I was told they sold the farm and nobody knew where they went from there.

I have often wondered if they are still alive. I wonder if they think of me and wonder the same.

TWO

Joshua had stayed up late, cleaning and arranging his new living quarters, but he still managed to arise before daybreak. His employer, the Widow Patterson, had said she would meet with him in the newspaper office at eight o'clock. That gave him time to wash, shave, and go to the South Fork for breakfast. Later today he must purchase supplies at the mercantile. Dining out would soon deplete his limited funds. Fortunately, his grandfather had taught him how to eat well, even on a meager income.

"It's important you learn to fend for yourself, boy," his grandfather had often told him. "Never depend on others to do for you what you can do for yourself."

Outside, dawn had lightened the sky enough that he could see Main Street below. How much, he wondered, had the town changed since his grandfather lived here? It had to be a great deal, for Richard Terrell had left Idaho in the winter of 1871, close to half a century ago. Joshua knew very little about his grandfather's life before he'd returned to St. Louis. The old man had rarely talked about it, except to say the Idaho Territory was where he'd found Christ.

"That's when my life really began, Josh," he'd told his grandson. "There I was, closing in on fifty years old, and God made me a new man. The old me, the old sinner, was gone and forgotten.

By God, anyway. Sometimes I remember, and it makes me all the more thankful for what He did for me. Without Jesus, I'd never have returned to St. Louis. Without the Holy Spirit's nudging, I'd never have met and married your grandmother, and I'd never have fathered Angelica or become your grandfather. So nothing before my life in Christ matters one whit to me. Everything good came after that."

There was no man, living or dead, whom Joshua admired more than his grandfather. Although Richard Terrell had passed away fourteen years ago, Joshua's memories of him were strong. He wanted to emulate his grandfather in every way possible — in his acts of kindness, in his generosity, in his integrity, in his faith, in his forbearance. Perhaps especially in his forbearance. Losing patience, allowing his temper to flare, was one of Joshua's greatest faults and was partly to blame for his being in Bethlehem Springs with little money in his pocket.

With a shake of his head, he turned from the window and walked toward the bathroom. Twenty minutes later, he entered the restaurant next door. Unlike the previous evening, the South Fork was doing a brisk business, and two waitresses were needed to see to the needs of the customers. The same girl who had waited on Joshua the night before showed him to one of the few empty tables.

"You must've liked your supper last night if you've come back so soon." She handed him a menu, and when he looked at her, she blushed scarlet and lowered her eyes. "Would you like coffee to start off with?"

"Yes, thank you. I would."

She scurried away.

Joshua studied the menu for a few moments and was ready to order by the time the waitress returned with his coffee. As she set the cup on the table before him, he said, "I wonder if you could help me with something. I'm looking for a D. B. Morgan. Can you tell me where I might find him?"

"Sorry." She shook her head. "Never heard of anybody by that name in these parts."

He thanked her, then gave his order. He would have better success finding Mr. Morgan once he spoke with his new employer. Newspaper folks knew everyone by name in a small town. It was the same everywhere.

❧

Bleary-eyed, Daphne made her way to the kitchen, where she set about making herself a pot of coffee. There were days when she wished she had a maid and a cook to take care of her. She could certainly afford such luxuries, but she would hate having others about the house while she worked.

Once the coffeepot was on the stove, she went to the door to see if a newspaper had been left on the front porch. There wasn't one. Again. Disappointment shot through her. How much longer would Bethlehem Springs be cut off from news of the country and the world?

"Maybe I should offer Mrs. Patterson my services," she said aloud.

Drawing the collar of her dressing gown together against the chilled morning air, she closed the door. But as she turned toward the kitchen, the thought repeated itself. Perhaps she *should* offer Christina Patterson her services. Before Gwen married Morgan, she'd written a regular column for the *Daily Herald*. Daphne could do the same. In fact, there were probably several roles she could fill, at least until Christina hired someone to manage and edit the newspaper for her.

The idea of tackling something new held more than a little

appeal. She could let Bill's next adventure sit and stew for a while. She'd hit another wall with her writing late last night and was back to wondering if she should kill Rawhide Rick or perhaps draw the chronicles to a close. Even that new unnamed character with the astonishing eyes couldn't seem to stir her creativity. It might do her good to step back from the story for a while. It would be temporary. A few weeks or a couple of months at most. That's all. She could help a widow in her time of grief and provide a service for the town, and when she returned to her latest story, she could do so with renewed enthusiasm and fresh ideas.

She sighed, thinking how nice it would be if she could talk to someone about this book and the problems she was having with it. Her sister-in-law would be the ideal person. Gwen was adept at looking at things from many different angles. She could probably come up with solutions for Daphne's latest novel in short order.

Two weeks ago, Gwen had asked Daphne if she wasn't bored with so little to do. She'd almost laughed aloud. So little to do? With another deadline hanging over her head? If only she could have told her sister-in-law about her writing. But she couldn't. The only way to make certain that the true identity of D. B. Morgan remained a secret was to be the only person who knew the truth. Someday, perhaps, she would tell others. But not yet.

She couldn't imagine how Morgan would react if he learned she'd authored a series of dime novels filled with buffalo, horses, trappers, cattle rustlers, mining disasters, wild Indians, gunfighters, and a hanging judge. But she was quite certain he wouldn't think it a proper occupation for his sister. She'd been groomed for a much different life. There were certain things expected of a well-educated, unmarried young woman of large fortune. Writing dime novels wasn't among them. And even if her brother reacted without censure, the news would cause a scandal among her friends and acquaintances in the East.

She glanced around her cozy little home and knew many of those friends and acquaintances would be equally scandalized by her living conditions, irrespective of the work she did there. As it was, none of them understood why she chose to remain in this small town in the mountains of Idaho, and no matter how many times she tried to explain how happy she was in her new life, they refused to believe it.

⌘

It didn't take Joshua long on his first morning at the *Daily Herald* to discover that Nathan Patterson had been a fine journalist but not the most organized of businessmen. Newspapers and file folders covered desktops and cabinets. More of the same were stacked on the floor. And while the printing press and other equipment were in good shape, the record keeping was almost nonexistent.

Joshua's first recommendation to Christina Patterson had to be that she change the newspaper from a daily—common in larger cities but difficult to maintain in any small town—to a triweekly. With the world at war, there was plenty of news for the front page seven days a week, but there wasn't a lot of local news or enough advertising to fill up the remaining pages. It wasn't financially responsible to continue as a daily. He didn't know how Nathan had kept the paper afloat before this.

His second recommendation would be that she retain the services of Grant Henley, the *Herald*'s press operator whom Joshua had met yesterday. In their brief conversation, he'd learned that Grant—a friendly fellow in his early fifties with salt-and-pepper hair and a crooked grin—had a wealth of experience in typesetting and printing-press operation. He was obviously worth the wage he received, even with only three editions a week instead of seven.

His third recommendation would be for Christina Patterson to begin searching for someone to permanently take over the position Joshua now filled. But that recommendation could wait until the time was right, until after he'd found D. B. Morgan and achieved his purpose.

It was after twelve o'clock when the door to the newspaper office opened, admitting a young woman. The same one he'd seen in the restaurant the previous night. A man wasn't likely to forget her. Her curly hair was abundant and as black as ink, and her large eyes were the color of rich, dark chocolate. Surprise crossed her pretty face as he rose from the chair behind the cluttered desk. It would seem she recognized him as well.

"May I help you?" he asked.

"I ... I'm looking for Mrs. Patterson. Is she here?"

"Not at present." He stepped around the desk, repeating, "May I help you?"

She recovered from her surprise. "I'm sorry. I don't know who you are." He could almost hear her unspoken question at the end: *And what are you doing back there, poking around where you don't belong?*

"No reason you should know me, miss. I'm new to Bethlehem Springs. Arrived only yesterday. Mrs. Patterson hired me to manage the newspaper for her."

"Oh."

"My name is Joshua Crawford."

There was something regal about the way she held herself, her spine straight, her shoulders back, her head held high. "I'm Daphne McKinley." She extended her right hand. "It's a pleasure to meet you, Mr. Crawford."

"Likewise." He shook her hand—and wished he knew for sure if there was a Miss or a Mrs. in front of her last name.

"Well ..." She took a step backward, her fingers slipping from his grasp. "I hope you shall find Bethlehem Springs to your liking."

"Thank you."

"Would you please tell Mrs. Patterson that Miss McKinley wishes to speak with her when she has a moment?"

Ah. *Miss* McKinley. "Of course."

"Good day, Mr. Crawford."

"Good day, Miss McKinley."

She turned away, and seconds later, the door closed behind her.

Joshua watched through the window until the sidewalk carried her out of sight. A slight accent—he had a good ear for such things—told him she hailed from the East. Massachusetts, more than likely. Everything about her appearance, carriage, and speech said she was a woman of privilege. She didn't fit Joshua's image of the sort of person who would choose to settle in a remote town like this one.

He returned to his cluttered desk, but his thoughts remained on Miss McKinley. He'd seen intelligence in those large, dark eyes of hers. Perhaps a hint of mischief as well? Yes, he thought so. And her mouth had seemed made for laughter. She was the sort of woman he would like to know better. Pretty *and* smart. He pictured her in his home in St. Louis, playing a parlor game with a group of his friends. It made a pleasant image in his mind.

However, if he were hosting an evening with friends, Mary Theresa would be there too. In which case, his attention wouldn't— and shouldn't—be focused on the lovely Miss McKinley from Bethlehem Springs.

Mary Theresa Donahue was the granddaughter of Richard Terrell's closest friend, Kevin Donahue. Joshua had a dim memory of the two men sharing a toast in his grandfather's parlor on the day Mary Theresa was born. He'd been five years old at the time. For as far back as he could remember, it had been assumed by everyone they knew that he and Mary Theresa would marry. And on most days, he assumed the same. They liked each other, had much in common — and, as a child, Mary Theresa had loved his grandfather almost as much as he had. That always endeared her to Joshua.

With a shake of his head, Miss McKinley was forgotten. He needed to remain focused on his reason for being in Bethlehem Springs. And once he took care of the business that had brought him here, he would return to St. Louis. Maybe by then he would even be ready to marry Mary Theresa. His grandfather had left a small inheritance that would come to him on the day he wed. It wasn't a great deal of money — Richard Terrell hadn't been a wealthy man at the end of his life — but it was enough to help a young couple set up a household and to live in a modicum of comfort.

"Joshua," his grandfather had said in one of their last conversations, "I'm leaving you a bit of money, but it won't come to you until the day you marry. I don't want you struggling to make ends meet when you take a wife, the way I see happen to many. You're too young right now for it to mean much to you. That's all right. You'll be glad when the time comes."

Had the time come? All of their friends had married long before this. If he was successful in finding D. B. Morgan, he would most likely win his job back. There wouldn't be anything hindering a wedding then — *if* Mary Theresa was able to forgive him. They'd had a heated argument the week before he left St. Louis, one in which she'd called him pigheaded. He'd deserved the name too.

From the printing room in the back came the sound of a closing door. A moment later, Christina Patterson entered the front office. When she saw Joshua, she said, "Mr. Crawford, are you back from lunch already?"

"I never left." He motioned toward the desk. "I've been going through your husband's record books. There are a few things we should discuss."

She removed her coat and hat and hung them both on the rack near the door. "I'm sure those matters can wait until you've eaten something."

It would probably be better if he stayed on task. He suspected it would take a solid week of very long days, maybe even more than a week, before he had things as organized as he would like them to be. Still, a man had to eat.

"Go on, Mr. Crawford. A half an hour or so won't make a difference."

"I guess you're right." He retrieved his hat, then slipped his arms into the sleeves of his suit coat that had been draped over the desk chair. "Oh, Miss Daphne McKinley dropped by. She would like to speak with you when you have a moment."

"Thank you. I'll give her a call."

With a nod, he headed out the door, making a shopping list in his mind as he walked toward the mercantile.

THREE

Daphne lifted her infant niece from the cradle in the front parlor and held her close to her chest. "Little girl, you are the most beautiful baby in the whole, wide world. Did you know that?" She brushed her lips across Ellie's forehead and breathed in the sweet scent of her.

Gwen laughed softly. "Keep that up, Daphne, and you'll have her head turned before she can walk."

Ellie cooed and waved a fist in the air.

"Impossible. She will always be just as precious and perfect as she is today."

"Hmm."

"Where's my nephew?"

"Andy's down for a nap. At last."

The two women settled onto chairs near the fireplace.

"I have news to share," Daphne said without taking her eyes from the baby.

"Good news, I hope."

"I think it is. I'm going to take up your mantle at the *Daily Herald.*"

"My mantle?"

Daphne lifted her gaze to meet Gwen's. "I'm going to write a weekly column for the paper. I met with Christina Patterson yesterday afternoon, and she seemed pleased with the sample writing I brought for her to see."

"That's wonderful, Daphne. And I assume that means Morgan will be able to read our local newspaper again soon?"

"Yes. Mrs. Patterson says they'll have an edition out on Monday."

"I'm glad about that. Bethlehem Springs needs its newspaper. I know things have been difficult for Christina, losing Nathan the way she did. So sudden and unexpected. It breaks my heart to think about it. He was a wonderful editor. So easy to work with. And when I ran for mayor, he encouraged and supported me in all the best possible ways."

"Do you miss writing your column?"

A soft smile curved Gwen's mouth as she shook her head. "Not really. At least not for now. I'm enjoying my role as a wife and mother too much. Perhaps that will change when Andy and Ellie are older."

Daphne understood Gwen's sentiments. But for herself, she had few incentives to change her life. She had money of her own and an occupation—although secret—that brought her pleasure. Before coming to Bethlehem Springs, she'd received two or three proposals of marriage a year. Did the men who'd asked for her hand do so because they loved her or because they loved her fortune? It was hard to know and, therefore, easy to decline. Perhaps if she fell in love, the way Gwen loved Morgan, it would be different. Never having loved a man, she couldn't say for sure.

A distant memory drifted into her thoughts. No, she'd never loved a man, but she'd lost her heart to a boy the summer she turned sixteen. Henry Townsend was his name, and he'd come to stay for the summer with his cousins, neighbors of the McKinleys. Seventeen, handsome, tall, strong, and alive with laughter, Henry had drawn the attention of every female around. Daphne had been smitten like the rest of them, and he'd seemed to like her too. She'd written his name in her diary at least a thousand times in the days and weeks that followed. He'd been her first thought upon awakening and her last thought before falling asleep. She'd been certain they would be together forever. Her fantasies had been filled with images of their future. But then her father had died, and by the time she'd looked up from her grief, Henry had gone away. She'd never heard from him again.

Sixteen and seventeen. They'd been hardly more than children. Daphne was a woman now. Did a man exist who could turn her head and win her heart the way Henry had?

"When can we expect to see your first column?" Gwen asked, drawing Daphne's attention to the present.

She gladly pushed away the perplexing question of love. "Next week, I think." A pair of startling blue eyes slipped into her mind, prompting her to add, "But I haven't told you all the news about the paper. Mrs. Patterson hired someone to take over the management of the *Daily Herald*. Only it isn't going to be a daily any longer. Mr. Crawford suggested that it be changed to a triweekly paper. Mondays, Wednesdays, and Fridays. And Mrs. Patterson agreed."

"Who is Mr. Crawford?"

"The new managing editor."

Ellie began to fuss, and Gwen held out her arms to take the baby from Daphne.

"He's from St. Louis and came here to work as a reporter for the paper at Mr. Patterson's invitation. But Mr. Patterson's death changed everything, and Mrs. Patterson offered him the position as managing editor."

Gwen drew a blanket over her shoulder, covering Ellie as she nursed. "Have you met Mr. Crawford? What's he like?"

"We've met. Briefly." In her mind, she saw Joshua Crawford looking at her, and she had to catch herself before she told her sister-in-law about his piercing, pale-blue eyes, about how they'd made her breath catch the other night in the restaurant, even before she could be sure of their color. Blue, as she'd confirmed yesterday in the newspaper office. A wonderfully unusual shade of blue. A color she had yet to be able to put into words for her book.

"And?" Gwen prompted.

She cleared her throat. "He seemed pleasant enough."

"Good heavens, Daphne. Surely you can tell me more about him than that. You, who notices everything."

She sighed, as if it were an effort to remember when, in truth, she remembered quite clearly. "As I said, he's from St. Louis. I'd guess he's close to thirty years old. Fairly tall. His hair is brown and his eyes are blue." Thank goodness she managed to say the latter without revealing how his eyes affected her. Gwen would totally misinterpret such an admission. "Oh, and he has a slight cleft here." She touched her chin with an index finger as she spoke. "He seems to know something about running a newspaper. I guess I shall find out for myself since he'll be my editor."

This information seemed to satisfy Gwen, and the topic of conversation soon turned to other matters.

⸙

Neither Christina Patterson nor Grant Henley came into the newspaper office on that first Saturday of Joshua's employment, which gave him the freedom to do more than simply get organized. Out of curiosity, he decided to look through the archived newspapers. Wouldn't it be something if he could find references to his grandfather's time in this town? What might he learn about the man who'd helped raise him?

Disappointment was his only reward. The oldest issue was dated July 1886—fifteen years after Richard Terrell left Idaho. A fire, the paper reported, had destroyed a number of businesses in Bethlehem Springs, including the office of the once-named *Weekly Herald* and the municipal building.

Well, he didn't need old articles about his grandfather to know that he was right about the man's character. Of more immediate concern was locating D. B. Morgan. His inquiries thus far had proven unsuccessful. Like the waitress at the South Fork Restaurant, Christina Patterson didn't know of anyone with the last name of Morgan living in or around Bethlehem Springs.

Very frustrating. Was the writer of those ridiculous novels a recluse with a hideaway in the surrounding mountains, a man who kept to himself—so much so that no one knew of his existence? But that couldn't be. *Someone* had to know him. D. B. Morgan, like everyone else, must buy food supplies on occasion. He had to use the post office to mail his manuscripts to the publisher, Shriver & Sons, in New York City. There had to be *someone* who could tell Joshua where to find the fellow.

"And the sooner I find him, the better."

He could comb through recent issues of the newspaper, but if Mrs. Patterson didn't know the name, it was doubtful her husband had written anything about the author. Surely she would have remembered it if that were the case. No, Joshua would have a better chance of learning what he wanted to know by making inquiries of the citizens of Bethlehem Springs. He would begin with the postmaster and the grocer.

He spent a few more hours working on the preliminaries for his first issue of the new *Triweekly Herald* that would go to press in the early hours of Monday morning. Then he locked the office and followed the sidewalk along Main Street.

The Bethlehem Springs Post Office, located at the corner of Washington and Main, wasn't large. The front area was divided in half by a tall counter. Behind it, he saw a man wearing a green visor handing a parcel and several letters to a woman in a yellow dress.

"Thank you, Mr. Finster," she said.

"*Ja.* A pleasure always to see you, Miss McKinley."

Daphne McKinley, Joshua's new columnist. He should have recognized the set of her shoulders and the black curls that showed beneath the wide-brimmed hat. The decision to hire her hadn't been left to him. It had been made by Christina Patterson, who assured him the young lady was an excellent writer. If Joshua had been planning to stay longer than a couple of months, he might have objected. A managing editor should be allowed to manage.

"It's a pleasure to see you too," Daphne said to the postmaster. "Your English seems to get better every week."

"*Ja.* Miss Thurber, she teaches me now."

"Good for you, Mr. Finster." As she spoke, Daphne turned around. When she saw Joshua, her smile vanished. "Oh. Mr. Crawford. I didn't know anyone had come in."

He was sorry his presence had removed her smile. "Good afternoon, Miss McKinley." He tipped his hat. "I understand from Mrs. Patterson that you and I shall be working together."

"Yes. I understood the same."

She was a little thing, the top of her head coming no higher than his chin, but if she was intimidated by either Joshua's height or his gender, she didn't show it. Once again he noted the regal way she held herself and the confidence in her unwavering gaze. It both appealed to him and challenged him, although he couldn't say why it should do either.

"I'll have my first column ready for you by Friday, Mr.

Crawford. I hope that's agreeable to you. Mrs. Patterson thought it would be."

"Friday will be fine." He wondered what she would write about. Cooking? Sewing? Gardening? Canning? He could ask, but there was a part of him that wanted to be surprised. "I look forward to it."

As she nodded, the hint of a smile returned to the corners of her mouth. "Good day, Mr. Crawford." She glanced over her shoulder. "Good day, Mr. Finster."

"*Ja*. You, too, Miss McKinley."

She held her parcel and envelopes close to her chest and stepped toward the door. Joshua was quick to open it with his left hand while touching the brim of his hat with his right. He caught a faint whiff of her perfume as she moved past him. A musky scent that seemed perfect for her.

He gave his head a slight shake as he closed the door. He wasn't the sort of man who noticed a woman's cologne. Or at least he hadn't been before meeting Daphne McKinley.

He turned toward the man behind the counter. "Sir, I have come to introduce myself." He stepped forward. "I'm Joshua Crawford, the new editor of the *Herald*."

Mr. Finster shook Joshua's proffered hand. "Dedrik Finster. I am the postmaster, *ja*. Pleasure to make acquaintance."

"A pleasure for me as well. I just wanted you to know who I am since I'm sure I'll begin receiving mail soon. I'm living in the apartment above the *Herald*'s offices."

"*Ja*, I have heard."

Of course he'd heard. This was a small town.

"We are glad to have newspaper again."

"Yes." Joshua cleared his throat. "I'm wondering if you can help me find someone. I'm looking for a man by the name of D. B. Morgan. Can you tell me where he lives?"

The postmaster frowned in thought. After several moments, he shook his head. "I do not know him."

"He doesn't get his mail here? I was led to believe Mr. Morgan lives in Bethlehem Springs."

Dedrik Finster shook his head again. "*Nein*. No Morgans." His eyebrows lifted. "Maybe you look for Morgan McKinley?"

"Morgan McKinley?" It didn't seem likely. His source in New York hadn't mentioned that D. B. Morgan was an assumed name. Of course, if Joshua wrote that tripe, he would use a pseudonym as well. "Perhaps that is who I mean. Could you tell me where he can be found?"

"*Ja*." The postmaster came around from behind the counter and walked toward the door, motioning for Joshua to follow him outside. Once there he walked to the corner, turned north, and pointed toward the hillside. "There, you see gray house. *Ja*?"

"I see it."

"That is McKinley home."

"And might I inquire if Miss Daphne McKinley is any relation to Morgan McKinley?"

"*Ja*. His sister."

Joshua almost asked if Daphne lived with her brother but stopped himself. The attractive young woman with the big brown eyes had nothing to do with the matter. He offered his hand once again. "You've been most helpful, Mr. Finster. Thank you for your assistance."

Once the postmaster had gone back inside, Joshua looked again at the house on the hillside. It was a stately two-story brick-and-timber structure, painted two shades of gray, with an attic and numerous windows. A wide piazza wrapped around at least two sides of the house, and tall, mature trees cast shadows across its many-angled roof. A residence that bespoke an owner of some importance in the town.

Before he tried to meet Mr. McKinley, it might be wise to learn more about him. Joshua would prolong his investigation for another day or two. Surely this time the newspaper archives would turn up the information he needed.

December 23, 1871

I am a married man of two weeks. I thank God for allowing me this happiness. I do not deserve a bit of it.

Annie and I returned yesterday from a brief honeymoon in New Orleans, and we have settled into our new residence in St. Louis. My wife is busy turning the house into a home and making plans for our first Christmas together. We have a small household staff to help her, including a cook whose ability has already impressed me. I fear I'll soon be fat and useless if she always feeds us so well.

And now to continue the record of my life.

It was the summer of 1835 when I left the farm and my surviving two brothers. Over the years that followed, I lived and worked in Louisiana, Kentucky, Tennessee, Arkansas, Indiana, and Illinois. I swept out saloons and I slopped hogs and I chopped down trees and I even spent a few months working a steamboat on the Mississippi River. I did just about anything I could do to put food in my belly. I stole when I had to, and it's a wonder I never got caught and thrown into jail.

The western migration had started by that time, men looking for land they could own and farm, a place where they

*could raise their families. I had no yearning to be a farmer.
I'd seen enough of that life when my parents were still alive.
But there were other stories I heard about the West that made
me decide to strike out in that direction.*

*That's how I found myself working a wagon train the
year I was twenty-four. That was in 1845. By that time, I was
good with horses and with a rifle. Still wet behind the ears in
many ways, but tough and not afraid to try something new.
That must have been why Gus, the wagon master, decided to
give me a chance. My main job was to drive the livestock that
wasn't being ridden or yoked to a wagon. It was hot, dusty
work, but that couldn't dampen my excitement as we followed
the Oregon Trail across the vast, mostly uninhabited country
that separated Missouri from the Pacific Ocean.*

*I will never forget the first time I saw a herd of buffalo in
the distance. So many it looked as if the land itself was rising
and falling like the sea. Who would have thought men would
kill so many of the great beasts from that day to this? God
forgive me, I slaughtered more than my share of them for their
skins alone.*

*I did make it all the way to the Oregon Territory by the
end of the summer of 1845. Even went on over to the rugged
coast and stuck my feet in the cold waters of the Pacific.
During the trip out, I'd decided I might just stick with
Gus and make a living bringing immigrants to Oregon or
California. But it turned out that I wouldn't make it back to
Missouri again for another quarter century. Once I'd seen the
mountains of the West, there wasn't any thought of going back.*

*For the next few years, I lived the life of a mountain
man. Probably would have frozen to death in a snowy pass
that first winter if I hadn't been befriended by a grizzled old*

man called Bearcat by friend and foe alike. If he had another name, one his mother gave him, I never heard it, and even so, I doubt he would have remembered it. Bearcat taught me a lot about surviving off the land. And once he moved on, I got used to the silence, the kind that says you're the only human being within five hundred miles in any direction.

I was living in a one-room log cabin that I built myself in what is now Idaho Territory when I met a Frenchman, Picard, and his daughter. The girl wasn't pretty in the conventional sense, but that didn't matter to me. I wanted her. Not as a wife, mind you. Not forever. Just a woman to ease a man's desire. And so I took her to live with me. Her father seemed glad to have her off his hands, and she didn't seem to mind staying with me.

I seem to recall feeling a twinge of guilt the first time I took her to my bed. It was as if my saintly mother was looking down from heaven and shaking her head in despair over her lost son. But since I didn't believe in heaven or hell and my mother was long dead, I didn't let the feeling linger for long.

The girl's name was Gemma. Gemma Picard. She was eighteen and soft in all the right places and had dark hair that, when it was unbound, fell past her plump bottom. She spoke only a little English and I spoke no French at all in the beginning. That was okay. I didn't take her in for the conversation. For close to a year, she kept the small cabin we lived in clean and tidy as was possible, cooked our meals, and kept my bed warm at night.

Then I heard about the gold strike in California. I put my earthly belongings onto a packhorse, saddled up my gelding, and rode away without a backward glance. I don't think I gave Gemma a second thought. Not for many, many years.

Did she love me? Did she want to be my wife? Did she consider us married even without some words spoken over us? What happened to her after I left? I guess I assumed she would reconnect with her father, but for all I knew some wild thing could have killed her.

May God forgive me.

FOUR

A cold wind whistled its way through Bethlehem Springs that Sunday morning. Daphne had to place a hand onto the crown of her hat to keep it from being blown away as she walked toward All Saints Presbyterian — accompanied by the sound of crisp leaves cartwheeling toward her — and even her best woolen coat couldn't stop gooseflesh from rising on her arms and legs.

Winter was coming to the mountains of Idaho. The glorious Indian summer had ended for another year. Daphne hoped it wouldn't be a harsh winter. As beautiful as it could be, heavy snows severely curtailed her ability to get about. Her automobile had to remain parked in the shed behind her house, and she became dependent upon the use of Morgan's horses and sleigh.

The wind pushed against her as she hurried along Wallula Street. She leaned into it, eyes on the sidewalk only a few paces before her. It wasn't a long walk to the church, but it seemed so this morning. She was grateful when she reached the steps leading to the church entrance.

She paused and glanced around as her right foot landed on the first step. No fellow worshipers lingered outside on this bitter morning as they often did when the weather was pleasant. She hurried to join them inside.

Before the door was closed again, she heard her brother's voice. "And here she is." She looked up, feeling windblown and unkempt.

Morgan grinned as he came over to help her out of her coat. "How are you this morning, dear sister?" He dropped a kiss on her cheek.

"Cold. And you?"

"The same. You should have called me to come for you in my automobile."

"Don't be silly. It's a short walk." She looked behind him. "Where are Gwen and the children?"

"Andy was ill in the night, so Gwen stayed at home to care for him."

"Oh, I'm sorry. I thought he seemed lethargic yesterday when he got up from his nap. So unlike him. It isn't influenza, is it?" The idea struck fear in her heart.

"The doctor says not. Otherwise, I wouldn't be at church myself." Morgan offered her his arm. "Shall we go in?"

With a nod, Daphne slipped her hand into the crook of his arm, and they walked together into the sanctuary, headed for what had become the McKinley family pew, third row, left side of the aisle. Brother and sister paused several times to speak words of greeting to various friends in the congregation. It wasn't until they were nearly to their pew that Daphne saw Joshua Crawford seated directly across the aisle — and he was looking over his shoulder. Right at her. Her heart made a strange little skittering motion in her chest. Those eyes of his. They were most disconcerting.

For a moment, she considered sliding into her pew without speaking to him. But that would be rude. Unforgivable. She stopped, drawing Morgan to a halt alongside of her. From the corner of her eye, she saw her brother looking at her, but she spoke first to Joshua.

"Good morning, Mr. Crawford. Welcome to All Saints."

He stood. "Thank you, Miss McKinley. It's good to be here."

"May I introduce my brother, Morgan?" She looked at her brother. "Morgan, this is Joshua Crawford, the new editor of the *Herald*."

The two men shook hands while Morgan said, "A pleasure to meet you, Mr. Crawford."

"Likewise."

"I was glad to hear we'll soon have another edition of the paper."

Joshua nodded. "Tomorrow morning, as a matter of fact."

The door to the small antechamber behind the altar area opened, revealing Reverend Rawlings in his black robes. Morgan must have seen him, too, for he gave a quick nod of acknowledgment to Joshua an instant before showing Daphne into their pew.

❧

Joshua was normally more attentive during a Sunday worship service. But today his thoughts were often on the man and woman seated to his left across the aisle. They were a handsome pair. No doubt about it. And although Morgan McKinley was tall and Daphne McKinley petite, the family resemblance was unmistakable, from the tone of their skin to the jet black hair and dark brown eyes. Both had a certain bearing that declared them people of good fortune and society.

Good fortune was a gross understatement. It hadn't taken much researching in the *Herald* archives for Joshua to learn that Morgan and his sister inherited great wealth from their parents, and Morgan's business acumen had increased his monetary worth even more. What Joshua couldn't understand was why they both had chosen to live in Bethlehem Springs, of all places. Competent managers could be hired to run the New Hope Health Spa, and

Morgan and his family could live anywhere else in the world that they pleased. New York. London. Paris. Athens. The Orient.

Joshua wasn't the type of man to covet, but it was hard not to envy people like the McKinleys. To travel abroad, to see the wonders of the world, to come to understand other cultures, to taste the foods of many nations, to broaden ones vision. But God had not chosen to give him such experiences, and he would do well to remember all he had to be thankful for.

With that mental chastisement, he focused his attention on Reverend Rawlings.

At the close of the service, Joshua rose and stepped into the aisle. It was impossible not to look toward Morgan and Daphne as they did the same. And when the men's gazes met, Morgan said, "Mr. Crawford, I wonder if you might join the family for dinner one evening this week. I would ask you to dine with us today, but out little boy is ill and I wouldn't want to surprise my wife with an unexpected guest on top of that. Perhaps Wednesday evening would be convenient for you?"

"That's very kind of you." Joshua couldn't believe his good fortune. Here he was, wanting to get to know Morgan McKinley, wanting to discover if he could be D. B. Morgan, and the opportunity had been dropped into his lap without him doing a thing.

"Not at all," Morgan said. "I remember what it's like to be a bachelor cooking for myself."

It took great resolve for Joshua not to show his surprise. When did a wealthy man have to cook for himself?

Morgan glanced at his sister, then back at Joshua. "Shall we say Wednesday at seven?"

"Thank you. Yes. I'd be delighted to join you and Mrs. McKinley for dinner."

"Wonderful. I look forward to it."

Joshua hung back and waited for Morgan to escort his sister toward the narthex. Then he followed at a slower pace, giving friendly nods to people he had yet to meet. If he'd planned to remain in Bethlehem Springs for an extended period of time, he would have made more of an effort to introduce himself. But he didn't plan to stay. Not any longer than necessary.

The outside temperature hadn't warmed up during the service, and it made him glad that his living quarters were catty-corner from the church. He hunched his shoulders, leaned into the wind, and dashed across the street and up the outside staircase.

☙

Daphne looked at the family gathered around the table in her brother's dining room and thought how blessed she was to be one of them. Too often in her life she'd felt alone and on the outside. Morgan was ten years her senior, and before she turned six, he'd been sent to boarding school, followed by college and then time abroad. Their father had died when she was sixteen, and soon after, their mother's illness had taken Morgan and Danielle McKinley to England and the Continent, to any place that offered some relief for the pain she suffered, while Daphne had remained in America to finish her schooling.

It hadn't been until Morgan moved to Bethlehem Springs — three years after their mother's death — that he and Daphne became close as brother and sister. His marriage to Gwen had made the circle of loved ones even wider.

Griff Arlington had become Daphne's surrogate father. The grizzled cattleman had a strong faith and a heart as wide as the western sky. Griff's daughters, Gwen and Cleo, had become the sisters Daphne never had. She admired them because of their courage to be true to themselves, to follow God and the path He set before them. And finally there was Woody Statham, Cleo's husband of two years. Who would have thought the wounded Brit, the fourth son of a duke, would fit so well into this American family? But he did, and now Daphne considered him a brother too.

"What do you think, Daphne?" Morgan's question brought her attention back to the Sunday dinner conversation.

"About what?"

"About the newspaper. Will it thrive under Mr. Crawford's guidance?"

"I have no idea. Mrs. Patterson must think so or she wouldn't have hired him."

Griff said, "I guess we'll have some idea tomorrow when the first edition of the *Triweekly Herald* is available."

"I invited Mr. Crawford to dine with us on Wednesday evening," Morgan said. "You're all welcome if you choose to come."

Woody exchanged a glance with Cleo, then shook his head. "The way my leg feels right now, I believe there is a good chance we shall see colder weather before Wednesday. Perhaps even snow. You had better not count on us."

Morgan looked at Daphne. "But you'll come. Right?"

"I never turn down one of Mrs. Nelson's delicious meals if I can keep from it." Daphne turned toward Gwen. "You really are fortunate to have such a wonderful woman in your kitchen. If I had a larger home, I would try to steal her away from you."

Gwen laughed softly. "I don't believe you'd succeed, Daphne, dear. Mrs. Nelson is too fond of our children to ever leave us."

With that, the conversation turned naturally to the youngest McKinleys, to Andy's sniffles and the words he was adding to his vocabulary and to Ellie's desire to be walked and rocked before going to sleep at night.

Yes, indeed. Daphne was blessed to be part of this family circle, and she said a silent thanks to God for making it so.

FIVE

Alone in the office, Joshua leaned back in the desk chair and stared at the front page of the *Triweekly Herald*'s Wednesday edition. He was proud of what he'd managed to accomplish in just seven days. And if the comments he'd received from townsfolk meant anything, the citizens of Bethlehem Springs were pleased with his efforts as well.

For Monday's edition, his editorial had been focused on himself. He'd tried to allow readers to know him in a small way, to feel comfortable with him. He expected to be compared to Nathan Patterson, an old friend to many. If he shared about his background and training, he hoped they would grow to accept him into their midst. Belonging was an important asset for an editor of a small-town paper.

Today's editorial was different. He'd written about the importance of staying informed, whether one lived in a large city or in a small town, and he'd given his pledge to bring the readers of the *Herald* the most up-to-date news about world, national, state, and local happenings. He hoped he could keep that pledge during his brief tenure with the newspaper.

His thoughts moved to the evening ahead. Tonight he would dine with Morgan McKinley and his family. With any luck, he would know without a doubt by the evening's end whether or not Mr. McKinley was the infamous D. B. Morgan.

Infamous, indeed.

It didn't matter to Joshua that the writer had maligned his grandfather's good name in fiction. People tended to believe what appeared in print. Even words that came between the covers of a novel.

He folded the newspaper in half, then in half again, before placing it on his desk. It was unlikely he would find the answers he needed tonight. Morgan didn't strike him as the sort of man to write melodramatic drivel.

Joshua's jaw clenched. He hated that Richard Terrell, the grandfather he'd so admired, had been turned into a one-dimensional cliché named Rawhide Rick in the hands and mind of some hack writer. He wanted Gregory Halifax to be forced to eat his words. He wanted the record set straight. Only D. B. Morgan could make that happen.

Feeling agitated, he got to his feet and walked to the front door, where he flipped around the sign that announced the newspaper office was closed. Then he headed toward the rear entrance, turning off lights as he went. Soon enough, the back door was locked behind him, and Joshua was climbing the stairs to his apartment. Overhead the sky was a slate gray, a solid blanket of moisture-laden clouds. He'd overheard many times since Sunday the prediction that snow was coming, and it looked to him as if those predictions might prove true today.

⚬₰

Daphne was driving her red McLaughlin-Buick — affectionately dubbed Mack — along Main Street when she saw a man on the sidewalk, leaning his head into the gusting wind. Joshua Crawford on his way to Morgan's house. She knew it even though she saw him only from the back.

She rolled the motorcar to a stop and called to him. "Mr. Crawford!"

He stopped in a pool of light from the streetlamp.

"Get in." She motioned for him to join her. "We're headed to the same destination."

He hesitated a moment before stepping into the street and hurrying around the front of her car, still holding onto his hat.

As soon as he was in the passenger seat, the door closed, Daphne said, "It's a foul night to be afoot."

"Indeed, it is."

She accelerated, and the motorcar continued up the street.

"It was good of you to stop for me, Miss McKinley. I've been shown nothing but kindness since my arrival in Bethlehem Springs."

"I know precisely what you mean." She glanced in his direction, smiling. "I felt the same way when I came here three years ago."

"What made you decide to live in Bethlehem Springs? It seems an odd choice. For both you and your brother. You could make your home anywhere."

Daphne heard the unspoken *"Because you're rich,"* a reminder she disliked. She often treated such comments with stony silence, but she decided to answer this time. "Morgan is here because of the hot springs. Of course, he could have built his resort any number of places, but he felt this was the right location. And when I came to visit him for the summer, I fell in love with the town and its people. Bethlehem Springs has a certain ... charm."

"Hmm."

Was that a sound of agreement or disagreement? "And what

brought you to Idaho, Mr. Crawford? There must be need for someone with your qualifications at newspapers closer to Missouri."

"I had a position with a newspaper in St. Louis, Miss McKinley, but I needed to come to Idaho on a personal matter. Nathan Patterson's job offer allowed me to make the trip."

On a personal matter. That sounded mysterious. Daphne wondered what it could be. Perhaps it was—

She cut off the "what-if" game before it could take hold.

For as far back as she could remember, she'd spun stories in her mind. About people she saw on the street. About words she overheard in a restaurant. About the horse pulling the iceman's wagon. About the stray dog begging for something to eat. The habit had caused her no end of trouble when she was in school. She'd be listening to the teacher and then something he said would spark a question or an idea and off Daphne would go into her imaginary world. More than once it had earned her a smack on the hand with a ruler.

She would have to give herself a mental smack with the ruler if she started making up stories about Joshua Crawford. After all, now that she was writing a column for the newspaper, he was her boss.

Thankfully, the ensuing silence didn't have a chance to feel awkward before they arrived at Morgan's house. She pulled the motorcar into the half-circle drive and cut the engine near the front steps. Joshua was quick to disembark, then offer her assistance. As she placed her fingers into his open hand, she looked up. Oh, my. That astonishing gaze of his. It *was* mesmerizing. Had she ever seen anyone with eyes that same piercing shade of blue? Surely not.

"Thank you," she whispered.

He continued to hold her hand until they'd climbed the steps onto the veranda. Would he have held on longer if her brother hadn't opened the door at just that moment? She would never know.

"Mr. Crawford. Daphne. Come in, the both of you. Come in before you blow away."

Joshua motioned for Daphne to precede him, and she didn't hesitate to oblige. Not so much from the cold as from the strange way she felt, her stomach all atwitter.

"What dreadful weather." Gwen welcomed Daphne with a kiss on the cheek before helping with her coat. "I'm afraid winter is upon us early." After hanging the garment on the nearby coat tree, she turned to meet her other guest.

Morgan made the introductions. "My dear, this is Joshua Crawford. Mr. Crawford, my wife, Guinevere McKinley."

"A pleasure to meet you, Mrs. McKinley."

"And you, Mr. Crawford. We're so glad you came to Bethlehem Springs. Our town was not the same without its newspaper."

After Joshua's coat and hat joined Daphne's on the tree, the small party went into the front parlor. While Daphne sat on the settee, Joshua expressed admiration for the grand piano.

"Do you play?" Gwen asked.

"No, I'm afraid not. Never had the opportunity to learn."

Daphne thought she heard regret in his voice.

Morgan must have heard it too. "It's never too late to learn. I should know. I got serious about it just three years ago."

"It didn't hurt that you fell in love with your piano teacher," Daphne said with a laugh.

Gwen blushed when Morgan turned his eyes on her. "No, that didn't hurt at all."

A rare feeling of envy rose in Daphne's chest as she watched her brother and sister-in-law, saw the unspoken thoughts of love pass between them. What would it be like to know someone so well you could communicate without saying a word?

Surreptitiously, she glanced at their dinner guest. She thought perhaps he might be wondering the same thing—and that thought elicited a fondness for him that she hadn't felt before.

❧

Joshua liked the McKinleys. For people of wealth and society, they were surprisingly down to earth. Not that Joshua knew many people of wealth and society. None, unless he counted the ones he'd interviewed for articles in the newspaper. Certainly he'd never been invited to dine in their homes.

And what a dinner he enjoyed with the McKinleys. He hadn't eaten this well in he couldn't remember how long. Maybe never. The roast beef was succulent, the vegetables flavorful, and the dessert—cherries jubilee over vanilla ice cream—delicious.

"Mrs. McKinley." He laid his napkin on the table next to his empty dessert plate. "I've never enjoyed a meal more. Thank you for including me."

"It was our pleasure to have you, Mr. Crawford. And I'll pass along your compliment to our cook. She'll be pleased to know you enjoyed it."

What must it be like to have a cook and a maid and other servants to tend to your every need, Joshua wondered. When his mother was young, her father was still a wealthy man. But God had called Richard Terrell to use his personal fortune to better the lives of others, and he had done so gladly for years, ministering to the needs of homeless men and orphaned children in St. Louis.

Thinking of his grandfather reminded Joshua why he'd accepted Morgan McKinley's invitation to dine in his home. He leaned back in his chair and, in as offhand a manner as he could muster, asked, "I wonder if you might know a man with the last name of Morgan. Supposedly he lives in the area. D. B. Morgan."

His host's eyes narrowed in thought, and then he shook his head slowly. "Sorry. I don't know him."

There was nothing about Morgan's expression that caused Joshua to think he wasn't telling the truth, and Joshua discovered he was relieved. He would prefer to have Morgan as a friend rather than a foe.

"Who is he?"

"A writer." Joshua swallowed the disdain he felt, keeping any emotion — beyond mild curiosity — from his voice. "I was told that Mr. Morgan lived in or near Bethlehem Springs, and I'm hoping I can speak with him about his books. I — "

Daphne began to cough, so violently that tears soon tracked her cheeks. With all eyes on her, she pushed up from her chair. "Excuse me," she choked out. "Something ... went down ... my windpipe." Napkin held to her lips, she left the room, staggering slightly when another fit of coughing overtook her.

"Gracious." Gwen rose to her feet. "I'd best make certain she's all right." She hurried after her sister-in-law.

Joshua's opportunity to ask questions had passed. But what did it matter? It was apparent none of the McKinleys knew anything about D. B. Morgan. Not even that he was a writer of dime novels. Which shouldn't surprise him. This wasn't the sort of family who read such tripe. The McKinleys' reading preferences probably leaned toward the great masters of literature.

"Why don't we await the return of the ladies in the front parlor," Morgan suggested.

Joshua nodded his agreement.

The two men rose in unison and made their way from the dining room, through the entry hall, and into the parlor where they had gathered before dinner. A fire burned on the hearth and electric lights chased shadows into the far corners of the room. Outside, the wind continued to whistle beneath the eaves and cause the near-leafless trees to bounce and sway.

"Do you have family in St. Louis?" Morgan asked as they settled onto chairs near the fireplace.

"Yes, my mother lives there." Joshua didn't usually talk about himself. He preferred to be the one asking questions. But he felt comfortable with Morgan — now that he knew he wasn't D. B. Morgan — and for some reason the words flowed out of him without additional encouragement. "With her new husband. They've been married six months. It's one reason I felt able to make this trip. My father died when I was an infant, and my mother and I lived with my grandfather until his death fourteen years ago. Then it was just the two of us until last year when she met Mr. Hanson."

Morgan nodded in understanding. "My mother was widowed, although I wasn't as young as you when my father passed away. I take it you approve of your stepfather."

"Yes." It was a simple response, but coming to the point of liking Charlie Hanson, of approving of his mother's marriage to him, hadn't been simple in the least. Joshua hadn't been sure Charlie could make his mother happy. He'd been wrong about that. Angelica Terrell Crawford Hanson had never been happier than during these past six months.

"And you? Is there a young lady waiting for you in St. Louis?"

Before he could respond, they were interrupted by the arrival of his hostess. Joshua stood, as did Morgan, as she walked toward them.

"Mr. Crawford, Daphne wishes me to express her apologies for her abrupt departure from the dinner table. She isn't feeling well, and I've put her to bed upstairs. She'll be staying here for the night."

"Then I should be going. Please tell Miss McKinley I hope she feels better soon." Joshua looked at Morgan. "I appreciate you and your wife's kind hospitality, Mr. McKinley."

"We enjoyed having you," Morgan replied. "Allow me to drive you home."

"That's kind of you, but I believe the walk will do me good after that fine meal." He turned a second time toward Gwen. "Thank you for the pleasant evening."

"You're most welcome. But are you sure you don't want Morgan to drive you? The wind is still so strong."

"Thanks for the offer, but I'm sure. It isn't far to my apartment."

❧

From her room upstairs, Daphne listened to the voices as Gwen and Morgan bid good evening to their guest. For herself, she couldn't wait for Joshua Crawford to be gone. She felt her secret was at risk as long as he was in the house.

How had he learned that D. B. Morgan resided in Bethlehem Springs? Shriver & Sons knew that information wasn't to be given out to a soul. She trusted Elwood Shriver hadn't leaked that bit of information. But someone had. Who? As soon as she returned home, she would write to Mr. Shriver to express her displeasure over this breach of privacy.

As for Joshua, why would he want to meet D. B. Morgan? The McFarland Chronicles had sold moderately well, considering the popularity of dime novels had been on the decline for a number of years. But it wasn't as if her books would earn her a Pulitzer Prize. She wasn't so prolific, nor were her books the type of novels that brought an author the notice of newspapers — unless someone had discovered they were written by a woman. More especially, by an heiress.

She closed her eyes, her head throbbing. She loved writing, loved spinning adventure tales, but the last thing in the world she wanted was to embarrass her family. What if Joshua intended to write some horrid exposé about her? What if he tried to smear her brother's good name or damage the reputation of the New Hope Health Spa? What if Joshua already knew who she was and had come to dinner under false pretenses? What if—

She drew a deep breath and forced herself to exhale slowly. There was no need to panic. No need to torture herself with what might happen in the future. This day had enough trouble of its own. Besides, Mr. Crawford didn't know D. B. Morgan was female. His inquiry had made that clear. No, there was no reason to panic. She would simply stay as far away from him as possible.

Let him ask his questions. Her secret was safe.

With the wind at his back, Joshua's walk into town from the hillside home of the McKinleys was an easy one. Still, he wished he could have shared another ride with Daphne. He would have enjoyed being in her company a little longer. There was something about her—beyond the loveliness of her face and figure—that made him want to know her more.

You don't plan to stay in Bethlehem Springs. Remember why you're here.

Find D. B. Morgan. Get him to agree to set the record straight about Richard Terrell. Help Mrs. Patterson find a new managing editor for the *Herald*. Return to St. Louis. Get an apology from Gregory Halifax and his job back from Langston Lee. Get on with his life. That was his plan.

But in his mind, he saw Daphne's smile, heard her laughter. She intrigued him, this woman of quality and privilege. At the dinner table tonight, he'd learned she was both witty and well read. He suspected she could hold her own in any conversation.

What would it hurt if some of those conversations were with him?

※

January 1, 1872

California! Gold!

The word was that you could walk around and pluck heavy gold nuggets off the ground. It wasn't far from the truth. There was lots of gold and it was easy to get to, not buried hundreds of feet below the ground's surface. Still, I was quick to learn that there were better ways to make my fortune than working a claim.

Men rushed to California from all over the world, eager to get rich quick, and there was more than women in short supply in that brave new land. Food was scarce, as were picks, tents, clothing, and just about anything else a man needed to work his claim.

I was twenty-eight and determined I wouldn't fail. I didn't care what I had to do to come out on top either. I had begun to hone the kind of character traits that would serve me well in getting what I wanted. I learned I could cheat at cards without getting caught, and I could tell a convincing lie with a straight face. Something else I discovered: I was a shrewd businessman.

What did the men in the hills of California want almost as much as gold? Women and liquor. I provided them with both.

In 1852, through a less than honest series of events, I became the owner of a dance hall called the Golden Nugget. The liquor wasn't the best, but it would get a man drunk quick enough. A customer had to pay premium prices for every swallow—to me.

I got rich. Not plucking nuggets of gold off the ground but by taking them from the men who worked their claims and came to town for supplies. I got richer still selling desperate young women for an hour to those same lonely, equally desperate men. The girls were young and pretty and smelled good. I told myself that what they did in those upstairs rooms wasn't my fault. It was their choice to go to work for me. I was just their employer. I convinced myself that I was protecting them from the hard, cruel world beyond the doors of the Golden Nugget. I even believed the lies I told myself for many years.

I would find them today if I could, those dance hall girls, and tell them I'm sorry. But the Golden Nugget burned to the ground soon after I left California, and those who once worked for me were scattered with the ashes.

⚘

March 30, 1872

Annie has given me wonderful news. She is with child. The baby is expected in September. It would be hard for me to adequately express the joy I feel. I am fifty-one years old, and although I secretly hoped when Annie and I wed that we might have children together, I knew that it might not happen.

God's grace is an amazing thing. That I, such a great sinner who deserves nothing good from the hand of the Lord, should be so blessed is beyond comprehension.

SIX

Daphne couldn't avoid seeing Joshua Crawford for long. Not if she wanted to write a regular column for the newspaper—and she did. Therefore, on Friday afternoon she pushed open the door to the *Triweekly Herald*, her heart beating faster than normal.

Relief swept through her when she saw Christina at the front desk. With any luck, Daphne wouldn't have to face Joshua today. Although she'd never felt guilty about her alter-ego before, since Wednesday evening she'd begun to wonder if using a pseudonym was more than a matter of privacy for herself and her family, more than an easy avenue to publication in a male dominated field. Was it also dishonest?

"Good afternoon, Miss McKinley," Christina greeted her.

"Good afternoon, Mrs. Patterson. I've brought my first column. I hope you'll be pleased." As she spoke, Daphne placed the carefully written pages on the raised counter.

Christina stood, her complexion looking pale against her stark black dress, and came around the desk. "I'll make sure Mr. Crawford sees it as soon as he returns. I believe he plans to run your columns in the Monday edition of the paper."

"It must be a relief to you, having Mr. Crawford here to manage the *Herald*. How fortuitous that Mr. Patterson already offered him a position before—" She regretted the words before they were out of her mouth. "—Before he fell ill."

The ever-present sadness in Christina's eyes deepened, and sorrow tugged at the corners of her mouth. Daphne wished she could offer words that would bring comfort to the young widow. But what help were words at such a time? All that came to mind were platitudes, and Daphne knew from personal experience how unwelcome trite phrases were when one was in mourning. She reached out and briefly touched the back of Christina's right hand. With her eyes she tried to convey her sympathy and understanding.

Christina nodded, as if hearing what had gone unspoken.

Softly, Daphne said, "Please have Mr. Crawford call me if the piece isn't to his liking."

"I will."

Without another word, Daphne turned and left the newspaper office.

It was a crisp, cool day, the golden sun overhead failing to provide much warmth. But at least the wind had died down, and the threat of snow had yet to be fulfilled. It would happen soon enough.

On her way home, Daphne stopped at the mercantile. She needed flour and salt, and hopefully the shipment of apples Bert Humphrey was expecting would have arrived by now. Although she wasn't much of a cook, she was in the mood to bake an apple cobbler.

"Miss McKinley!" Bert said when he saw her. "That Royal Typewriter you ordered arrived today."

The apples, flour, and salt were forgotten in an instant. "So soon? I thought it would take several weeks."

"Surprised me too. Came in on this morning's train. I was gonna send Owen Goldsmith down with it as soon as he gets out of school." Bert leaned his beefy forearms on the counter. "Mind tellin' me what you're gonna use it for? Makes sense to have those machines over at the municipal building, I guess, and for lawyers and such, but I've never known anybody to buy one just to have around the house."

"I'm writing a weekly column for the newspaper, Mr. Humphrey. I thought it would be good for me to learn to use a typing machine."

The grocer shook his head as he straightened and took a step back. "Waste of money, far as I can see."

"Not at all, sir," came a male voice from behind Daphne.

Her heart skipped a beat as she turned to look at Joshua Crawford—who stood much too close for her comfort. Would he be able to look her in the eyes and guess that she was D. B. Morgan?

"Every writer will one day use typing machines," Joshua continued with a smile and a nod in her direction. Then he looked at Bert. "Did you know, Mr. Humphrey, that Mark Twain wrote *The Adventures of Tom Sawyer* on a typewriter?"

"Do tell."

"Yes. It's a fact."

"Miss McKinley's not writin' a book."

Daphne felt color rise in her cheeks. Of all things for Bert Humphrey to say. He couldn't be more wrong. Hoping to hide the sheepish blush from Joshua, she turned to face the grocer again. "I'll await the typewriter's delivery at home. Thank you for seeing to it."

"No need to wait for it to be delivered, Miss McKinley," Joshua said. "Please allow me to carry it for you."

Her cheeks burned even hotter. She looked down at her hands, her fingers tapping restlessly on the counter. "I wouldn't want to put you out."

"I assure you, it won't put me out in the least. After all, you were kind enough to drive me to your brother's house the other night. This would only be returning the favor."

What could she do but accept? To keep refusing would only bring more attention that she didn't want, both from Joshua and from Bert. She took a deep breath, composed her expression, and turned around. "That's very kind of you, Mr. Crawford. If you're sure it won't be an imposition."

Joshua smiled. "Quite sure."

"The crate's in the back," Bert said. "I'll bring it right out."

❧

With the grocer gone, silence settled over the storeroom. Joshua didn't mind the silence. Nor did he mind being alone with Daphne. It gave him a few moments to study her. That she was nervous was unmistakable. What he didn't know was why. Where were her usual self-confidence and that regal carriage? Did *he* make her nervous?

The idea that he might be the cause of her display of nerves brought him unexpected satisfaction. Because if he were the cause of those nerves, there was only one reasonable explanation — she was attracted to him. What a perfectly fine state of affairs. Hadn't he hoped to learn more about her, to spend more time in her company? How much easier that would be if she hoped for the same.

"Here you go." Bert reappeared from the storeroom carrying a good-sized crate in his arms. He set it on the counter, then patted the top of it with his left hand as he looked at Joshua. "Hope you appreciate her getting a machine like that for writing her columns."

"I assure you, I do appreciate it. I've used a Royal Typewriter for some time and highly recommend it." He lifted the crate off the counter. "Shall we go, Miss McKinley?"

"Yes," she answered as she moved toward the door. "Good day, Mr. Humphrey. Thank you again."

Joshua followed, watching her departure over the top of the crate. The now familiar posture was there—head high, shoulders squared, pint sized but regal. And he saw something he hadn't noticed in their previous encounters—a rather mesmerizing feminine sway of her hips. What a pleasant observation.

Daphne opened the door and stepped out of his way so he could exit first. Since he couldn't see around the crate, he felt for the step down to the sidewalk with his foot. Her attraction to him—if that's what it was—wouldn't last long if he fell flat on his face in front of her and damaged her new typewriter in the bargain.

"Which way?" he asked.

"We'll turn right on Wallula. My house is almost at the end of the street."

Facing west, he waited on the sidewalk until she appeared at his side, then they walked together, Joshua shortening his stride to accommodate hers.

After a brief silence, he said, "I trust you're feeling better."

"Feeling better? Oh, the other night. Yes, I am. It was nothing, really. But thank you for asking."

Joshua wished he weren't carrying the awkward container. He would have liked to see her from a better angle than the one afforded him now.

"By the way, I've written my first column. I left it with Mrs. Patterson a short while ago." She glanced over at him, the color in her cheeks high once again. "I hope you'll approve of it, Mr. Crawford."

He found himself disappointed. It would seem Daphne's case of nerves had everything to do with pleasing her new editor and nothing to do with the man himself. But wasn't that just as well?

A romantic entanglement wouldn't be desirable for either of them. His stay in Bethlehem Springs was temporary and—God willing—would be of brief duration.

"Did you know my sister-in-law used to write for the *Daily Herald*?"

"Yes. As a matter of fact, I read a few of her columns last week while I was acquainting myself with the paper. Although I didn't know at the time that Guinevere Arlington was the present Mrs. Morgan McKinley."

"Here," she said, pointing the way. "We need to cross the street. That's my home over there."

The house was a single-story bungalow made of red brick, surrounded by trees, shrubs and flower bushes. There was a broad front porch with a swing and several wooden chairs off to the right side. It didn't look at all like the home of an heiress. He'd expected something more along the line of her brother's house. It made him wonder again why Daphne had chosen to settle in a small town in the mountains of Idaho when she could have lived anywhere in the world. Was it because, as she'd stated, she'd fallen in love with the town and its people? Or was there another reason?

"Careful of the steps." She moved ahead to open the front door for him. "You can set down the crate anywhere. Right there on the floor will be fine."

"Why don't I take it into the room where you intend to use it?"

"Oh, but I—"

"I've carried it this far. A few more steps won't matter."

"Very well."

She led the way to one of the bedrooms. Only it wasn't a bedroom. It was an office with several bookcases, the shelves lined with books. Dozens upon dozens of books. Thin ones, thick ones, and everything in between. A writing desk stood in the center of the room, a neat stack of paper on the left side, a collection of pens and pencils on the right side. It seemed she was more than a little serious about writing, and he doubted the column that awaited him back at the office was her first attempt.

He stopped, leaned down, and set the crate on the floor while Daphne moved to stand with her back to the window, her hands resting on top of the bookcase that sat beneath the sill.

"Would you like me to open the crate for you?" he asked as he straightened.

"Heavens, no. I've imposed upon you enough already."

"Not at all." He stepped over to one of the taller bookcases, and his gaze scanned the titles at eye level. It was an eclectic collection — biographies, histories, scientific studies, poetry, novels, short story collections. Old books. New books. Authors like Mark Twain, Edith Wharton, Willa Cather, Jack London, Jane Austen, Gertrude Stein, O. Henry, and Robert Frost. "Have you read many of these?"

"Most. I'll read them all eventually. I like to learn."

He glanced over his shoulder. "Your interests are rather varied."

"For a woman?"

"I didn't say that."

She gave him a tight smile. "Maybe not, but you thought it."

He wanted to deny the accusation.

"You'd be surprised by the things that interest me, Mr. Crawford."

"Perhaps you'll share some of them with me while I'm in Bethlehem Springs."

Her dark eyebrows arched. "You make it sound as if that won't be for long."

"One can't predict the future, Miss McKinley."

"No, one can't."

She was more than just another pretty face, more than a woman of wealth and privilege. There was intelligence behind those chocolate-colored eyes of hers, and he realized that he really would like to learn about her interests.

"Are you sure you don't want me to open that for you?" He glanced down at the crate as he spoke.

"Quite sure." She stepped toward him. "Thank you for carrying it home for me. I'm obliged to you."

As he lifted his gaze, he caught sight of a number of slight volumes on the lower shelf of the bookcase behind her. Unmistakably dime novels. It surprised him that she would have such poor reading material among the rest of her fine collection.

She shifted her position, and the books were once again hidden from view by her skirt.

Was it intentional, he wondered, as he met her gaze. Was she trying to hide those books from him? Perhaps she was embarrassed for him to know she read such disgraceful literature. As well she should be.

"I know you're a busy man, Mr. Crawford. Don't let me keep you any longer."

No matter the reason for her earlier case of nerves — whether an attraction she felt toward him or because she wanted to impress her editor — she had apparently overcome it. He was being shown the door. Without question. He made his way to the front entrance. She followed right behind.

As he opened the door, he bid her good day. "Do let me know how you fare in learning to use your new typewriter." He pushed the screen door open and stepped onto the front porch. Then he turned to look at her again.

"Of course." She smiled, but it was a fleeting, uncertain one. "And I look forward to learning your opinion of my first column.

I do want to make a good impression on the newspaper's readers." After a quick nod, she all but closed the door in his face.

Joshua stood there, still holding the screen door open with his left hand while mulling over what had transpired, from the moment he'd run into Daphne in the mercantile until now. He wasn't easily confused, but this particular woman baffled him. Did she like him or not? Did he like her or just find her curious?

With a shake of his head, he let the screen door fall closed, then turned and went down the porch steps. Better to drive thoughts of Miss McKinley from his mind. Better he concentrate on the matter that had brought him to Bethlehem Springs.

Strange that he had to keep reminding himself of that.

When he reached the corner of Wallula and Lincoln—and with that reminder upmost in his thoughts—he decided not to return to the newspaper immediately. Instead, he headed for Thurber's Feed Store at the end of the block.

An earthy scent filled his nostrils when he entered the store a short while later. Unlike the general store that was crowded with items of all kinds, narrow aisles between fully stocked shelves, the feed store had a wide open feel to it. Bags of grain were stacked against the far wall. Another wall displayed harnesses and other tack for horses, including a couple of saddles.

"Howdy." The man behind the counter wiped his hands on the green apron he wore over his shirt and trousers. "Can I help you find somethin'?"

Joshua introduced himself.

"You're the newspaper fellow," the man said before Joshua could add that detail. "Right nice to meet you. I'm Mark Thurber." Thurber was tall and beanpole thin with orange-red hair on his head and a red-and-gray close-cropped beard. He moved from behind the counter, holding out his hand.

Joshua shook it. "I'm hoping you can help me."

"Do my best."

"I'm looking for someone who is supposed to live in or near Bethlehem Springs. His name is D. B. Morgan."

Mark Thurber rubbed his chin between the thumb and index finger of his right hand. "Hmm. Can't say as I've ever heard of a Mr. Morgan anywhere hereabouts. But I'll tell you what. If'n anybody'd know, it's Griff Arlington. He's lived in these mountains more'n thirty years now and knows just about everybody, young and old."

"And where might I find Mr. Arlington?" The name sounded familiar. He was sure he'd run across it before. In the newspaper. Arlington ... Arlington ... *Gwen* Arlington. Perhaps Griff was her brother. No, not if he'd lived here for more than thirty years. More than likely her father or grandfather or maybe an uncle.

"Griff's got a ranch about ten miles or so east of town."

Ten miles. That wasn't walking distance. He would have to rent a horse at the livery. He mentally counted the money that needed to last until he drew his first salary from the *Herald*. It wouldn't stretch very far.

"I could draw you a map," Thurber offered.

"Thank you. I'd greatly appreciate it."

"'Course, it'd save you riding out there if you just tried to meet up with him day after tomorrow. There's not much short of a blizzard that keeps him and his family from bein' at church on Sundays." Thurber jerked his head to the right. "He goes to the Methodist Church across the way there, if'n that's what you choose to do. Service starts at ten in the mornin'."

Relief washed through him. He wouldn't need to rent a horse after all. "Thank you again, Mr. Thurber. I'll follow your suggestion." Joshua touched the brim of his hat. "Good day to you."

Perhaps on Sunday he would have the answers he sought.

With her chair facing the bookshelf beneath her office window, Daphne stared at the tangerine-colored spines of The McFarland Chronicles. Had Joshua seen them? Had he been able to read the titles? Would he wonder why she hadn't mentioned that she'd read D. B. Morgan's work? Would he be intrepid enough to search until he discovered the truth? And worse still, what would he think of her should that happen?

Pangs of conscience tightened her chest again. But why should she feel guilty? She wasn't the first female author to write under a male pseudonym, nor would she be the last. The main reason she used one was the same as it had been for others of her sex: because readers wouldn't accept a western adventure novel from a Daphne McKinley the way they did from a D. B. Morgan.

She reached for one of her novels and stared at the cover. *The Predicament of Dorothy Milford*. Her fourth novel and one of her favorites. The illustration showed Bill McFarland protecting the fair heroine while punching out Rawhide Rick. Oh, what wonderful exploits Bill and Dorothy experienced in that book. Daphne had been totally enthralled with her characters, and the story had seemed to write itself. Perhaps she should have let the two of them get married and settle down. Only that would have put an end to the Chronicles. After all, what adventures awaited a couple after wedlock?

The question brought her up short. Was that truly how she viewed marriage?

She considered her closest friends, Gwen and Cleo. Both of them were independent, strong-minded women who had been content while single. Content, that is, until they'd met the men they would marry. Falling in love had changed everything for them.

And she was certain, were she to suggest to them that their lives lacked excitement, they would heartily disagree.

With a shake of her head, she slipped the book into its place on the shelf before spinning the chair toward her desk. The new typewriter sat directly in front of her. With her index fingers, she pressed down on a few keys, one at a time, watching as they left black letters on the paper rolled into the platen.

Better she get her thoughts back into her next book than to muse about marriage, pseudonyms . . . or Joshua Crawford.

SEVEN

Daphne rose along with the rest of the congregation of All Saints Presbyterian and drew her first decent breath since entering the sanctuary ten minutes earlier. Joshua hadn't come to church this morning, and she was glad of it. Being around him made her nervous, made her afraid that something she might say or do would give away her secret. Oh, how she wished he'd never come to Bethlehem Springs.

She glanced to her right where Morgan stood, holding Andy against his hip. On the other side of her brother were Gwen and the baby. Ellie slept soundly in her mother's arms, unaware of the loud organ music or the voices raised in a song of praise.

Would it embarrass Morgan or Gwen should her secret be revealed? Perhaps not. She might even discover they would support her writing endeavors. Was *she* the one who was embarrassed by the stories she wrote?

She mulled the question around in her mind until she was certain of the answer. No. She wasn't embarrassed. Perhaps at times her writing was a little overwrought, but wasn't that what readers wanted? Was it awful to provide a few hours of escape to those who read her books?

Morgan closed the hymnal as the last strains of music lifted toward the rafters of the church, and Daphne realized she hadn't sung a single word. Shame on her. She should be thinking about God, not about her books. Here of all places her thoughts should be on those things above.

She bowed her head as Reverend Rawlings began his opening prayer. *Lord, help me to do what's right in your eyes.*

✑

Joshua had wondered how he would discreetly find Griff Arlington among the other worshipers who attended the Bethlehem Springs Methodist Church, but he needn't have worried. Mark Thurber, the fellow from the feed store, made certain the two men were introduced as soon as the service was over.

"A pleasure to meet you, Mr. Crawford. My son-in-law told me the two of you had met. We're all glad you're here and that we have a newspaper again."

"Thank you, sir."

"And this here," Thurber continued after Joshua and Griff shook hands, "is Griff's daughter, Cleo Statham, and her husband, Sherwood. But everybody calls him Woody."

"How do you do?" Joshua said with a nod to Cleo and another handshake for her husband.

Thurber spoke again. "Griff, Mr. Crawford's lookin' for somebody name of Morgan. D. B. Morgan. He's supposed to live around these parts. You ever heard of him?"

"No, I can't say that I have."

Anticipating that Griff might ask why he wanted to find Mr. Morgan, Joshua said, "He's a writer of novels. I'm familiar with his books and was hoping I might speak with him about them."

Griff glanced at his daughter—Joshua noted that Cleo looked little like her sister, Gwen McKinley—and said, "Do you know anyone by that name?"

She answered with a slow shake of her head.

Thurber patted Joshua on the shoulder. "If'n Griff's never heard of your Mr. Morgan, then you can bet your bottom dollar that he just don't live around here and never did. Whoever said he did's got it wrong, for sure."

"It would seem so." Joshua let his gaze move to each person in the nearby semicircle. "I thank you all for your help."

He tried to sound as if failing to discover Mr. Morgan's whereabouts meant little to him, but inside frustration began to build. He clenched and unclenched his hands at his sides. He *had* to find the man. If he failed, there would be no righting of wrongs, there would be no apologies from Langston Lee or Gregory Halifax, no restoration of the job he'd lost.

Griff's voice broke into Joshua's thoughts. "If you don't have other plans, Mr. Crawford, please join me and my family for Sunday dinner. A man shouldn't have to eat alone on the Lord's Day, not when he's got Christian brothers and sisters to make him welcome at their table."

"That's a kind invitation," Joshua answered.

He might as well dine with them. It would be a long, quiet afternoon in his apartment on his own. Too much empty time to think about his failure to find D. B. Morgan. Besides, it might be interesting to see the cattle ranch and learn some of its history. Maybe he would discover something worthwhile to write about.

"Good." Griff's smile carved deep creases in an already craggy face. "Then come along. You can ride to the house with us in our buggy. Gwen and Morgan's cook hates it when we're late."

Gwen and Morgan? But he'd thought—

"Don't concern yourself, Mr. Crawford," Woody Statham said in a low voice, his accent identifying his British roots. "You aren't the first stranger Griff has invited to dinner after Sunday services.

However, I married the last Arlington daughter. Perhaps you'll take an interest in Daphne McKinley. She'll make some lucky man a fine wife."

Where on earth did Woody Statham get the idea Joshua was in the market for a wife?

Woody laughed and gave Joshua a pat on the back. "You'll have to forgive me, Mr. Crawford. I've become a romantic since meeting my Cleo. You will see what I mean when you get to know her."

He was beginning to regret accepting Griff's invitation. A quiet afternoon in his apartment above the newspaper office might have been preferable after all.

&

Daphne was standing in the parlor, rocking a dosing Ellie in her arms, when the front door of the McKinley home opened and Griff walked in, followed soon after by Cleo, Woody . . . and Joshua Crawford.

The breath caught in her throat. What was *he* doing there? Gwen hadn't said anything about Joshua joining the family for Sunday dinner. Hospitality was one thing. But to invite him to eat with them twice in the span of four days? Well, it was just . . . just . . .

"Of course not." Morgan's voice carried into the parlor. "We're glad you've joined us."

Daphne turned, walked to the far end of the parlor, and stopped at the large window that overlooked Bethlehem Springs. As she stared down at the town, snowflakes began to fall, at first so few and so fine she wondered if she imagined them.

Cleo appeared at Daphne's right shoulder. "I told Dad we'd get snow for sure today, and there it comes. Woody thought it would come last week, but I told him he was wrong." She reached over to stroke the top of Ellie's head. "I see you've got our little angel. Doesn't she look pretty in her Sunday dress?"

"Mmm. Very pretty." Daphne sent a quick glance over her shoulder, then looked out the window again. "I didn't know Mr. Crawford was joining us today."

Cleo laughed softly. "Neither did he. He was at our church service, and Dad invited him to come eat with us."

Daphne couldn't help wondering if she was the reason he'd chosen to attend the Methodist Church over All Saints Presbyterian that morning. But why? He had no reason to avoid her. It was *she* who had something to hide, *she* who had a secret, *she* who didn't want to be in his company for fear he would find her out.

"Do you mind if I take Ellie?" Cleo held out her arms, anticipating Daphne's compliance.

"Of course I mind. I always hate to give her up when she's sleeping. Why don't you ask to hold her when she's fussy?" She smiled to let her friend know she was teasing.

It was no secret that Cleo longed for a baby of her own. After she'd married Woody in the summer of 1916, she'd spoken openly about wanting to begin a family right away. But as the months passed without any sign of pregnancy, she'd said less and less to others. Now she spoke of it to no one. Only she couldn't hide her desire when around her niece and nephew. It was there in her eyes for all to see, and seeing it made Daphne's heart ache for her friend.

Tenderly, she placed the baby in Cleo's arms. As she took a step back, she saw Woody's approach. She thought it best to give them some privacy, and so she left them and joined the rest of the family and their guest, who were seated near the fireplace.

Joshua stood. "Good day, Miss McKinley."

"Mr. Crawford."

"Have you mastered the typewriter since I saw you last?" There was a hint of a smile in the corners of his mouth and a sparkle of jest in his eyes.

She felt herself relax a little at his teasing. "I believe it will take me more than two days to master it, but I'm learning."

He motioned to the overstuffed chair where he'd been seated. "Please, take mine."

"That's not necessary. I—"

"Please." He smiled—a smile that was almost as remarkable as the blue of his eyes.

Confusion replaced her unsteady nerves as she sank onto the chair, suddenly helpless to do anything other than comply.

⁂

Joshua walked across the room to retrieve one of the straight-backed chairs set against the wall near the entrance. As he carried it toward his host and the others, his gaze returned to Daphne and his mind replayed Woody's earlier comment: *"Perhaps you'll take an interest in Daphne McKinley. She'll make some lucky man a fine wife."*

There was no disputing that Miss McKinley was a beautiful girl. No, not a girl. She was, without question, a woman. And when he looked at her, it was easy for his mind to stray to places he didn't want it to go. Like what that abundant mass of curly black hair would look like tumbling free down her back or spilling over a white pillowcase. Like how soft her mouth would feel against his if he kissed her.

He gave his thoughts a mental shake. The world would come to an end before he saw Daphne's hair unbound. As for kissing her? More likely he would become the editor of the *New York Times* or the head of a leading publishing house before the end of the year.

Wealth and privilege set Daphne McKinley apart from ordinary folks, and Joshua was unquestionably ordinary. He came from common stock. His father had been a man of trade. One of his great-grandfathers had been a farmer. And Richard Terrell, despite growing long in years, had worked to provide for his widowed daughter and only grandson. Daphne lived alone and had no need of employment, no concerns about how she would put food on the table. She'd traveled all around the globe, according to newspaper reports, while Bethlehem Springs was the farthest Joshua had been from St. Louis in his entire life.

No, he might be welcome as a guest in her brother's home, but there was a vast chasm that separated Joshua from Daphne. To think otherwise was to be a fool. And besides, he was all but engaged to someone else. All the more reason for him to bring such thoughts about Daphne McKinley to an end. Once and for all.

❧

Sunday, 27 October, 1918

Dear Mary Theresa,

I write this letter, hoping that you have found it in your heart to forgive me for the things I said in the heat of the moment. I regret losing my temper with Mr. Halifax and that he and I came to blows. I regret that my fight with him caused me to lose my position. But above all, I regret that I took out my anger and frustration upon you. You didn't deserve to bear the brunt of my ill humor. Please forgive me, Mary Theresa.

I arrived at my destination on the seventeenth of this month, only to learn that Mr. Patterson, the man who offered me employment as a reporter at the Daily Herald, had passed away. Fortunately, before his passing, he instructed his wife to offer me the position as managing editor of the paper. Since my funds were nearly depleted, I didn't hesitate to accept, knowing full well that I will need to find my replacement before I can return to St. Louis. I was provided with living quarters above the newspaper office as part of my compensation, a circumstance for which I am grateful. It would have cost more if I had to hire a room in the boarding house for the duration of my stay.

I have been made to feel welcome by many. All are glad that their newspaper is available once again. Twice I've been invited to dine at the home of the town's most influential (in my opinion) citizen, one Morgan McKinley. I have come to admire him as I've learned the reason he came to Idaho. Perhaps because he reminds me of Grandfather. Although his wealth far exceeds anything Grandfather had, his generous spirit seems to be quite genuine.

Unfortunately, I have been less than successful in my search to find D. B. Morgan. No one in Bethlehem Springs seems to know or have heard of the man. I wrote to my source at Shriver & Sons, hoping to obtain more information that will assist me in finding Mr. Morgan.

Bethlehem Springs is a sleepy little town, set right in the middle of tree-covered mountains. The terrain is very different from where you and I grew up. It's more arid. Certainly there is nothing like the mighty Mississippi River flowing nearby. The elevation of the town is better than five thousand feet, almost three times the highest point in all of Missouri but under half that of the highest point in Idaho. The population of Bethlehem Springs is miniscule compared to St. Louis. I miss the hurry and bustle of our thriving city.

Tonight, with snow falling outside my apartment's windows as it has done much of the day, I feel isolated from *the rest of the world. However, I've begun to adjust to the tempo of the town, and my stay will be worth it once I find and confront Mr. Morgan.*

Your grandfather has been much on my mind. How is he? I know you were afraid his last illness might be the influenza. Fear over the dreaded disease is everywhere these days. The conductor on the train told me that fewer people are traveling, and whenever he hears a passenger cough or sees one who looks ill, he wonders if he will soon join the thousands who have died from the Spanish flu. I admit, I've had similar thoughts. I learned from my employer, Mrs. Patterson, that there have been no outbreaks of the influenza in Bethlehem Springs. They are grateful, and so am I.

When you see my mother and her husband, please tell them I am well. I intend to write to Mother next, but she will be reassured if you convey the same message to her.

I remain affectionately,

Joshua

July 1, 1872

It's a shame that I'm not more disciplined in writing down the record of my life, but for the present, my past doesn't seem as important as my future. Our future.

I'm pleased to say that my new business ventures in St. Louis are thriving. Doing far better than I had reason to expect. But my involvement with them does keep me very busy during the day. When I return home in the evening, I much prefer spending the time with Annie than writing about days gone by.

My beloved wife has grown large with the child she carries. She frets about being fat, but I tell her daily how beautiful she is. It's not a lie. She is beautiful, and the life inside of her is a miracle for which I will always be thankful to God. Annie is convinced the child will be a boy, but I secretly hope for a girl. One who will look exactly like her mother.

✧

Looking back to those years I was in California and owned the Golden Nugget, I see nothing to recommend myself. I was dishonest and disreputable to the core. I put on airs of respectability, but it was an act. I considered the welfare of no one other than myself. If something would benefit me, I went after it. What I couldn't buy, I took by force. I wasn't above threats or blackmail. It's a wonder I never killed anyone to advance my fortunes.

At least I don't have murder on my conscience. Another circumstance for which I am grateful to God.

But death is not always the worst thing that can happen to a man. I destroyed many in other lasting ways. I took their money. I ruined their businesses. Sometimes I dallied with their wives just for the novelty of it.

I have no defense, no way to justify the man I was then. Sin ruled me to the core. Even now, so many years later, I have to battle against my old ways of doing things. I have to keep myself in check when making business decisions. Old habits die hard, and I find I must plead for God to break those patterns, those temptations. I beg Him to control every area of my life. Without Him, I am most surely lost.

I take comfort in the words that Paul wrote in Romans 7:

For I know that in me (that is, in my flesh,) dwelleth no good thing: for to will is present with me; but how to perform that which is good I find not. For the good that I would I do not: but the evil which I would not, that I do. Now if I do that I would not, it is no more I that do it, but sin that dwelleth in me. I find then a law, that, when I would do good, evil is present with me. For I delight in the law of God after the inward man: But I see another law in my members, warring against the law of my mind, and bringing me into captivity to the law of sin which is in my members. O wretched man that I am! who shall deliver me from the body of this death? I thank God through Jesus Christ our Lord. So then with the mind I myself serve the law of God; but with the flesh the law of sin.

Indeed. Thank God. Jesus Christ is the One who shall deliver me from the body of this death. Amen.

EIGHT

Daphne found her column on page 2 of the Monday edition of the paper, upper right-hand side. And there was her byline—Daphne McKinley—beneath the heading *A Woman's Words*. A thrill of excitement shivered up her spine. Although she didn't care much for the title Joshua Crawford had given her column—it seemed rather dull and ordinary to her—at least others would know she was the author of the piece that followed. No cloud of secrecy. No worry about being discovered. For better or worse, there was her name for all to see.

Her eyes scanned the column, which was about woman's suffrage in America and in Idaho and how Bethlehem Springs should be proud that they'd elected a woman as their mayor three years earlier. As far as she could tell without comparing it word for word to her copy, Joshua had made only a few changes. She hoped that meant he was pleased with her effort. He hadn't told her so, and until this moment she hadn't known how much she desired his approval. He was, after all, a professional editor. He must love words as much as she did.

She folded back the paper so her column was on the top page, then folded the paper in half and placed it on the kitchen table. What should she write for next Monday's column? Her debut piece had come to her in a flash. Writing about Gwen's accomplishments as mayor hadn't been difficult. But what next? A woman's view of the war in Europe. The need for quarantine efforts in order to stop the spread of influenza around the globe. Or perhaps a piece about something closer to home, such as the effect of prohibition in Idaho.

Instinct told her Joshua wanted her columns to be more personal, less news and more opinion. Something softer, perhaps.

She released a sigh. Despite her many frustrations with her current novel — Was she ready to end the life of Rawhide Rick? Should Bill McFarland be allowed to fall in love and marry? Was it time to bring The McFarland Chronicles to an end? — she had to admit she found it easier to write fiction than opinion pieces. Could she come up with enough engrossing topics on a weekly basis?

Oh, my. Writing for the newspaper had seemed an excellent idea when it first came to her. Would it turn into a disaster instead?

She left the kitchen and went to her office. The typewriter awaited her, a clean sheet of paper rolled into the platen. With practice each day, she was getting the hang of typing. She did wonder why the keys weren't lined up alphabetically. Wouldn't that have made more sense?

She sank onto her desk chair, shoving her loose flowing hair behind her shoulders. She would practice a little while before changing out of her dressing gown. Perhaps she might even manage to write a page or two about Bill McFarland's latest adventure, just to prove it was, indeed, easier than coming up with an idea for her second column.

Dry Creek was a town as uninviting as its name. The buildings lining Main Street were weather beaten and sun-bleached, and any small breeze sent dust devils whirling every which way.

It was said only the most desperate characters lived in Dry Creek, a wide patch in the road halfway between Boise City and the gold towns of the Boise Basin. Even government officials gave the town a wide berth, believing it was better to let the ruffians kill each other than to risk their own lives enforcing the law.

But Bill McFarland wasn't the kind of man who backed away from danger. He wasn't about to start backing down on this day ...

A knock on Daphne's front door drew her out of her fictional world. Who on earth would come calling so early in the morning? Except it wasn't early. When she looked at the clock on her desk, she discovered it was almost noon. And there she sat in her dressing gown, the floor of her office littered with crumpled pages.

The knock sounded again. It seemed her visitor wasn't going away. Probably Edna Updike wanting to borrow a cup of flour or sugar. Or perhaps her neighbor wanted to give Daphne a scolding because of her column in the newspaper. Daphne remembered how disapproving Mrs. Updike had been when Gwen ran for public office. What a fussbudget!

"Oh, my." She released a sigh. "And I was doing so well."

She rose from the chair, once again shoving her hair over her shoulder. Whatever it was Mrs. Updike wanted, Daphne would not let her come inside. She would make certain her neighbor's visit was brief. Then she would change into a day dress and return to writing while her muse was cooperating.

She pasted on a smile as she opened the door. It vanished in an instant. Her caller wasn't Edna Updike. Joshua Crawford stood on her front porch, his hand raised to rap once more upon her door.

"Mr. Crawford." Her fingers fluttered to the neck of her dressing gown. She was perfectly covered, of course. As modestly and adequately as any of her day dresses. Still ...

"Miss McKinley." He bent the brim of his hat in greeting. "Might I speak with you for a moment?"

⁓

Looking at Daphne, her thick mass of curly black hair tumbling over her shoulders and down her back—appearing much as he'd imagined it would—Joshua almost forgot what had brought him to her door.

"I ... I'm not prepared for company." Color rose in her cheeks as she fingered the collar of her pale yellow dressing gown.

He hunched his shoulders inside his coat. "I won't take up much of your time."

"Well ..." She reached out and pushed on the screen door. "Come inside. We're letting the heat out."

"Thanks." As he moved by her, he caught the faint scent of her cologne. It was different from the last time he'd noticed her fragrance. Honeysuckle, if he wasn't mistaken, and he wasn't. It was his mother's favorite.

The door closed behind him.

"I would offer you a cup of coffee, Mr. Crawford, but I'm afraid it will be bitter. It's been on the stove for several hours. Still I—"

He removed his hat as he turned to face her again. "That's kind, but I promised I wouldn't keep you."

Yesterday he'd wondered what it would be like to kiss Daphne. Later, he'd written to Mary Theresa, partly because of the need to remind himself that he shouldn't think about kissing another woman. But how could he help it, seeing her as she was now?

He swallowed. "Miss McKinley, I'm here—" His voice

cracked, like a nervous schoolboy. He cleared his throat. "I'm here about D. B. Morgan."

She moved away from him, walking from the small living room into the kitchen. "Are you sure you don't want some coffee?"

"I'm sure." He shouldn't have come. It was a crazy notion that had brought him here today. And yet, he had to try. If there was any possibility she could help him ... "Miss McKinley, I couldn't help noticing your collection of novels when I was here the other day."

She arched an eyebrow and tipped her head slightly to one side. The look in her eyes bade him continue.

"The McFarland Chronicles, in particular."

The blush that had colored her cheeks moments before drained away. "What about them?"

So he was right. The books he'd seen were not only dime novels, but they were those *particular* dime novels, the ones that had caused him so much anger and grief. "You must know they were written by D. B. Morgan."

"Yes."

"But you didn't say anything when you heard me ask others about the author." He walked forward, stopping when he reached the table.

"No, I didn't say anything."

"Why not? You knew I wanted to find him."

She drew a deep breath and released it, her chest rising and falling with it. "I said nothing because there is nothing I can tell you."

"Perhaps you don't want others to know you read those kind of books. There isn't much to admire about them, that's for certain."

If she'd looked pale and uncertain moments before, now she looked perturbed. "I'm afraid I disagree, Mr. Crawford. I find a great deal to enjoy about The McFarland Chronicles. They're entertaining and filled with history of the Old West."

"They are ridiculous and filled with inaccuracies."

"Mr. Crawford, you may be a fine newspaper editor, but you obviously know little about fiction or the people who love to read it."

His own temper was on the rise. "I know Mr. Morgan has no regard for facts, no respect for the truth. He's ruined the good name of a good man in his novels."

"What good man?"

"My grandfather!"

Silence enveloped the kitchen.

Breathing hard, Joshua turned away. Why take out his frustration on Miss McKinley? She had a right to read what she wanted, and it wasn't her fault what the author had written. *Practice patience*, he reminded himself. *Be like Grandfather.* But his annoyance remained. Daphne was the closest thing he had to a lead, and he was certain she knew more than she was saying.

"I don't understand what your grandfather has to do with The McFarland Chronicles."

Joshua faced her again. "My grandfather's name was Richard Terrell, and when he was a young man living out West, he was sometimes called Rawhide Rick. He lived in Bethlehem Springs before moving to St. Louis, where he married and raised his daughter. My mother."

"Oh, dear," she whispered, her hand covering her mouth.

"I didn't learn about the nickname until after his death, so I don't know how he came to be called by it. But I do know my grandfather was not the scurrilous villain portrayed in Mr. Morgan's novels."

"They *are* novels, Mr. Crawford. Just fiction."

"Should that make the insult less?"

"Perhaps the use of his name is a coincidence?"

Joshua shook his head. "If it was only my grandfather's real name or the nickname, perhaps. But both? No, it's no coincidence. I don't know why the writer wants to twist the truth about my grandfather in his novels, but I'm certain it's intentional."

"Is that the reason you want to meet D. B. Morgan?"

"Yes."

She was silent for a long while before saying, "You must have loved your grandfather a great deal." Her expression seemed kind, sympathetic, compassionate.

"There was a great deal about him to love. He was a good man, respected by everyone who knew him."

"How long has he been gone?"

"Fourteen years."

Again she was silent for a long moment before speaking, softly this time. "How can the words in a novel hurt him after so many years?"

His mother had asked him the same question when he'd announced his plans to find and confront D. B. Morgan. "They can't hurt him," he answered now, just as he had then. "But I don't want anyone believing that disreputable character was anything like the real Richard Terrell. I can't let the lies stand unchallenged. I owe my grandfather too much not to fight for his good name."

Daphne continued to look at him but didn't say anything more. Perhaps there was nothing more she could say. Perhaps she really didn't know anything about the author.

Joshua slid his fingers around his hat brim. One circle. Two circles. Finally, he set the hat on his head. He was wasting his time. "Thank you, Miss McKinley. I won't trouble you any longer." He turned on his heel and strode to the door, where he let himself out.

❧

As the door closed behind Joshua, Daphne sat on the nearest chair and drew a deep breath into her lungs. What a terrible predicament. She had included Rawhide Rick in her books for historical accuracy. In hindsight, perhaps that hadn't been the best choice. But she hadn't written anything about him that wasn't true — or at least that she hadn't *believed* was true.

Oh, dear. What if Griff's stories of early Idaho and Bethlehem Springs weren't true at all?

She covered her face with her hands.

Joshua Crawford had come all this way because he felt his grandfather's good name had been besmirched in the novels of D. B. Morgan. *Her* novels. She hadn't actually *lied* when she said there was nothing she could tell him. She wasn't ready to reveal that *she* was D. B. Morgan. Her work had been a secret from the start. How could she tell him and not tell everyone else? Or at least tell her family and closest friends.

"Father in heaven, whatever am I to do now?"

❧

Joshua's frustration continued to build throughout the afternoon, and by the time he flipped the sign in the office window to Closed, frustration had turned to a simmering anger. Had he come to Idaho for nothing?

"How can the words in a novel hurt him after so long a time?"

It seemed he was the only person who understood the importance of setting the record straight. He'd loved his grandfather. He'd grown to admire him even more as he'd grown into adulthood. Joshua needed to honor his memory. If even one reader believed that the character in those books was a true representation of Richard Terrell, that was one too many.

He pictured a smirk on Gregory Halifax's face. One that plainly said Joshua was a complete failure. At the thought, his anger boiled over, and he slammed his fist into the door jamb. Pain shot up his arm and into his shoulder. He released a mild oath.

"You all right, Mr. Crawford?"

Joshua drew in a quick breath. He'd forgotten Grant Henley was still in the back room. "I'm fine," he called, though he wasn't. He'd taken the skin off his knuckles, and his head had begun to pound. Not to mention the disgust he felt over losing his temper once again.

Would he never learn?

Grant appeared in the doorway. "Calling it a night?"

"Yes. And you should too."

"I won't be far behind you. Got to finish a few repairs to the old girl." *Old girl.* That's what Grant called the press.

Joshua nodded as he slipped his arms into his coat. "All right, then. I'll see you in the morning."

A few moments later, he stopped at the base of the stairs that led to his apartment. He was hungry, but he didn't feel like cooking for himself. The quiet of the apartment would allow him too much time to consider the different ways he'd failed, and he might find himself punching another door jamb because of it.

He turned away from the stairs and walked to the South Fork. Inside the restaurant, he was hailed by several other diners.

"Enjoyed your editorial today, Mr. Crawford."

"Heard you went to the Methodist Church yesterday. Hope you'll be back to All Saints next Sunday."

"Mr. Crawford, you're doing a fine job. Mrs. Patterson's lucky to have you."

Funny, wasn't it? Less than two weeks ago, he'd come into this restaurant a stranger. Now he was treated as if he were one of them. To his surprise, he felt the same. He was even able to respond to each one of them by name. Neighbor to neighbor.

Not that he truly belonged in Bethlehem Springs. His would be a short stay.

NINE

On Thursday, with the snow gone from the roads, Daphne joined her brother, sister-in-law, and their children for the family's weekly visit to the Arlington ranch. By the time they arrived, everyone's cheeks and noses were rosy from the cold and no one felt like dawdling outdoors.

"We liked your column in Monday's paper," Cleo said after giving Daphne a warm embrace. "I reckon most everybody'd have to agree with you too. Gwennie was the best mayor Bethlehem Springs ever had and ever will have."

Gwen lowered Ellie into Griff's arms before glancing over her shoulder. "I'm certain Edna Updike doesn't agree." Her gaze met with Daphne's. "Has she said anything to you about what you wrote?"

"Not yet."

"Sure as shootin', she will." Cleo chuckled. "Mrs. Updike's never been one to hesitate expressing her opinion to anybody who'll listen."

"No, indeed," Gwen agreed, her laughter joining her sister's.

Gwen and Cleo drifted into the living room, their conversation switching to the children, while Woody challenged Morgan to a game of chess in the sitting room.

Before Griff could follow the men, Daphne stopped him with a hand on his arm. "Could we talk? Privately."

"Of course." A frown wrinkled his brow. "Is something wrong?"

She shook her head. "No. It's just, I have some questions and you're the only one I know who might be able to answer them."

With his free arm, he motioned toward the dining room. Daphne led the way and took a seat on the first chair. Griff settled into the one at the head of the table. Although his gaze revealed his curiosity, he waited patiently for her to continue.

If only she knew what to say, how much to say.

At last she drew a deep breath and began. "You know that Mr. Crawford is interested in finding D. B. Morgan."

Griff nodded.

"Well, the reason is because ... the author has included a character called Rawhide Rick in his—" She almost choked on the masculine pronoun. "—books. As it turns out, Joshua Crawford is a descendent of the real Richard Terrell."

Griff's eyes widened. "You don't say."

Daphne nodded. "His grandson."

"Well, isn't that something."

"Mr. Crawford objects to the way his grandfather is portrayed in the D. B. Morgan books. But I—" She cleared her throat. "—But I'm familiar with the books in question, and nothing in them appears to contradict the stories you've told me about the man. The ones about the early days in Idaho. Do you ... do you think the stories you heard were true?"

Griff was nobody's fool, and there was something about the way he looked at Daphne that made her fear he'd seen through the little half-truths she'd told. But if he had, he didn't tell her so. "I haven't read the books, so can't say for sure if what was written is accurate. But I can vouch for the things I told you. The men who shared those stories with me were straight shooters. Honest men. They aren't the kind to tell tall tales. They knew Rawhide Rick. Knew him well, and I'd take whatever they told me as gospel."

"Too bad Mr. Crawford can't speak to them," Daphne responded on a sigh.

Ellie whimpered, and Griff shifted the baby from the crook of his arm to his shoulder where he began to pat her gently on the back. "No reason he couldn't if he cared to take a little trip. The Coughlin brothers are both alive and kicking. They're over in Stone Creek. We keep in touch every now and again. I'll be glad to tell Mr. Crawford how to find them if he wants the information."

"I'm sure he would appreciate it."

Ellie began to cry in earnest.

"I believe she wants her mother." Griff rose to his feet. As he headed for the living room, he added, "Before you leave today, I'll write down the information and you can give it to Mr. Crawford."

Daphne stood, but instead of following Griff, she moved to the dining room window and stared outside. A bright sun beamed down from a cloudless sky, promising warmth without giving any. The horses in the corrals already sported thicker coats. Soon winter would arrive in earnest. But it wasn't the weather or the animals that occupied Daphne's thoughts.

It was knowing she would have to tell Morgan about her writing.

Worse, she would have to tell Joshua Crawford that she was D. B. Morgan.

❧

Seated at his desk, Joshua took a bite of the sandwich he'd made for himself while his eyes scanned the newspaper open before him. He'd decided to read through a few random issues every day to make himself more familiar with the town and its citizens. This one was from more than three years ago, June 1915. On page four, there was a society piece about Daphne McKinley, newly arrived from the East on a visit to her brother.

> Daphne Bernadette McKinley arrived in Bethlehem Springs on Friday last for a visit with her brother, Morgan Alistair McKinley. The daughter of Alistair and Danielle McKinley, deceased, Miss McKinley is a graduate of ...

Daphne had been on his mind a lot this week. Mostly he remembered the last time he'd been with her and wondered why he'd made such a fool of himself over those books on her shelf. It was her business what she liked to read. Who was he to act as judge and jury? And liking to read dime novels didn't make her responsible for what was in them.

He owed her an apology.

> Miss McKinley told this reporter that she is looking forward to learning more of the history of Idaho. "I am fascinated by the men and women who settled the West. How very courageous they were. What an exciting time that was in the history of our country." She went on to say that ...

Joshua's eyes returned to the beginning of the piece.
Daphne Bernadette McKinley.
Morgan McKinley.
Daphne Bernadette.
D. B.
Morgan.
D. B. Morgan.

It couldn't be. It was mere coincidence. If it was difficult to believe that a man like Morgan McKinley could author dime novels, it was impossible to believe it of his sister. Only, the more Joshua considered the possibility, the less improbable it seemed. If she liked to read them, why couldn't she like to write them?

"I find a great deal to enjoy about The McFarland Chronicles. *They're entertaining and filled with history of the Old West."*

Were those the words of a fan of dime novels? Or were they the words of the writer of dime novels? Great Scot! It must be the latter. Daphne McKinley *was* D. B. Morgan. The name was a pseudonym, and to anyone with an ounce of deductive powers, a rather obvious one at that. He should have realized it long before this.

And to think she'd let him go on about the author, about the inaccuracies, about his grandfather, and she hadn't confessed the truth. Did she believe wealth and privilege gave her a right to lie? Well, he meant to be the one to tell her it didn't.

He spun his chair away from the desk and got to his feet. He would give that young woman a piece of his mind, and he wasn't going to delay doing so a minute longer.

❦

"Is something wrong?"

Daphne looked at her sister-in-law, seated beside her on the sofa. The men had gone outside after lunch, and Cleo had taken Andy upstairs to play while Ellie slept in a cradle in the living room.

Gwen continued. "You've seemed distracted all day."

"Have I?"

"Mmm. Not to mention that frown you're wearing."

Daphne released a sigh. "There's something troubling me. Something I need to tell Morgan."

Gwen lifted an eyebrow.

"You, too, but I need to tell my brother first."

"That sounds rather mysterious."

Daphne offered a weak smile. "I know, but it can't be helped."

"Perhaps you should go talk to him now."

"Now?"

"If it's bothering you so much, yes. Delaying something you know must be done never seems to make things better."

Ever since her conversation with Griff that morning, Daphne had played out a dozen different scenarios in her head, imagining the moment when she told Morgan about her writing. She'd envisioned him angry, amused, appalled, proud, disappointed, accepting. But the only way she would know for sure would be to tell him and see for herself.

"You're right." She rose from the sofa. "I'll do it now."

After putting on her coat, she went outside and walked across the yard to the barn, where she found Morgan and Griff standing with their arms resting on the top rail of a stall. Woody was inside the stall with a young horse, running his hands over the colt's flank.

"He shows great promise," Woody said. "Cleo prefers training the smaller horses that can make quick turns. This horse is built to fly. Look at those legs."

"So have you convinced her to go with you to California?" Morgan asked.

"I do believe so. But we won't make the final decision until spring."

"Who's going to California?" Daphne asked as she drew near the stall.

Morgan and Griff turned their heads to look at her.

Woody answered, "I am. And Cleo."

Griff added, "They think they may have a horse worth racing."

Daphne looked through the rails at the black colt inside. "He's beautiful. How old is he?"

"Still a yearling."

"Really? My goodness but he's tall."

"Indeed." Woody beamed with pride, as if he were responsible for the horse's height.

Morgan said, "I suppose it's about time we left for home."

Daphne gave a slight shrug.

"Then I'd best see what mischief I can get into with my grandson before his mother spirits him away." Griff pushed off the stall rail and headed for the barn door.

"You'll find him upstairs with Cleo," Daphne called after him.

"Thanks." He waved without looking behind him.

Daphne laid her hand on Morgan's arm and said softly, "I'd like to speak with you before we go in."

Woody must have heard her, for when she glanced at him, he nodded and followed his father-in-law from the barn.

Confession, the old saying went, was good for the soul. But Daphne had never confessed anything like this before.

Morgan leaned his back against the rails and crossed his arms over his chest, waiting. Her brother was by nature an exceedingly patient man. Not that she'd known that fact three and a half years ago. She hadn't known much at all about him until she'd come to live in Bethlehem Springs. They'd been separated by age and distance for much of their lives. Perhaps that's why she was so nervous about this. She still didn't know him well enough to predict his exact response.

"So what is it you need to talk about?" he asked after a lengthy silence.

She glanced toward the barn door, almost wishing they would

be interrupted. They weren't. With a sigh, she began. "Have you ever wondered how I spend the better part of my days?"

A smile tugged at the corners of his mouth. "No, Daphne, I must admit I haven't given that much thought. I suppose with the usual feminine pursuits."

"Not quite."

His eyes widened in question.

"I write novels."

"Novels?" He straightened away from the stall.

She couldn't decide whether to laugh at the incredulous tone of his voice or to be insulted by it.

"But why, Daphne?"

"So others can read them, of course."

"You mean your novels have been published?"

Insulted. Definitely insulted. "Yes. Ten of them so far."

"Great Scot!" He shook his head. "How have you managed to keep it a secret? I would have thought people around here would — "

"I use a pen name." She inhaled deeply. "D. B. Morgan."

For a moment, he didn't react. But the instant he put the name together with the inquiries of a certain newspaper editor, Daphne saw his expression change. She rushed to tell him the rest, that the books were adventure novels, that Joshua didn't yet know she was D. B. Morgan, that Mr. Crawford was convinced her stories had damaged the name of his grandfather, and last but not least, that Griff had reassured her the information he'd given was true and accurate.

"I suppose I could have misunderstood something," she finished, her words slowing at last, "but I don't believe that's the case."

Her brother raked the fingers of one hand through his hair and once again said, "Great Scot," this time in a whisper.

"I love writing, Morgan. I cannot imagine having all of these stories running around in my head and not being able to write them down to share with others. But I wouldn't want to become an embarrassment to you or Gwen or the children. Really I wouldn't. That's why I used a pseudonym. That—and knowing it might be harder to sell my stories under my own name." A shudder moved through Daphne, and she pulled her coat more tightly about her.

Her brother was silent for a long time, and his expression no longer revealed surprise—or any other emotion. The waiting was torturous. Daphne heard every creak the barn made, heard each rustle of straw as animals moved in their stalls.

At last he said, "And what do you intend to do now?"

"I don't know." She remembered the look of frustration on Joshua's face, the day he'd asked her about the dime novels on her shelf. She recalled the tinge of anger in his voice. Without question, his frustration and anger would soon be directed at her. Oh, how she wished she could avoid that. "I suppose I shall have to tell Mr. Crawford."

"Yes. I suppose you shall."

"I don't believe he'll take it very kindly."

"Can you blame him?" Her brother cocked an eyebrow.

She sighed. "They're only novels." She'd said something similar to Joshua a few days ago. The excuse sounded even weaker now.

"How would you feel if you picked up a novel and discovered a disreputable character by the name of Alistair McKinley, who resembled our father in countless other ways? Same family. Same hometown. Same work. But devious and dishonest and wicked instead of the god-fearing man we knew."

"I wouldn't like it."

"No. Neither would I."

"But what if the real Richard Terrell was the same as the

character in my books? What if I'm right and Mr. Crawford is wrong? I shouldn't have to apologize for telling the truth. Should I?"

Morgan shrugged. "You'll have to sort that out for yourself, Daphne."

"Some help you are."

With a grin, her brother put his arm around her shoulders. "I do what I can." He turned her toward the barn door. "Come on. We'd best help Gwen get the children ready for the drive home."

She supposed she should be glad that he hadn't scolded or lectured her. Now if she could only believe Joshua Crawford's reaction would be as mild as her brother's.

γ

August 25, 1872

"For as the body without the spirit is dead, so faith without works is dead also." James 2:26

It occurs to me that I must do more than explore my past in order to avoid making the same mistakes. God requires more of me than that. I must somehow give back. I must give to others. I came to St. Louis with money that has been tainted by the choices I've made. While legally mine, much of it remains ill-gotten gain, and I would now like to use it to help others less fortunate. I wish to turn it over to the Lord for His use.

Thus, I am in the process of purchasing two buildings in the city. One will become an orphanage. I know what it is like to be left an orphan. I want to give poor fatherless and motherless children a chance to thrive, even if they must do so in an orphanage. The other building will become a home for men who are without work, without income or an ability to earn a living.

A recent acquaintance of mine from our church has partnered with me in this new venture. Kevin Donahue is thirty-nine, a father of three, and respected in the community. Best of all, he also wants to serve God and desires to help those less fortunate.

I believe Kevin and I shall become good friends, and even though he is younger than I am by more than twelve years, I trust he will give me some good parenting advice once Annie gives birth to our first child.

TEN

Daphne waved as Morgan pulled his automobile away from the curb. Then with a sigh, she turned and walked toward the front porch, silently debating whether she should go to see Mr. Crawford at once or if she should finish polishing her next column instead. It might be good to take it with her. Perhaps they could discuss it first, before she told him what else she'd written. Perhaps she should wait until—

"Miss McKinley."

She gave a little shriek and spun toward the sound of her name.

Joshua rose from the chair at the end of her porch. "Sorry. I didn't mean to startle you. I've been waiting for your return."

Her heart hammered in her chest. It seemed God had chosen the time and place for her to tell him the truth. She wasn't to have the luxury of putting it off another hour or to another day.

"There's a matter I need to discuss with you," he said as he moved toward her. His eyes seemed cold, his mouth a hard line.

Nerves tumbled in her stomach. "There's something I need to discuss with you as well, Mr. Crawford. Do come inside. It's too cold to linger out here." She opened the screen door. "I hope you haven't been waiting long."

He made no reply as he followed her inside.

How should she begin? Should she simply blurt it out? Or

should she apologize first and then try to explain the choices she'd made?

Tea. She would make some tea first. It was the hospitable thing to do. And hopefully, by the time it brewed, she wouldn't feel her insides shaking the way they were now.

"Please be seated, Mr. Crawford, while I make a pot of tea."

But he didn't sit down in the parlor as invited. Instead, he followed her into the kitchen. "Don't bother with the tea on my account."

"To be honest, I'm chilled from the drive back from the Arlington ranch and could use something warm to drink."

After raking live coals from the back to the front of the firebox, she added wood until she had a blaze going. Then she filled the kettle with water and set it on the stove.

"It won't take long to prepare the tea, Mr. Crawford." She took the fine-bone china teapot, the one painted with royal-blue roses, from its place on the shelf near the window. Soon the teapot was joined by the canister that held her favorite tea leaves, the china strainer, and two delicate cups.

Only when everything was ready and waiting for the water to boil did she turn toward her guest again. He remained standing, his hands now resting on the back of one of the kitchen chairs. The way he scowled at her sent a shudder up her spine and caused her mouth to go dry.

He knows already. He's learned the truth before I could tell him.

There was no point in dragging it out another moment. "Yes, Mr. Crawford."

"Yes?" His frown deepened.

"I'm D. B. Morgan." She drew in a breath and released it. "I'm the author of The McFarland Chronicles."

He muttered something under his breath.

Daphne moved toward the table, stopping opposite him. "I'm sorry for the injury you feel my books have done to you."

"Not to me. To my grandfather."

"I have something for you." She reached into the pocket of her skirt and withdrew the slip of paper Griff had given to her, holding it out to Joshua.

He took it, read it, then looked at her again. "Are these names supposed to mean something to me?"

"Frank and Lawrence Coughlin knew your grandfather when he lived in Bethlehem Springs. I understand they worked for him. They're the ones who told Griff about Richard Terrell."

"And then Mr. Arlington told you?"

She nodded. "But he didn't know what I did with the information. He thought he was just telling me stories about the early days of Bethlehem Springs and Idaho. That's how it started. I was so curious about everything and was always asking him questions. He's a fount of knowledge about the early settling of the West. But he never knew I would put those stories into my books because he didn't know about my writing. No one knew I'd written any novels until today when I told Morgan." She pointed at the slip of paper in his hand. "The Coughlins can verify what I ... what I wrote in my books about Richard Terrell."

❦

Joshua wished Daphne hadn't admitted her guilt before he could make his accusations. Now the anger inside him had no place to go, no way to be spent, and it left him aggravated beyond description. To make matters worse, she seemed certain that these two men — "Frank and Lawrence Coughlin, Stone Creek, Idaho," the slip of paper said — would *verify* the stories she'd written about his grandfather. If so, they were liars.

"Where is Stone Creek?" he asked through a clenched jaw.

"Griff told me it's about fifty miles southeast of here."

He folded the paper in two before sliding it into his coat pocket. He wanted more than an apology from the author. He needed evidence to take back with him so he could shove the truth down Gregory Halifax's throat. Only then would he have a chance of being reemployed by the newspaper.

And if Daphne wouldn't provide what he needed, maybe he would sue her for libel. She was worth a fortune. Why not reap a reward? It was her fault he'd lost his temper with Halifax, her fault — in an indirect way — that he'd lost his job. He would surely win in a court of law, and she wouldn't miss the money.

On the heels of that thought came convicting words of Scripture. Better he be wronged, First Corinthians told him, better he be defrauded, than that he take a fellow believer to court. Which only served to make his anger increase. Was he to have *no* justice, *no* satisfaction, *no* righting of the wrong?

The kettle began to whistle, and Daphne turned toward the stove. Joshua watched for a moment as she poured water into the teapot, then he walked to the door, letting himself out without a word of farewell. Anger quickened his stride and carried him quickly along the sidewalk toward the newspaper office.

"Mr. Crawford! Mr. Crawford, wait!"

He stopped and turned, surprised that she'd followed him. She hadn't even taken the time to put on a coat before leaving her house.

"Mr. Crawford." She stopped a few feet away. "Please believe me when I tell you I meant no one any harm. I wrote only what I believed to be true about Richard Terrell. He's part of the history of Idaho."

"But what you wrote *isn't* history. That man in your books isn't my grandfather. Your stories are based on fables or gossip. Nothing more. And your books haven't just caused my grandfather's name to be maligned. They cost me my job back in St. Louis."

"I don't understand." Daphne hugged herself. "How could my novels do that?"

He felt a tug of guilt for stretching the truth. If he'd kept his temper in check, if he hadn't punched Halifax, he would still have his job. But he wasn't ready to let her off the hook for any part of this. Not yet. "Words have power, Miss McKinley. Even words in a novel. You may think your stories are simply for entertainment, but they still have the power to build up or tear down."

"What if everything I wrote about Richard Terrell turns out to be true?"

"It won't."

She took two steps closer to him. Her cheeks and the tip of her nose were pink from the cold. "But if it does?"

"I suppose I'd have some apologies of my own to make." He imagined Gregory Halifax's smirk and his blood began to boil again. "But I won't have to apologize because none of it's true. I knew my grandfather. You didn't. The only part that's true is that he once lived in this area and was called Rawhide Rick by a few people."

"I'll go with you to Stone Creek to speak to the Coughlin brothers."

He shook his head. "No. That's not necessary." There was no way he wanted to go anywhere with Daphne McKinley.

"I need to know the truth as much as you do, Mr. Crawford. How else can I correct the errors?" She arched her brows. "If any exist."

The challenge in her eyes was not lost on Joshua. "All right,

Miss McKinley. We'll go together, just as soon as I can arrange to be away from the newspaper for a few days."

Friday, 1 November 1918

Dearest Mother,

At last I write to you with what I believe is good news. Yesterday afternoon, I discovered the identity of the author of The McFarland Chronicles. To my great surprise, the writer I sought is not a man but a woman, and she writes her books under a pen name. It is my understanding that no one in Bethlehem Springs is aware of her writing endeavors. Even her own family didn't know until my inquiries forced her confession.

Miss M is a woman of some means and high position, not only in this town but elsewhere. (It is no wonder she uses a pseudonym.) To my great relief, she has agreed to correct the scurrilous assertions made in her novels about Grandfather once I prove that they are, indeed, erroneous. I shall keep her name in my confidence unless she otherwise forces my hand.

Today I was able to make arrangements to meet with the two elderly gentlemen who claim to have known Grandfather in their youth and who were the sources for the material used in Miss M's novels. They live in another town about fifty miles from Bethlehem Springs, and I will be traveling there next week. I trust that I will be able to reason with them and convince them to tell the truth I seek. If all goes well, I should be able to return to St. Louis early in the New Year.

Has Mary Theresa been to see you? I wrote to her earlier and expect to receive a reply next week. I continue to hope that she has forgiven me for allowing my anger at Mr. Halifax and

D. B. Morgan to spill over onto her. How often as a youth did Grandfather warn me about my quick temper? Even now I can hear him quoting Ephesians: "Let all bitterness, and wrath, and anger, and clamour, and evil speaking, be put away from you." I am sorry that I seem unable to practice those same disciplines with greater success in my Christian life.

Give my regards to Charles. I pray that this letter finds you both in good health.

Your devoted son,

Joshua

ELEVEN

When Daphne and Joshua set out from Bethlehem Springs on the following Wednesday, the mood inside the automobile felt as chilly as the frosty November morning outside of it. That Daphne's passenger was less than happy to spend today and tomorrow in her company was plain as the nose on her face.

Would Joshua feel different toward her after they'd met with the Coughlin brothers? Or perhaps that would only serve to make things worse. She fully expected the elderly gentlemen to confirm all that Griff had told her. If Griff Arlington trusted them to be honest, so did she.

Driving her automobile to Stone Creek had been Daphne's idea. Another reason for Joshua's foul mood, no doubt. Taking the train would have left them more than twenty miles from their destination, which would have precipitated hiring a horse and carriage and most likely staying a second night in the Stone Creek boarding house.

"It's unnecessary," she'd told Joshua. "My motorcar is sound and the weather is supposed to remain dry all week long."

"It's my experience that weather predictions are often incorrect, Miss McKinley. Remember there was snow on the ground only a week ago."

She had merely smiled at him, and in the end, he'd acquiesced— as men tended to do when she was determined to have her way.

They traveled south without a single word passing between them for three quarters of an hour. That was when Daphne spied five elk drinking at the river's edge, the lone bull sporting a massive rack. She quickly brought the motorcar to a stop.

"Look." She pointed across the river. "Isn't he magnificent?"

Several moments passed before Joshua answered, "Indeed."

"I never tire of seeing the wildlife in these mountains." She glanced at Joshua. "As long as we're stopped, would you care to get out and stretch your legs?"

"Sounds like a good idea." He opened the passenger door and disembarked, then assisted her out as well.

Pulling her coat close against the cool air, Daphne walked to the edge of the road to watch the elk on the opposite side of the low-running river. The animals had stopped drinking and were returning the stare.

She heard Joshua step up beside her. Without looking his way, she said, "Do you know what that bull elk is thinking? He's thinking, 'Do *we* come into your home and watch while *you* eat and drink? Please go away.'" She laughed aloud, and it was her laughter that seemed to cause one of the cows to turn, unhurried and unafraid, and stride gracefully into the forest, followed soon by the others.

"Do you do that a lot, Miss McKinley?"

"Do what?"

"Imagine the thoughts of wild animals."

She grinned. "I'm afraid it's the curse of a novelist, Mr. Crawford. To put oneself into the head of another. To try to think what they think and feel what they feel. To always imagine what will happen next."

"Hmm."

"You're a writer." Now she looked at him. "Surely you understand what I mean."

"I'm a journalist, Miss McKinley. I deal in facts, not fairy tales."

She ignored the note of condescension in his voice and mimicked his previous response, a low and gravelly sound in her throat. "Hmm."

This, at last, brought the hint of a smile to his lips, and in response, her heart thrummed. Perhaps in time he would be able to forgive her for the wrongs he believed her writing had done him. She hoped so. She wanted him to forgive her. She wanted him to like her, although she couldn't think why it should matter to her that he did.

"How much farther have we to go?" he asked, bringing her attention to the present.

"Better than an hour and a half. It's been mostly downhill so far, but after we turn east, we'll have a few mountains to climb. That will slow us down considerably."

"Would you like me to drive the rest of the way?"

"If you wish."

A short while later, the crank was turned, the engine was running, and both driver and passenger were in their seats.

Unwilling to allow silence to fill the motorcar again, Daphne asked a question that she was certain would begin a conversation. "Would you tell me about your grandfather? I know you admired and loved him, but tell me why. What was he like in his latter years?"

Joshua glanced in her direction as he pressed on the accelerator and the automobile rolled forward. His gaze returned to the road before he spoke. "Grandfather was sixty-nine when I was born, and he never seemed to change in the years I remember him. His skin was wrinkled and a bit leathery. The hair on his head was white as snow, and he wore it long enough to brush his shoulders. My mother was always after him to cut it, saying it was too long for the fashion, but she never persuaded him to change. He had a bushy white beard too. He looked a lot like the illustrations of Santa Claus. He seemed tall to me when I was a child, but by the time he passed away, I was already taller."

Daphne noticed the small smile had returned to the corners of Joshua's mouth as he spoke.

"He was a strong man, even into his eighties. Almost to the time of his death, he could lift and carry things that many younger men couldn't."

"Do you look like him?"

He nodded. "He had only a few photographs from his younger years. One was taken of him in California, close to the time the Civil War began. He was a lot leaner then than in his later years and the photograph wasn't very good, but the resemblance to me today at about the same age is unmistakable."

"And that pleases you. I can tell."

"Yes, I guess it does." He rubbed his chin with his right hand as his smile broadened. "Maybe I should consider growing a beard."

Daphne preferred Joshua clean-shaven but didn't share her opinion with him.

"Grandfather liked to suck on peppermints. His breath always smelled of them. That's my earliest memory of him. Sitting on his lap and smelling peppermint."

She envied that kind of memory. Her grandparents, both paternal and maternal, had passed away either before she was born or while she was still too young to remember them.

"Above all, Miss McKinley, he was nothing like the character you portrayed in your books. You couldn't have written a more opposing character if you'd tried."

Daphne pressed her lips together, swallowing a reply while turning her gaze out the window to her right. There was no point starting another argument. Nothing would be resolved until they reached Stone Creek and met with the Coughlins.

⇛

Joshua didn't need to look at Daphne to know she wanted to protest, to stand up once again for the stories she'd written, and he wished he could call back his words. Why bait her? He would prove the truth soon enough.

He decided to aim the conversation in a different direction. "I believe it's your turn."

"My turn?"

"Tell me something I don't know about the McKinleys."

"Gracious. What could be left for you to know? You've already ferreted out my well-kept secret."

He glanced at her quickly, wondering if he'd upset her. But she was watching him with a twinkle in her eye and a smile on her lips. Had he ever met a woman with as much self-confidence as she seemed to possess? He thought not. His mother was the shy, retiring sort. And Mary Theresa? She liked to cling to his arm when they were in social settings. Not so Daphne. He had the feeling she was utterly fearless, wherever she found herself.

His gaze back on the road, he couldn't help but smile as well. "I imagine you have more than one secret, Miss McKinley."

She answered him with laughter. A sound almost as lovely as she was.

His reaction was instantaneous and unexpected. The desire to take her in his arms and kiss her until he'd left her breathless was so strong he could hardly think straight, let alone remember how to drive. He tried to swallow, but his mouth was as dry as dust.

What was wrong with him? Yes, he'd felt an unwelcome attraction to the lovely Miss McKinley before this. But now that he knew she was D. B. Morgan, he should feel nothing more for her than ... than contempt. Or at the very least, indifference. Certainly he should have more self-control than to allow a woman's laughter to stir such a strong response. Particularly *this* young woman.

"I believe, Mr. Crawford, that I am mostly an open book." Her voice was soft, barely audible above the putter of the engine.

Her beauty was indisputable. In the short time he'd known her, he'd been captivated by her wit and charm — which she had in abundance. Even when he was angry because of her irresponsible portrayal of his grandfather in her silly little books, he'd found he still enjoyed her company. How could that be?

"Except for my writing, I've tried not to keep secrets."

He cleared his throat. "Wise words, indeed."

"I've learned keeping secrets can complicate one's life." She paused for a moment, then added, "And they often hurt those you love too."

Have you ever been in love, Miss McKinley? The question that popped into his head was not the kind a gentleman could ask aloud, but he wished he had the answer to it all the same.

❧

The necessity of backing an automobile up steep hillsides to avoid flooding the engine was both bothersome and time consuming, and it took them longer to reach Stone Creek than Daphne had expected. It was already suppertime when Joshua stopped the motorcar in front of the boarding house.

The proprietress of the Stone Creek Boarding House was

a Mrs. Hannigan, a plump, short, buxom woman with graying brown hair and a friendly smile. She took them straight to the dining room. "You'll be wanting to eat first, and I'll show you to your rooms when we're done."

Daphne would have loved a few minutes to freshen up, but it seemed she wasn't to have that option.

Mrs. Hannigan made quick introductions of the three other people at the table—her sixteen-year-old daughter, Fiona Hannigan; Mr. Pratt, a traveling salesman; and Miss Conner, who had come to Stone Creek to marry the manager of the bank. "And this is Miss McKinley and Mr. Crawford, who'll be with us for one night."

"How do you do," Daphne said with a nod to each person before slipping onto one of the empty chairs.

Joshua sat beside her.

"And what brings you and Mr. Crawford to Stone Creek?" Mr. Pratt passed Daphne a bowl of mashed potatoes.

She thought about her response for a moment, not certain how much she wanted to reveal to a perfect stranger.

Joshua answered before her. "I'm the editor of the Bethlehem Springs' newspaper, and I've come to interview two men about some early Idaho history. Miss McKinley writes a column for the *Triweekly Herald* and is along to observe."

Daphne couldn't decide if she should be irritated with Joshua for speaking when Mr. Pratt had addressed his question to her or if she should admire him for the careful yet truthful reply. She decided on the latter for the sake of peaceful coexistence.

As Joshua slid a slice of meatloaf from a platter onto his plate, he asked Mr. Pratt about the products he sold, and throughout the remainder of the meal, he peppered the others with questions, easily drawing out information from each one of them. It was quite the artful display. Daphne couldn't help but be impressed. He must have been a crackerjack reporter back in St. Louis. She had the feeling their interview with the Coughlin brothers wouldn't take long. Whatever they knew about Richard Terrell, Joshua would have it out of them quickly—and perhaps even more than they intended to tell.

And judging by the way Fiona Hannigan stared across the table at Joshua, she would have told him anything he wanted too. The girl wore a star-stuck expression. Dazzled no doubt by Joshua's charisma and good looks. Or maybe it was the intense blue of his eyes. Whenever he looked at Daphne, she felt—

No, she wouldn't allow her thoughts to go there again. In the weeks since she'd first seen Joshua Crawford in the South Fork Restaurant, she'd given far too much thought to his eyes. Of course it was only because she wanted to include a character with similar eyes in her book. Purely a literary interest. That was all.

⁂

September 9, 1872

Thanks be to God! Our daughter, Angelica Ruth, was delivered safely today. I would not have thought it possible that one glimpse at her beautiful little face would cause me to be overwhelmed by such indescribable joy. I am a father. I had a part in giving this child life. She is in my care. I am responsible for her well being, for her education, for helping her to know Christ from an early age. It is my duty to show her how to live a righteous and honorable life, to grow into a giving and caring young woman. It is not a charge I take lightly. May she never know what a wretched man her father was in the early years of his life.

Annie had a difficult time of it. The labor lasted more than forty-eight hours, and the doctor told me it would be unwise for her to have more children. He warned that another labor like this one might take her life and the life of the child too. I haven't had the heart to tell Annie that news yet. Tomorrow or the next day will be soon enough. I know she will be heartbroken, for she has spoken often throughout these months of wanting several children. Not impossible for a woman of thirty-six, but it appears now that it is not God's plan for us to have a full quiver. ("As arrows are in the hand of a mighty man; so are children of the youth. Happy is the man that hath his quiver full of them: they shall not be ashamed, but they shall speak with the enemies in the gate." Psalm 127:4–5)

During Annie's labor, while I waited, worried, and prayed, I thought of my parents. My mother was Annie's age when she died, my father just two years older. I had not considered before how young they were when their lives ended. But at least I know, now that I am in Christ, that I shall see them again. What a blessed hope that is.

TWELVE

Despite Joshua's hopes to the contrary, Daphne did not rest well. She tossed and turned much of the night and arose before dawn with a headache that pounded in her temples and made her eyes squint. She hoped a hot cup of tea would ease the pain. Otherwise, the long drive back to Bethlehem Springs would be a miserable one.

She was surprised to find Joshua already in the dining room when she entered it. Apparently she wasn't the only one who hadn't slept well.

"Morning," he said when he saw her.

"Good morning."

He pointed to the sideboard that held several covered plates and bowls. "Mrs. Hannigan said to help yourself."

Daphne's stomach rolled at the suggestion of food. She would begin with tea. A couple of minutes later, she sat at the table, holding a cup between both hands.

"Frank Coughlin said in his reply that we were welcome to call early this morning. If you think you can be ready—" He checked his pocket watch. "—I thought we would leave here at eight o'clock."

She took a sip of the hot beverage before answering, "I'll be ready whenever you say."

"It seems our drive back to Bethlehem Springs will be a cold one. The temperature dipped sharply during the night."

A headache *and* frigid weather. Oh, how she longed to be home in her own cozy cottage. She hoped Joshua's interview with the Coughlins wouldn't take long. At the moment, she couldn't care less what they had to say. She didn't care whether or not her portrayal of Rawhide Rick was accurate. She just wanted to go home.

She continued to take slow sips of tea, her gaze focused on the centerpiece on the table, a rather strange-looking glass object that seemed determined to worsen the pain behind her eyes.

"Are you feeling all right?"

She blinked, then looked at Joshua. "A bit tired is all."

He arched an eyebrow, as if to say he didn't believe her.

Forcing a smile, she said, "I'm not an early riser by nature." That wasn't entirely true. When she didn't write into the late hours of the night, she often rose before the sun.

"That's unfortunate. Morning is the best time of the day."

She shrugged and sipped more tea. If it weren't for this pain in her head, she would have gladly conversed with him.

"Well." He slid his chair back from the table. "I'll meet you at eight at the front door."

She nodded, knowing she must appear to be in a foul mood but unable to do anything about it. She could only hope the hot beverage would work its wonders before they called upon the Coughlin brothers.

⧼

Per Mrs. Hannigan's directions, Joshua turned the automobile left at the first street he came to and followed it north out of the small town of Stone Creek. Fifteen minutes later, he spied the single-story log house set back from the road, surrounded by lodgepole pines.

"There it is," he said to Daphne.

He slowed the motorcar and drove into the clearing in front of the cabin. As the engine fell silent, Joshua said a silent prayer, asking that truth would prevail during his meeting with Frank and Lawrence Coughlin. Then he and Daphne got out of the car and walked to the cabin's front door. His knock was answered after a few moments by a man with thinning white hair, pale blue eyes, weathered skin, and slightly hunched shoulders.

"Mr. Crawford?"

Joshua nodded. "Yes." He removed his hat. "And this is Miss McKinley. Her brother is Griff Arlington's son-in-law."

"Pleased to meet you both. I'm Frank Coughlin." He threw the door open wide. "Come in out of the cold and set yourself by the fire."

Joshua placed his hand in the small of Daphne's back, a brief touch that drew her gaze before she stepped away from him.

"This here's my brother Larry."

Lawrence Coughlin bore a strong resemblance to Frank, although he stood a few inches taller and his shoulders were unbent.

Joshua nodded at the other man. "I appreciate that you agreed to speak with us."

"Glad to have you," Lawrence Coughlin said as he motioned toward four chairs near the stone fireplace. "We don't get many visitors out this way. Besides, your message made us kind of curious. Nobody's asked us about Richard Terrell in more years than I can remember."

Daphne took the chair closest to the fireplace. Joshua sat beside her and the two Coughlin brothers quickly joined them in the other chairs.

Frank looked at Daphne. "How's Griff? We haven't seen him in ... What? Maybe twenty, twenty-five years. His girl Cleo was about seven or eight when we left Bethlehem Springs to come to Stone Creek to work. And she's your brother's wife. Imagine that."

"No." Daphne shook her head. "My brother is married to Cleo's sister, Gwen."

Lawrence rocked back in his chair and crossed his arms over his chest. "That's right. I remember now. Griff wrote us about it. Gwen came out from the East where she was livin' with her ma and ended up as mayor of Bethlehem Springs a few years back."

"Yes, that's right."

Joshua wanted to interrupt, to turn the conversation to the purpose for their visit, but he reined in his impatience. Better to let the Coughlins grow comfortable with him before he began quizzing them about his grandfather. He hadn't long to wait. After a few more questions concerning long time residents of Bethlehem Springs, most of which Daphne was able to answer, Frank Coughlin turned his gaze upon Joshua.

"So tell us what it is you want to know about Richard Terrell. Been a lot of years since he left Idaho. I didn't suppose anybody but us old-timers even remembered his name."

Joshua drew a deep breath. "I'm his grandson."

"You don't say." Frank and Lawrence exchanged looks of surprise. "Legitimate? Never would've expected Judge Terrell would get hitched. He didn't seem the kind."

Judge Terrell? Gregory Halifax had written in his article that Richard Terrell had been a judge, but Joshua had thought that was just more fiction. "Yes," he answered. "My grandfather married soon after moving to St. Louis."

"And he had children too. Never would've believed it."

"One child. My mother. After my father died, my grandfather helped raise me."

"Well, I'll be." Frank Coughlin shook his head slowly. "Just goes to show you never can tell what'll happen in the future."

A frown creased Lawrence's forehead. "I'm guessin' he passed away or you'd be askin' him whatever it is you want to know."

"He's been dead fourteen years now."

"Fourteen. Must seem a long time to somebody as young as you."

"Mr. Coughlin." Resting his forearms on knees, Joshua leaned forward and looked from Frank to Lawrence and back again. "There have been things written about my grandfather that simply don't seem possible. The man I knew, the man my mother knew, was a kind, caring, hardworking, and God-fearing individual. He cared for the less fortunate and did all he could to alleviate suffering wherever it existed." Joshua paused, searching for the right words. "But he was portrayed as a very different kind of man in some stories about the Old West that came to my attention a short while ago. I came to Idaho to discover the truth."

❧

Daphne saw the look that passed between the brothers, and she felt her heart sink. Joshua wasn't going to hear what he wanted about his grandfather. These men were about to confirm everything D. B. Morgan had written in The McFarland Chronicles. She could see it in their eyes. While a part of her was grateful to know she hadn't written falsehoods about Richard Terrell, another now larger part of her was heartsick for Joshua. This mattered to him a great deal. Far more than it mattered to her. A fact she found surprising. Hadn't she come with Joshua because she wanted to be vindicated?

"This might take a spell," Frank answered Joshua. "Why don't I pour us all some coffee? Miss McKinley looks like she's still feelin' a mite chilled."

She offered a brief smile; she was cold, despite the nearness of the fire on the hearth. "Thank you, Mr. Coughlin. I would be obliged."

The elder of the brothers rose and went into the kitchen, a smaller area off the parlor of the four-roomed log house. A few minutes later, he returned with mugs of coffee on a tray. He offered it first to Daphne, then Joshua and Lawrence, before settling onto his chair again.

"About my grandfather," Joshua said.

Frank nodded. "My brother and me was workin' in the mines back when Terrell first came to Bethlehem Springs. That was in —" He scratched his grizzled jaw. "— I reckon about sixty-six. The Boise Basin gold rush brought lots of men to Idaho durin' and after the Civil War. Men lookin' to make new lives for themselves after all that fightin' and destroyin'. That's what we were doin' too. Me and Larry."

Lawrence took over the narrative from his brother. "Richard Terrell came to Idaho from California, but he'd lived in the Oregon Territory twenty years before that. Came west on a wagon train. Did some buffalo huntin' and fur trappin'. That's where he came by the nickname of Rawhide Rick. Minin' in California. Gamblin' and who knew what all before he wound up in Bethlehem Springs, where he got himself appointed as judge."

Joshua shook his head. "He never mentioned to me that he'd been a judge."

"Yep. Served three years on the bench," Frank said. "And let me tell you, he wasn't the kind of judge you wanted presidin' over a case if'n you weren't rich."

"What are you implying?" Joshua's voice was hard.

Frank grunted. "Ain't implyin' nothing, Mr. Crawford. Sayin' it right out: if a man wanted justice, he needed to pay for it in Terrell's court."

"You got to remember somethin'," Lawrence added. "Bethlehem Springs—just like most towns that sprang up during the gold rush days—was a wild and lusty place. Plenty more saloons and gamblin' establishments than churches, that's for sure. Not many women—least not ladies like you, Miss McKinley. All the men carried guns, and they weren't shy about using them either. Vigilantes were quick to hang a man. Justice wasn't easy to come by, with or without gold linin' your pockets."

Frank took a long sip of coffee. "Your grandfather knew how to survive in such a place."

Daphne watched Joshua shake his head again, as if refusing to believe what the men had told him. Into the silence, she asked, "Did you know Mr. Terrell by more than reputation?"

"Yep," Lawrence answered. "Did some work for him on his place a time or two. And one thing was sure true of the man: he loved to tell his stories. If somebody was there to listen, he'd tell you all about the things he done and the places he'd been. Ain't that right, Frank?"

"That's right."

Lawrence continued, "Said he grew up in Missouri but left the farm when he was still a young pup. Fourteen, fifteen maybe. Made his way out west anyway he could. Survival of the fittest. Ain't that what they call it? I reckon he done whatever he had to to get by."

"He was right fond of telling the story about the time he killed a grizzly. Winter of 1848, I think he said it was."

Daphne smiled. Griff had told her that story, and she'd used it in her fourth book. She would love to know if she'd gotten the facts right. But now was not the time and this was not the day to ask.

Joshua stood. "Gentlemen, I thank you for sparing us the time, but I believe Miss McKinley and I should begin our drive back to Bethlehem Springs. If I have more questions, perhaps you would be so good as to answer them in a letter."

"Sure thing. We could do that." Frank rose to his feet as well. "But it seems you came a long way just to hear the little we've told you."

Daphne happened to agree with Frank. She could think of another dozen or so questions to ask about Richard Terrell. But one glance at Joshua silenced them in her head. He was in no mood to listen to whatever else the Coughlins had to say.

After quick handshakes and another word of thanks, Joshua headed for the door.

Daphne wondered if he would leave without her if she didn't follow at once. Taking no chances, she stood. "Thank you, Mr. Coughlin." She nodded to Frank. "Mr. Coughlin." She nodded to Lawrence. "You've been very kind."

"Our pleasure." Frank walked beside her. "Give Griff our regards, you hear?"

"I will."

A blast of cold air struck her in the face when Joshua opened the door, but he didn't wait for her before striding toward the automobile.

~

A man could change. Coming to Christ caused a man to be born again, to be raised up new in the Lord. Changed forever. But even when Joshua acknowledged that truth, he couldn't reconcile the Richard Terrell of the Coughlin brothers' memories — and the one of D. B. Morgan's books — to the Richard Terrell he'd known as a boy. It simply wasn't possible that his grandfather had done those things, had lived that kind of life.

Perhaps his grandfather had gone west on a wagon train as a young man. Perhaps he'd even hunted buffalo and panned for gold in California and Idaho. But a dishonest judge? It stretched the boundaries of believability to the breaking point.

I came here for the truth. This can't be the truth.

Neither Daphne nor Joshua said a word as he drove the motor-car into Stone Creek. At the boarding house, they stopped for their bags as well as the lunch Joshua had paid Mrs. Hannigan to pack for them. They were on the road again fifteen minutes later.

Thankfully, Daphne seemed inclined to leave him to his own thoughts. Thoughts as dark as the steadily darkening sky.

THIRTEEN

Daphne awoke with a start, feeling disoriented and confused, her body aching from head to toe. She heard the wind blowing before she realized the motorcar's engine was silent. They were stopped in the middle of the road, and Joshua was no longer behind the steering wheel.

How long had she been asleep? A quick glance at her watch told her it wasn't yet noon.

She straightened and looked about, only then realizing how dark it had become. Clouds hung low over the mountains, turning the world the color of slate. She shivered. It was unbelievably cold inside the automobile.

Where's Joshua?

As the question passed through her mind, he appeared over the edge of the road, climbing up an embankment. He walked straight to the passenger door and opened it. "Good. You're awake."

"Why have we stopped?"

"There's something wrong with the car, and you're too sick to stay out here while I figure out what."

Sick? Why would he say that? She'd fallen asleep, was all.

"I found shelter down below. There's a cabin near the creek. Can you walk?"

What a ridiculous question. Of course she could walk.

"Come on." He took hold of her arm. "We'll take it slow."

She stood ... and immediately crumpled to the ground. A moment later she was cradled in Joshua's arms, her head upon his chest.

"You're burning up. We need to get you inside."

Who was he talking to? If it was her, he was crazy. She wasn't burning up. She was freezing half to death, so cold she couldn't keep her teeth from chattering. Each step he took jarred her bones, made her muscles ache more than before, caused her head to swim. She clasped her hands behind his neck and held on tightly lest she plummet into some black abyss.

Cold. She was so terribly cold.

⁂

The fire Joshua had started in the wood stove before returning to the stalled automobile hadn't begun to warm the one-room cabin yet. After setting Daphne on the tick mattress and covering her with his coat, he checked to make sure the fire hadn't gone out, then headed back to the motorcar for the lap blanket, the lunch Mrs. Hannigan had prepared, and their satchels. Later he would have to see if he could ascertain why the automobile had died, but he held out little hope of success. He had few mechanical skills.

But that wasn't his first concern. He was far more worried about Daphne. He should have guessed she wasn't feeling well. She hadn't been her vivacious self when they were at breakfast or later with the Coughlins. If he'd known she was ill, he might have suggested they stay in Stone Creek another night or two.

This time when he returned to the cabin, the fire had taken some of the chill from the room. But Daphne was shivering even harder than before. He placed his hand on her forehead. He'd never touched anyone who felt this hot.

A shudder passed through him. Not from the cold but from a recent news report that had said nearly two hundred thousand Americans had fallen victim to Spanish flu during the previous month. Larger cities had seen three hundred, five hundred, even eight hundred people die in a single day.

Did Daphne have the Spanish influenza? God help her if she did. God help them both. He began to pray hard as he laid the blanket he'd brought from the car over her. She stirred, her eyes fluttering but never opening, and then she rolled onto her left side and curled into a fetal position, still shivering. She mumbled something unintelligible.

He leaned closer. "What do you need, Daphne?"

She didn't answer.

A feeling of helplessness washed over Joshua. He had little experience with sick people. Even his grandfather had remained hale and hearty until almost the last day of his life. As for himself, Joshua was healthy as a horse. Rarely even had so much as a head cold.

He racked his brain for what he'd learned about influenza in recent months. The disease was most dangerous to the young and the elderly. However, the Spanish flu had also proven deadly to those in the prime of life, people in their twenties and thirties—people like Daphne. Since the first outbreak in the spring of that year, hundreds of thousands around the world had died from it, although because of the war it was hard to get the full truth about the pandemic. Government censors and all that.

He rose from the side of the cot and began a more in-depth exploration of the cabin. In one cabinet there were cooking and eating utensils, a few pots and pans, and mismatched plates, bowls, and cups. In another he found food supplies—canned and dried goods. In a large trunk he discovered bedding and, in a smaller one, men's and women's clothing. There was a box on a table with some bandages, ointment, hydrogen peroxide, and other first-aid items. Several fishing poles were leaned in a corner.

A fine layer of dust covered everything indoors, but it was obvious the cabin hadn't been abandoned. Perhaps the people who owned it came into the mountains from Boise or another town to the south for several weeks or even a couple of months in the summer. The owners must not worry about others using it, for he'd found a key to the door without difficulty. Thank God for that. The little house would keep them warm and fed until they were able to travel again. He hoped that would be soon.

~

Her throat was on fire. Her body ached. Every joint. Every muscle. The backs of her eyelids felt like sandpaper. She couldn't stop shivering, despite the blankets that covered her. Heavy blankets, a weight that seemed to crush her bones.

A few times she thought she heard what seemed like familiar voices, but the words were indistinguishable. Once she cried out, "Mother!" Even as she said the name, she knew it wasn't possible. Her mother was dead ...

Maybe so was she.

~

The wind came first, whistling through the canyon and slamming into the sturdy log cabin. Then, just before nightfall, the wind silenced and it began to snow. Large lazy flakes at first, followed by smaller ones that fell in a dense curtain to the ground.

Joshua stood at the window, wondering how long it would last. He'd counted on someone seeing their stalled automobile on the road and looking inside where he'd left a note, giving their location. But how much traffic did this mountainous route see in the winter? Not much, he'd wager. And even less when the snows came.

He turned, his gaze moving to the bed where Daphne lay shivering and moaning. The soft sounds that escaped her throat were torture to hear. He wanted to help ease her misery, but he didn't know how to do that beyond applying cold compresses to her forehead in an effort to bring down her fever.

He prayed she'd told her brother or sister-in-law where they were going and when they would return. If so, someone ought to come looking for them within a day or two. If not? That didn't bear thinking about.

He returned to the stove, opened the front, and put in more wood. Then he crossed to the tall table under the far window and poured creek water he'd boiled earlier into a cup. Returning to the cot, he sat on the edge and lifted Daphne's head with one hand while holding the cup to her lips with the other.

"Drink, Daphne."

She tried to turn her head away.

"Just a few sips. Come on. You need to drink at least a little."

Her eyes fluttered open and she looked at him. "Where are we?" she whispered at last.

He put the cup against her lips again. "Sip."

This time she obeyed.

"We're in a cabin maybe a quarter mile from the road. We're about halfway between Stone Creek and Bethlehem Springs. At least I think so."

His words were wasted. Her eyes had closed before he'd finished answering her question.

❧

It snowed for days. It snowed so much, it buried the automobile. Not that it mattered. The road saw no traffic. There was no one going or coming who would have discovered the motorcar even if it were in plain view.

But the blizzard wasn't Joshua's first concern. He was more afraid that Daphne would die here in this cabin, far from friends and family. Her illness had left her weak and listless. Sometimes she talked nonsense, muttering to herself or perhaps to someone she thought was there. Other times she barely seemed to breathe.

On their first day in the cabin, seeing no other option — he was the only one who could care for her — Joshua had set aside worries about modesty and had removed her clothes down to her undergarments. He'd bathed her brow, her cheeks, and her throat with cool water. He'd piled more blankets on top of her when she'd shivered so hard it seemed the log house would fall down around their ears from the shaking. He'd encouraged her to drink. He'd encouraged her to eat. She'd done little of either. There had been times during the first two days of her illness when her breathing was so labored, so torturous, it had been agony to listen to it. He'd been certain the sound was what doctors called the *death rattle*, and the certainty had terrified him. Would he have to bury Daphne McKinley in a shallow grave, the ground too frozen to do more than that? Would he have to be the one who related her last hours to her family?

Even now, days later, he feared that would be their fate — her to die, him to live with her death on his hands. And so he gathered her into his arms, as he had done numerous times during her illness, and held her close to his chest. Placing his lips against her dark tangle of hair, he whispered, "Don't die, Miss McKinley. Live. Please God, help her live."

⚘

October 1, 1872

Annie is fully recovered from childbirth, and Angelica Ruth — our little angel — is thriving. She has become the center of our universe.

*I left off the story of my life while I was still in California.
It is time I resumed putting it to paper.*

*For ten years I owned the Golden Nugget and added
numerous other businesses as well. I began to educate myself,
although at first it was without purpose beyond wanting
to prove myself smarter than the next man. But eventually
I read for the law. I grew wealthier than I ever dreamed
I might, but I took little pleasure in all I acquired. I was
restless and looking for something that would ease my
dissatisfaction. I looked in the wrong places for an answer to
my discontentment.*

*When news arrived of a gold strike in what would soon
become the Idaho Territory, I felt a strange longing to return. I
even thought of looking for Gemma Picard when I got there—
not that I believed she would still be waiting for me in that old
cabin we'd shared. It had been thirteen years since I left her
for the promises of riches in California.*

*I sold the Golden Nugget and my other properties,
including a mercantile and a bank, and I headed north.
Certainly I was going back to the high country in better style
than I had traveled on my way to California. I no longer wore
tanned animal skins for my clothes. My suits were tailored, my
shoes of the best quality. For all appearances sake, I was a man
of quality and some importance. Inside, I know now, I was a
man consumed by the maggots of sin.*

*I settled in West Bannock in the very heart of gold
country. Two years later, the town was rechristened Idaho
City. It was a bawdy place where whiskey was cheaper than
water. Just the sort of place where men like me belonged. But*

again, I wasn't there to pan for gold. I was there to take the gold from others the easiest way I knew how. Before I left Idaho City, I owned four of the eventual forty-one saloons that sprang up. Two of mine had fancy billiard rooms. I also had my own law office. For a while, I thought the place might end up with more lawyers than all the other laborers added together because there was plenty of call for them. All of the law offices were kept busy with disputes over mining claims.

The year before I left Idaho City, a fire destroyed eighty percent of the buildings. I was one of the lucky twenty-percent. My home and businesses survived unscathed, and during the time it took folks to rebuild the many other saloons, mercantiles, breweries, barber shops, dress shops, bakeries, livery stables, banks, and drug stores, I made another small fortune.

And it got me to thinking about how much competition there was in Idaho City. I decided that another place might suit me better. A town where they had fewer lawyers and definitely fewer saloons.

In 1866, at the age of forty-five, I sold everything once again, making another tidy profit, and moved to Bethlehem Springs, Idaho. It would prove a life-altering decision.

FOURTEEN

Daphne felt as if she were crawling up from a bottomless pit. When she opened her eyes, she found the room dark. Black as ink and eerily silent. Not a sound disturbed the stillness.

Where was she? She couldn't seem to recall, but she was certain she wasn't home in her cozy bedroom. Something was different. Quite different.

That's when she felt it. Warm air upon her neck.

She rolled her head to the side on the pillow — and came nose to nose with ... with someone. She sucked in a breath of surprise.

It came back to her then, little by little. Stone Creek. The Coughlin brothers. She'd taken sick on the drive back to Bethlehem Springs. Cold. Such unbelievable cold. A cup of water to her lips. A bite of fruit from a spoon. Joshua, always nearby. Joshua's touch. Joshua's voice.

His breathing changed slightly, and she knew he'd awakened, that he was looking at her.

"Where ... are we?" she whispered.

"I'm not sure. We hadn't yet reached the main road to Bethlehem Springs when the motorcar broke down."

"Broke down? I ... don't remember that. I've been ... ill, haven't I?"

"Yes."

He didn't need to tell her that it had been serious. She felt it all through her body.

"I'll fix you something to eat. You need nourishment." He rolled away from her and rose from the bed.

It was only then she realized he hadn't been beneath the blankets. At least not the one that was closest to her skin.

Her skin?

She drew her hand from her side and touched her collarbone, then drew her fingers downward until they touched the fabric of her chemise. She had no recollection of removing her outer garments. Was it possible Joshua Crawford had undressed her before putting her into this bed? Heat rose in her cheeks. Of course it was possible. He'd taken care of her. For how long she couldn't say. One day. Two days. Five days.

Rather than contemplate the possibilities of what his care had entailed, she asked, "Whose house is this?"

Joshua opened the door to the stove and shoved in more wood. Sparks flew upward, and the fire cast an orange light into the darkened room.

"Joshua?"

He turned toward her, his face captured in the firelight.

"Whose house is this?"

"I don't know. Someone's summer place. It's a cabin below the road. I found the key to the door on the front porch."

She closed her eyes, too weary to keep them open any longer. "Will they find us?"

"Don't worry. We won't be here much longer."

She wondered, as she drifted back to sleep, if he was as sure as he sounded.

The sun came out the next morning, beaming down through frosted trees, turning the snow a blinding white. But there was no warmth in the golden rays. When Joshua went outside to bring in more wood, his breath froze in a white cloud before his face. The cold nipped his nose and made his jaw ache. The snow on the ground was as high as the raised porch in front of the cabin. Deeper where the wind had blown it into drifts.

How long before the road was passable, he wondered. How long before Daphne's family sent someone to look for her? He prayed it would be soon. Although the worst seemed to be over, she wasn't out of danger yet. She needed a doctor. She needed better food. She needed better care than he could give her.

And I need someone else to care for her.

Something had happened in Joshua as he'd nursed Daphne through the worst of her illness. Things had been tense between them ever since he'd deduced she was D. B. Morgan, but it was difficult to remain angry with her while at the same time praying for God's mercy, while asking for healing, for a miracle. It was good that the anger was gone, but he didn't want to feel anything for her beyond Christian compassion. Certainly not anything . . . tender.

With a sigh, he carried the wood inside and dropped it into the box near the stove. When he turned, he found Daphne awake again and sitting up in bed for the first time since he'd laid her on it nearly a week before. Her fingers clutched the blanket beneath her throat.

"What day is it?" she asked, her voice soft and scratchy.

"Tuesday."

"I've been sick that long?"

He nodded as he took a couple of steps toward the bed. "Yes."

"What . . . what was wrong with me?"

"I think you've had the Spanish influenza."

Small patches of pink appeared in her cheeks, color in a face that had been deathly pale only moments before. "You've cared for me this whole time?"

"Yes."

The flush in her cheeks deepened as her gaze lowered to the blanket covering her.

"There was no one else to attend to you, Miss McKinley. I promise, your honor has not been compromised."

She looked at him again. "You mistake my silence. I ... I'm very grateful for your care, and I don't doubt you behaved as a gentleman at all times."

True enough. He'd taken no liberties. But now that the risk of her dying seemed behind them, he felt a troubling desire to take her in his arms again — in a much different way than before. Look at her! Dark hair tumbled over her shoulders, thick and unruly. Her chocolate-colored eyes seemed to hold a world of wonderful secrets in their depths. And the cabin suddenly felt too small and too warm.

He turned on his heel and crossed to a large trunk that held blankets, sheets, and towels. From it, he withdrew a bright, multi-colored blanket that he'd spotted several days ago. Then he grabbed the broom from a corner in the kitchen area and took it and the blanket outside without a word of explanation to Daphne. It was better this way. He didn't trust himself to speak to her.

Making his way through the snow up to the road was an arduous task. Every few steps, he broke through the crusty surface and sank to his thighs. What he wouldn't give for a pair of snowshoes. His breathing became labored, and although the air was cold, sweat beaded his forehead by the time he reached the automobile. He could barely make out its shape beneath the heavy snow.

After a few moments rest, he drove the broom handle into the snow near what he presumed to be the front of the motorcar. With both hands and feet, he packed the snow around the handle in the hopes it would remain upright until someone came looking for them. Finally, he tied the colorful blanket to the top of the broom.

As he straightened, his gaze looked west, then east. *Send someone soon, God. I need them here soon.*

❧

Exhaustion forced Daphne to slide down on the bed even as mortification burned hot in her chest. She had only a hazy memory of the details of the past several days, yet she understood Joshua had to have helped her in ways no man should help a woman who wasn't his wife. Knowing that, how on earth was she to bear being in his presence from here on out?

Stomping sounds from the porch alerted her to his return moments before the door opened, giving him entry. Daphne closed her eyes and feigned sleep, scarcely daring to draw a breath until she heard him walk to the opposite side of the one-room cabin. She opened her eyes again, but just enough to look at him through her lashes. His back was to her, so she opened her eyes a little more, watching as he took a bowl from a nearby cupboard and set it on the raised table. He took a jar from another cupboard—peaches, she guessed, judging by the color of the contents.

Then he paused, the heels of his wrists resting on the edge of the table, and he lowered his head. There was something about his shoulders that bespoke of weariness, helplessness, perhaps even hopelessness. She felt a strange need to rise and offer him comfort. But the simple act of pushing herself up into a sitting position for the second time sapped what little energy she had.

"Mr. Crawford."

He straightened and turned to face her.

"Are you well?"

"I'm fine, Miss McKinley." He motioned to the table behind him. "Can you try to eat something?"

She didn't have an appetite, but it would seem ungrateful to refuse. After all, it seemed she owed him her life. "I'll try."

"Good. We've got peaches, and I can cook some oatmeal too."

"The peaches should suffice."

"You need more than that. You haven't eaten more than a few bites since we left Stone Creek."

"All right." She offered a brief smile. "I'll try to eat some oatmeal too."

He returned the smile before making himself busy.

Daphne watched in silence as he prepared the oatmeal in a pot on the stove, not speaking again until he carried a tray to the bed and sat in the chair beside her. "Who taught you to cook, Mr. Crawford?"

"My grandfather." He set the tray on her lap. "He was a man of many talents."

"And interests."

"What do you mean?"

She shook her head, regretting her words. Why had she brought it up? After all he'd done for her . . .

"Ah, you mean the things you wrote about him."

"I'm sorry. I shouldn't have —"

"No, it's all right, Miss McKinley. I've had plenty of time to think things over, and while I don't believe my grandfather was the sort of man you portrayed in your books, it does seem there were things he didn't choose to share about his past. At least not with me. As much as I hate to admit it, he seems to have been a different man when he lived in Idaho."

"I'm sorry," she repeated.

Pointing at the tray, he said, "Please. Eat."

Obediently, she dipped the spoon into the oatmeal and raised it to her lips. The cereal needed milk and some honey to make it taste good, but she was determined to eat as much of it as possible as a way of showing her gratitude.

Joshua rose from the chair and walked to the window by the front door. "I wish you could have met him, Miss McKinley. I never knew Grandfather to see a need in another that he didn't try to meet. We weren't wealthy by any stretch of the imagination, but he always found a way to give to others." He clasped his hands behind his back as he looked out the window. "You know the many ways the Bible tells us to live as Christians? Abhorring evil. Cleaving to what's good. Being kind to another with brotherly love. Being patient in tribulation. Praying without ceasing. Distributing to the necessity of the saints. Being hospitable. Rejoicing with those who rejoice and weeping with those who weep. In everything giving thanks. Richard Terrell embodied those traits. Those and so much more."

The oatmeal seemed to have stuck in Daphne's throat, making it impossible to reply.

"I have a hard time reconciling that godly man with the Richard Terrell the Coughlins knew or the one you portrayed in your books."

She couldn't help remembering what he'd said to her before they'd made the trip to Stone Creek: *Words have power, Miss McKinley. Even words in a novel. You may think your stories are simply for entertainment, but they still have the power to build up or tear down.*

I'm sorry. Tears welled. *I never meant to harm anyone with my stories.*

Many years before, when Daphne had been caught in a tall

tale, her mother had said something similar: *"What we say, my child, has an impact on those around us. Words can spread darkness and hate or shed light and love. Don't misuse them, Daphne."*

She'd wanted the Coughlin brothers to prove what she'd written was true, and that's what had happened. But being right, she was discovering, wasn't always enough.

And being right didn't always make a person feel good either.

❧

That night, Joshua bedded down on the floor on the opposite side of the wood stove. It wasn't likely Daphne would need his help—or his body heat—as she had in the worst hours of her illness, and it was his wish to give her as much privacy as possible now that she was on the mend.

Sleep didn't come easy. He told himself it was the hardness of the floorboards, but the truth was it bothered him that he couldn't hear her soft breathing, that he wasn't able to reach out and touch her forehead to see if it was feverish. What if her condition took a sharp turn for the worst? It took great willpower to remain on the floor, to resist the urge to rise and go to her bedside, if only for a few moments.

A log shifted in the stove, and the pipe echoed with the flurried sounds of sparks striking metal. Joshua rolled onto his side and watched the dancing orange light that slipped around the edges of the iron door.

The temptation wasn't simply to go to her bedside to check on her health, and he knew it. Earlier today he'd ceased thinking of Daphne McKinley as someone in need of care and had started thinking of her as a woman, a beautiful woman alone with him in a remote, snowed-in cabin.

There hath no temptation taken you but such as is common to man: but God is faithful, who will not suffer you to be tempted above that ye are able; but will with the temptation also make a way to escape, that ye may be able to bear it.

Joshua closed his eyes and prayed that God would make that way of escape available soon because he wasn't sure how many more nights like this he could take.

FIFTEEN

Behind a curtain that Joshua had rigged to allow Daphne a measure of privacy, she gave herself a sponge bath. She longed to wash her hair as well, but such a luxury would have to wait until she was home again. God willing, that wouldn't be too long.

From the other side of the curtain, she heard the crackle of the fire in the stove and the sizzle of meat warming in a frying pan. Joshua had told her it was the last of the tinned beef in the cupboard. After it was gone, they would have to make do with the canned fruit and vegetables — which were also in dwindling supply. Not that she cared that much for herself. She hadn't much of an appetite yet.

A fit of coughing overtook her. Tears ran from her eyes as she bent over at the waist, wondering if she might suffocate before she could draw another decent breath.

"Miss McKinley?"

She didn't answer. Couldn't answer.

"Daphne?"

From the sound of his voice, she guessed he now stood just on the other side of the curtain. Feeling exposed, she grabbed her blouse and managed to slip it on over her chemise, coughing all the while.

"Do you need some water?"

"Please," she answered at last, her voice soft and hoarse.

He didn't move away at once. She knew he didn't because she could see his shoes beneath the blanket that separated her space from his. Her fingers fumbled with the closure of her blouse, not managing the small round buttons until she saw Joshua's feet turn away.

Mercy! This cabin felt altogether too small. And as her health improved, little by little, and as she remembered more of the days and nights of her illness, the smaller the cabin became. Joshua had taken good care of her, and she was grateful to him. All the same, no one outside of her mother or her nanny had nursed her through sickness the way he had. Certainly no other man—not even her father—had seen her in such a state of undress. She understood that their confinement and her illness hadn't given Joshua Crawford any other options, but that didn't alleviate her embarrassment.

She suppressed the groan that rose in her throat as she stepped into her skirt and fastened it at the waist. Rather than sinking onto the edge of the bed as she wanted, she moved to the makeshift curtain and slid the blanket to one side.

Joshua had returned with the glass of water. He held it toward her, a smile of encouragement on his lips. She couldn't help but return the smile as she reached for the glass.

"Better?" he asked.

She nodded, then took a sip of water.

"I think there's a little more color in your face today."

"I'm feeling stronger." That was stretching the truth, but she didn't want him to feel obliged to continue to wait on her every need.

His single cocked eyebrow told her he knew she wasn't being one hundred percent honest.

Carrying the glass of water, she walked to the stove and sat on a nearby chair.

"Ready to eat?" he asked.

"Yes."

He retrieved the pitcher, washbasin, cloth, and towel from beside the bed and carried them to the kitchen area. After setting them on the table beneath the window, he dished up the food he'd prepared—pan-warmed slices of tinned beef, a bowl of applesauce, and a cup of black coffee—and brought the meal to the dining table. As she turned her chair around, he settled on its mate.

"Aren't you eating too?"

"In a minute."

She wanted to tell him to quit watching her so intently, but it seemed easier to lower her own gaze to the food set before her. She picked up the fork and took a tentative bite. The meat was too salty, but at least it had flavor.

⁓

It surprised Joshua, the pleasure he took in watching her eat, the relief he felt over the fresh hint of color in her cheeks and the new sparkle in her eyes. Silently he thanked God one more time for sparing her life, as well as for keeping him in good health. The ending could have so easily gone another way.

Not that they were out of danger yet. There was still the matter of being found before they ran out of food to eat. He would have to trust God for that, for he was helpless to do anything about it himself. His grandfather had said that was always the best place to be. At the end of oneself was the best place to discover the Lord at work.

What he wouldn't give to be able to talk to the old man again. Not just to clear up the questions about his past either. Joshua could have used his grandfather's wisdom in several different areas of his life—work, love, faith, family. Not all that long ago, he'd felt he was on the right path. But now?

"A penny for your thoughts."

He blinked, surprised that his attention had drifted so far from the present.

"Where did you go?"

He answered with a shrug.

She glanced down at her bowl, moving the spoon through the applesauce in small circles. "This experience will give both of us something to write about, once we're back in Bethlehem Springs."

That was putting a good light on their situation, he thought. "I believe you're an optimist, Miss McKinley."

She smiled briefly, her gaze meeting his again. "Yes, I suppose I am. I get that from my mother. She always saw the cup as half full, even in her darkest days."

"Do you favor her in other ways?"

"Some. Not as much as I would like. She was a beautiful woman. Very striking."

"Then you favor her more than you think." He spoke the compliment before he had a chance to wonder at the wisdom of it.

Her cheeks grew rosy and her gaze lowered.

The temptation to rise and draw her into his embrace was nearly irresistible. He would just about give his right arm to kiss her lips, to drink in her sweetness, to lose himself in the soft curves of her body. Reasons existed why he shouldn't do anything of the kind, but at the moment he couldn't remember what they were.

God, help me.

❦

His desperate prayer was answered the next day. He was outside, chopping more wood for the stove, his fingers stiff with the cold, when he heard someone shouting their names.

"Daphne! Joshua!"

A man's voice. It sounded like Morgan McKinley.

"Daphne! Joshua!"

Joshua dropped the ax and struggled through the snow to the porch. "Down here! We're here!" He yanked open the front door and looked in at Daphne. "They've found us." He closed the door again. "Down here!"

A moment later, Morgan appeared at the road's edge. Joshua whipped off his hat and waved it madly.

Morgan turned and called something Joshua couldn't make out. A short while later, he was joined by another man and a woman, and the threesome started down the hillside toward the cabin. As they came closer, Joshua recognized Morgan's companions as Woody and Cleo Statham.

"Thank God you've found us," he called to them.

"Where's Daphne?"

"Inside. She's been ill."

Morgan exchanged a glance with his sister-in-law.

"Don't worry. She's out of danger." Joshua took a step back as the others arrived at the porch.

Morgan didn't waste time asking more questions. He quickly went inside. Joshua waited for Cleo and Woody to follow Morgan before he brought up the rear. Already, Morgan was at his sister's bedside, kneeling on the floor, holding both of her hands in his.

"We've been worried half to death. And now I'm told you've been ill."

"I'm all right," Daphne answered him with a smile. "Truly, I am." She glanced toward Joshua, then back at her brother. "Mr.

Crawford found this cabin after Mack broke down, and we've had food and water and plenty of firewood to keep us warm."

Joshua had a feeling that Morgan wouldn't accept such a simple reply. He didn't seem the sort of man to be easily fooled, not even by his lovely younger sister. The hard questions would be sent in Joshua's direction, not Daphne's.

"Next time you leave town, dear girl, I expect you to let me know where you're going and when you'll return. If it weren't for Mrs. Patterson, we wouldn't have had a clue where to start looking for you."

Daphne leaned over to kiss her brother on the cheek. "Don't scold me today, Morgan. Wait until we're back in Bethlehem Springs and I'm feeling stronger. Then you can say all you like to me, and I'll listen to every word."

"She's right, you big lug." Cleo moved to the other side of the bed and sat on the edge. "Leave her be. Can't you see she's weak as a kitten." She squeezed Daphne's left hand between both of hers.

As he rose to his feet, Morgan's gaze met with Joshua's.

Joshua motioned with his head toward the kitchen table. A moment later, he settled onto one of the hard-backed chairs and waited for Morgan to do the same in the other.

"What's been wrong with her?" her brother asked in a low voice.

"My guess is the Spanish influenza."

"And you?"

Joshua shook his head. "No signs of me getting sick with it."

"Well, thank God for that."

"What about others in Bethlehem Springs? Has there been an outbreak?"

"As far as I know, no one's been ill with the flu in town."

Joshua felt a rush of relief. Good to know they weren't facing a local epidemic.

Morgan looked around the cabin. "How did you find this place?"

"Providence. The motorcar broke down straight up the path from it. Before the snowstorm started, it was easily visible from the road. Your sister was already running a high fever by then. Even if I'd known how to repair the car . . ." He allowed his words to drift into silence.

"What were the two of you thinking? Winter comes suddenly in these mountains. What if you hadn't found this cabin? The both of you would have frozen to death in that automobile."

Joshua could have made excuses for himself, could have said that driving the touring car had been Daphne's idea, that he'd wanted to take the train, that he hadn't even wanted her to accompany him on the trip. He swallowed back the words. He deserved whatever dressing down Morgan decided to give him.

But apparently Daphne's brother thought better of doing so here. Instead he walked back to the bed. "Do you feel able to travel? I'd like to get you home before the weather turns ugly again."

"I can travel, Morgan. I'm stronger than I look."

SIXTEEN

At Daphne's insistence, the rescue party stopped at Doc Winston's office before taking her to Morgan's home. Only after the physician promised she was no longer contagious was she willing to stay with her brother and his family, even for one night.

It was Doc Winston who told her the Spanish flu had spread across Idaho at a rapid rate in the past two weeks, shutting down schools, movie theaters, and churches. Authorities continued to stress there was no need for panic, but many communities were frightened. As it seemed they should be. The death rate in some towns was as high as fifty percent. But they had been fortunate in Bethlehem Springs. The worst of the pandemic seemed to have past them by.

As with many survivors of the Spanish flu, Daphne's convalescence was protracted, her weakness and general fatigue lingering for what seemed an eternity. And with each passing day, she grew a little more depressed. The malaise settled around her like a gray cloak, making her world seem grim, cold, and lifeless. Not even knowing that a ceasefire in the Great War had taken effect and that troops were being withdrawn on the Western Front lifted her spirits.

She thought on occasion of the novel her publisher awaited—the one that was only half written—but such thoughts failed to stir her to action, failed to entice her to take up her pen again. Nor did they make her wish to leave her brother's home for her own cozy cottage on Wallula Street. She hadn't the energy or the will to leave.

It was a cold but sunny day, shortly before Thanksgiving, when Joshua Crawford called upon her. She was reclining on the sofa in the front parlor, her legs draped with a blanket, watching the fire flickering in the fireplace, when she heard his voice in the entry. In response, she felt an odd quickening in her chest. A moment later, Gwen appeared in the parlor doorway, Joshua by her side.

"Look who's come to visit you," Gwen said, her smile bright.

It was as if Daphne's heart had begun to beat again after too many days of quiet.

"Miss McKinley." Joshua crossed the room to the sofa. "I'm sorry to learn you haven't returned to your usual good health as yet."

"Thank you, Mr. Crawford." She'd missed him, she realized — and wondered why it had taken so long for him to come to see her.

He settled onto a nearby chair.

"And you've been well?" she asked. A silly question. He looked wonderful.

"Yes, I've been well. But Stone Creek wasn't as lucky as Bethlehem Springs. Did you hear?"

She shook her head.

"Quite a few deaths reported. Twenty, last I heard. Mrs. Hannigan from the boarding house and her daughter were among them. That must have been where you contracted it. The incubation period's fast with this flu."

Daphne covered her mouth with her hand. What if she and Joshua had made it back to Bethlehem Springs that first day? What if she'd exposed Morgan and his family to the disease before she'd known she was ill? Oh, she never would have forgiven herself if anything had happened to them because of her actions.

"I'm sorry, Miss McKinley. I didn't mean to cause you distress." He moved as if to rise. "Perhaps I should go."

She reached out a hand toward him. "No. Please. You haven't distressed me. Truly."

"Well ... if you're sure." He settled back in the chair. "I did wish to speak with you."

"Yes?"

"I wondered if you felt up to writing your column for the newspaper again. You're a welcome voice for our readers, and they've missed seeing it in their Monday papers these last three weeks."

Daphne suspected Joshua of exaggeration. After all, she'd only written two columns for the paper before she'd fallen victim to the Spanish influenza. Readers of the *Herald* couldn't possibly have become accustomed to it, at least not enough to miss it.

"The *Herald*'s received a number of letters in response to your last column." He reached into his breast pocket and withdrew some envelopes. "I brought them for you to read. Perhaps they'll give you some ideas."

She accepted the proffered envelopes.

"What do you say?" he persisted, leaning toward her. "Are you ready to write for me again?" He grinned.

She felt so strange all of a sudden. The room seemed to spin, and her heart had begun to flutter as rapidly as a hummingbird's wings. An unwelcome memory flitted through her mind. A memory of the morning she'd awakened to find Joshua asleep beside her on the small bed in the cabin, his breath warm upon her neck. There had been nothing improper about it, and yet ...

"Thank you, Miss McKinley."

She wished he would call her Daphne, as he'd done a few times when they were trapped in that cabin. Calling her Miss McKinley seemed so formal now.

He stood. "I look forward to receiving your column this Friday."

"This Friday," she echoed softly.

He looked as if there was more he wanted to say to her. There was something in his eyes, something about the set of his mouth. She found herself holding her breath. But in the end, he only gave his head a nod before turning and striding toward the entry.

Daphne lay back on the sofa, trying to quiet the odd sensations churning inside her.

⤗

Gwen McKinley smiled at Joshua as she handed him his hat and coat. "Thank you for doing this, Mr. Crawford," she said in a near whisper. "We've been quite worried about our dear Daphne. Her spirits have been low, and that's completely unlike her."

He remembered suggesting Daphne was an optimist and her agreeing with him, saying she got it from her mother. "I'm glad I could be of service, Mrs. McKinley." He set his hat on his head. "I hope her writing will do the trick." He reached for the door.

"Mr. Crawford, have you plans for Thanksgiving?"

"Plans?" He shook his head.

"Then would you be good enough to dine with us?"

"I wouldn't want to put you out."

She laughed softly. "Don't be silly, sir. You will be just one of several guests in our home for the holiday. Hardly an imposition. We have so much to be thankful for, having our Daphne returned to us safely and the rest of the family in good health. And you're responsible for saving Daphne's life. How could we not include you?"

Gwen McKinley's effusive words made Joshua uncomfortable. Yes, he'd cared for Daphne through the worst of her illness, but if he hadn't allowed her to go with him to Stone Creek, she wouldn't have fallen ill in the first place. If he hadn't been so set on proving her wrong, she wouldn't have had cause for wanting to accompany him.

"Please join us, Mr. Crawford." Gwen placed her fingers lightly on the back of his hand. "No one should be alone on Thanksgiving Day."

There would be no refusing her, he realized. He could tell by the look in her eyes that she had no intention of accepting any excuse he made. And truth be known, he didn't want to refuse. "All right, Mrs. McKinley. I shall be delighted to accept your invitation."

"Wonderful. Everyone will come to the house immediately after attending the community Thanksgiving service at the Presbyterian church."

With another nod, Joshua opened the door and went out into the frigid November air. He bent his head into the wind as he walked along Skyview Street, down the hillside, and through the center of town to the newspaper offices. By the time he opened the door to the *Herald*, his face and ears felt half frozen from the cold.

He hung his hat and coat on the rack. At his desk, he picked up that morning's edition of the newspaper. Glancing through the pages, he made mental notes to himself about changes he wanted to make in future editions. And those thoughts made him think of Daphne again.

Naturally.

She'd rarely been out of his thoughts since their return to Bethlehem Springs.

When Morgan had dropped by the newspaper office early that morning and shared his concerns about his sister's health and lethargy, Joshua had been glad for a reason to call upon her at the McKinley home. He'd wanted to visit before now, but he'd always stopped himself from going. Perhaps because whenever he thought of her, he pictured her sitting up in bed, her dark mass of hair falling around her shoulders.

He rubbed his hands over his face, as if he could wipe away that image. But he couldn't. It was burned into his mind, and it troubled him. Deeply troubled him. For the truth was, now that the danger was over, now that they were safely home, he couldn't help wishing they were back in that cabin, just the two of them, under much different circumstances.

⁓

October 15, 1872

Bethlehem Springs is like Idaho City in many ways. Gold strikes in 1863 brought hordes of people into the mountains of the Boise Basin. When I left Bethlehem Springs nearly two years ago, there were several mining enterprises to the west still in operation and a new lumber mill to the south. The town also had at least a half dozen saloons and numerous other businesses. There remains a lot of promise for a better future for the citizens of Bethlehem Springs, but it will never grow to be the size of Idaho City. At least that's what I predict.

When I arrived in Bethlehem Springs in the spring of 1866, I acquired an existing saloon, purchased the livery stable, and opened my law office. I also took it upon myself to build an opera house. I aspired to refinement—or to, at the very least, have others think me refined.

I guess it worked, for the following year I was sworn into office as a judge. Judge Richard Terrell, the very same man who'd been dubbed Rawhide Rick when he first arrived in California seventeen years earlier. I was a self-made man without any formal education. (At least I considered myself self-made at the time. Now I see things somewhat differently. I believe God was altering the course of my life even then.)

I wish I could write that becoming an arbiter of justice changed me for the better, but that would be a lie. Another lie in a long string of lies. Truth was a relative thing in my mind. I told it when it was convenient or beneficial to me. I twisted it when to do otherwise wouldn't be convenient or beneficial to me. What mattered to Richard Terrell was the only thing that was important.

As a lawyer, I was interested in one thing—winning. As a judge, I was interested in doing whatever would help me in the present or the future. Plenty of men paid me to find in their behalf.

It wasn't that I needed the money. I was already a wealthy man. I'd been a wealthy man for many, many years by then. I owned the largest, most elegant house in town. I had the best horses and the finest carriage. But no matter how much I had, it was never enough. Enough wasn't a word in my vocabulary. I was greedy.

Perhaps I became that way because of the poverty I experienced in my early years. Or perhaps it's the sin-nature I was born with. Who besides God can know our hearts and minds?

I can sleep at night now only because I know that I didn't sentence any innocent men to death or to long prison terms. But did I mete out true justice in my court? Not often. Maybe not ever.

SEVENTEEN

Daphne finished reading the article, then laid the sheets of paper on the writing desk with a sigh of satisfaction. She'd done it. Her next column was ready to turn in. She hoped Joshua would be as pleased with it as she was. After all, he'd inspired the topic. Not that anyone other than she and Joshua would know.

She pushed the chair back from the desk. Lifting her arms above her head, she stood and stretched.

Her gaze moved around the second-story bedroom of her brother's house. It was comfortable and familiar to her, and yet it wasn't home. She missed her own little office and her many books and even her brand-new typewriter. She missed the freedom that came with living alone. While she was grateful for the care Morgan and Gwen had given her during her illness and recovery, she was ready to be out from under their watchful eyes. The depression, the lethargy, seemed to have lifted at last. Perhaps because writing the article on the desk had required her to think and act.

She crossed the room and sank onto the edge of her bed, lifting her Bible off the nightstand as she did so. She opened it to 1st Chronicles, the twenty-eighth chapter, and read aloud the words that had spoken to her heart that morning: "And David said to Solomon his son, Be strong and of good courage, and do it: fear not, nor be dismayed: for the LORD God, even my God, will be with thee; he will not fail thee, nor forsake thee, until thou hast finished all the work for the service of the house of the LORD."

Do it. Do the work. God will be with thee.

It seemed so clear. The Lord was telling her to get on with her work. He would be with her in whatever He called her to do. And hadn't Paul told believers that whatever they did, they were to do it as unto the Lord and with all their might? She was a writer, and she should be writing.

She closed the Bible and set it on the bed beside her.

It was time she went home and got back to work. She was well. God had restored her to good health. She would return to her own home tomorrow night, as soon as all of the McKinley Thanksgiving guests had departed.

Feeling energized by her decision, she left the bedroom, following the sound of Gwen's voice into the nursery, where she found her sister-in-law seated on the floor, Ellie held in the crook of her left arm and Andy held in the crook of her right arm as she read to him from an open book.

Thank You, Father, that they didn't take sick. It was a prayer of gratitude she'd sent up daily in the two weeks since she and Joshua were brought back to Bethlehem Springs in her brother's sleigh.

She entered the nursery and sank down beside Gwen. "Can I be of help?"

Her sister-in-law smiled as she passed the dozing infant into Daphne's waiting arms.

"Mama's reading," Andy offered, turning the page of his book.

"I see that. What's the story?"

"Tom Sum."

"Tom Thumb," Gwen corrected.

Grinning, the boy said, "He's littler than me. He's even littler than Ellie."

Daphne laughed. "I know. Tom Thumb's only this big." She held up her right thumb.

Andy tugged on his mother's arm, demanding that she continue with the story. Gwen obliged, and Daphne was content to listen as she gently rocked Ellie from side to side, her gaze fastened on the baby's sweet face. She had little notion how much time passed before she realized Gwen had fallen silent. She glanced up to find Andy had fallen asleep like his sister.

"You're feeling stronger today," Gwen whispered. "I can tell."

Daphne nodded. "Much."

"Good." Gwen looked at Andy. "Let's put these two down so you and I can relax."

A short while later, with the children both in their beds, the two women slipped out of the nursery, Gwen closing the door behind them.

"I finished my next column for the newspaper." Daphne slipped her arm into the crook of Gwen's. "I think it's rather good if I do say so myself."

"May I read it?"

"Do you mind waiting until Mr. Crawford says whether or not he likes it?"

"Not at all. I remember what I was like when I was writing a column for the paper."

They began down the stairs, taking each step in unison.

"Do you miss it?" Daphne asked when they reached the bottom step.

"Writing? Not really. I've found other things more satisfying."

"I fear I would miss it horribly."

They walked into the front parlor, and Gwen settled onto the settee. Daphne sat on a nearby chair.

"I read one of your books."

Daphne felt a shiver of nerves. She'd known Morgan had told his wife about her novels, but the two women hadn't spoken of them before this moment. There hadn't been an opportunity before Daphne's trip to Stone Creek, and after the trip she'd been too ill. "Which one?" she asked softly.

"The first one. *The Fate of Phoebe Tate*."

"Did you like it?"

"It was quite the adventure, wasn't it?"

That wasn't a real answer to her question, but Daphne let it pass. "Would you be embarrassed if others knew I was the author?"

"No." Gwen frowned thoughtfully. "I wouldn't be embarrassed. Neither would your brother. But whatever made you decide to write that kind of story? A dime novel doesn't—" She gave a small shrug. "It doesn't seem like you."

Daphne felt a sting of disappointment, realizing then that she'd hoped for words of praise. "I love all the legends of the Old West. After I came to Idaho and had the opportunity to listen to so many of Griff's stories, I discovered I wanted to write about some of them. That's what got me started. When I wrote *The Fate of Phoebe Tate*, I never dreamed it would actually get published."

"And what about Rawhide Rick? Did you portray him accurately?"

"According to the Coughlins, yes."

"Poor Mr. Crawford. I suppose now that he knows the truth about his grandfather he'll go back to St. Louis."

Daphne caught her breath. She hadn't thought of that. Was learning about his grandfather's past the only thing that had brought Joshua to Bethlehem Springs? Hadn't he come for a job with the *Herald*? Would he really leave so soon? And why on earth did the notion of his leaving make her feel bereft?

Wednesday, 27 November 1918

Dear Mary Theresa,

I regret that it has taken so long for me to reply to your letter of 4 November. It arrived when I was out of town, and I have been much occupied with other matters since my return to Bethlehem Springs.

Perhaps Mother told you that I was to interview a couple of elderly gentlemen who purportedly knew my grandfather when he lived in Idaho. At the time I met with them, I wasn't satisfied with what they had to tell me and didn't give them sufficient time to tell me everything they knew. I have since written to them with additional questions. I am also querying the Idaho Daily Statesman in Boise City as well as applying for information from the state. I'm told that Grandfather served as a judge for three years here in Crow County. A fire in Bethlehem Springs in 1886 destroyed county government records along with the newspaper archives, but I hope I can get the information I desire from other sources.

It is clear to me that I will be obliged to remain in Idaho longer than previously planned. Perhaps until spring. I have determined not to leave until I am convinced of the complete facts regarding my grandfather. Naturally, I also hope that my findings will allow me to prove that what Mr. Halifax suggested about him was unfounded and untrue.

Bethlehem Springs has had one case of the Spanish influenza, but so far there have been no new cases reported. Every one of my acquaintance here is understandably thankful to God that the town hasn't suffered a worse outbreak.

I pray that this letter will find you well.

I remain affectionately yours,

Joshua

❧

Joshua looked at the closing words and wondered at their accuracy. *Was* he affectionately hers? He'd thought so for a number of years. After all, it had been the wish of both of their grandfathers that the two families would be joined through the marriage of Joshua and Mary Theresa.

"But I don't love her," he whispered as he signed his name. "I don't desire her."

It hadn't bothered him before, the lack of passion between them. He and Mary Theresa were fond of each other. They had grown up together and had countless shared memories. They were both believers in the saving grace of Jesus Christ. Weren't those things enough to build a good marriage upon?

He tried to picture Mary Theresa in his mind, to remind himself of the many things he liked and admired about her. But it wasn't Mary Theresa's image he recalled. It was Daphne's, her thick black hair cascading about her shoulders, her brown eyes wide and inquiring, her generous mouth bowed in a smile.

Why, he wondered, had the beautiful Miss McKinley never married? He suspected it was because no man had come along who'd swept her off her feet. She had a zest for living that was revealed in her dark eyes and her joyous laughter and her wondrous smile. A marriage lacking in ardor and zeal would never do for her.

He knew it then. He wouldn't be able to give his heart to Mary Theresa in the future. He'd already lost it to Daphne.

EIGHTEEN

Morgan and Gwen tried to convince Daphne to stay home from church on Thanksgiving morning, insisting she should rest since there would be a houseful of guests the remainder of the day, but she wouldn't be dissuaded. She wanted to thank God in His sanctuary for the life she still enjoyed. It had come upon her suddenly yesterday, the realization of how close she'd been to dying and the mercy that God had shown in restoring her to health and to the loving arms of her family.

And so, a little before 10:00 a.m., she walked into All Saint's Presbyterian Church for the community Thanksgiving service. The narthex had been decorated with white and brown ribbons and bouquets of dried flowers. The voices of friends and neighbors greeting one another filled the entry and reached to the rafters.

"You look well, Miss McKinley."

"So good to see roses in your cheeks, Daphne."

"Thank God they were able to find you after that snowstorm, Miss McKinley."

She shook hands and thanked folks for their good wishes and kind words. There were a few who refused to speak to her. They were the ones — like her neighbor, Edna Updike — who had publicly criticized her decision to take such a trip, an unmarried woman with an unmarried man and without a proper chaperone. The ones who thought her character compromised, her reputation sullied, by the days she'd been in that cabin with Joshua Crawford. Her brother and sister-in-law had done their best to shield her from the gossip, but she'd heard of it anyway. Her critics were the same folks who always thought the worst of others, and she was determined not to allow their censure to spoil this day for her.

As the family moved through the doorways into the sanctuary, she saw Joshua standing near one of the stained-glass windows on the right side of the spacious room, deep in conversation with Christina Patterson. Her chest tightened at the sight of them. It took her a moment to recognize the sensation.

Jealousy? For heaven's sake. She'd never felt jealous of anyone or anything in her entire life. Why ever would she feel it now?

True, Christina was comely, even in her mourning attire, and Joshua seemed to be hanging on her every word. The two of them worked together at the newspaper every day. They must have come to know each other well by this time. It was also true that Daphne could not be the only single woman in Bethlehem Springs who found Joshua attractive. How could anyone not notice his gorgeous blue eyes that seemed able to look straight into a person's heart or the attractive smile that made a girl's heart quicken?

But still ... Jealousy? That wouldn't do.

When the McKinleys reached their regular pew, they found Griff, Cleo, and Woody already seated there. Daphne slipped in first and sat beside Cleo. Gwen followed next with Ellie, and Morgan brought up the rear with Andy.

Immediately, Cleo took Daphne's left hand in both of hers and squeezed it. "You look like you're feeling lots better than the last time I saw you."

"I am."

"Looks like our prayers for you were answered."

Daphne nodded. "I'm returning home tonight or tomorrow morning. I don't want to be under Morgan's and Gwen's feet any longer."

"I reckon they don't feel you've been in the way."

She smiled, knowing Cleo was right. She would be welcome to stay in the McKinley home just as long as she liked. Forever, if she chose. But she was ready to leave. She was ready to get back to her writing and to her own life. A life God had graciously granted back to her.

※

From his seat two rows back and across the aisle, Joshua observed Daphne. Wisps of hair curled along her neck beneath the umber-colored hat she wore. It was the exact same shade as her jacket and skirt. A color too somber for Daphne. She should wear more vibrant tones, he decided. Colors as vibrant as she was.

He closed his eyes and tried to shove the thoughts away. Daphne had been too much on his mind since he'd written his letter to Mary Theresa yesterday. Thoughts of Daphne had hounded him during his waking moments and plagued his dreams while he slept. He half wished the anger he'd once felt toward her would return. He knew what to do with his anger. He hadn't a clue what to do with the emotions roiling inside him now.

The church organ began to play. Joshua rose with the rest of the congregation to join in the singing of the familiar hymn and for the next hour or so was able to successfully—for the most part—focus his thoughts on God rather than the beautiful young woman two rows up and one aisle across from him.

※

The delicious scent of roasting turkey greeted family and guests as they entered the McKinley home a short while before noon. Inez Cheevers, the housekeeper, was near the front door to take hats and coats and was half buried beneath them before Morgan insisted on helping with the rest. The maid, Louise, took command of the two children, escorting them upstairs to the nursery, while Gwen invited everyone into the front parlor.

Daphne had always admired the way her sister-in-law made others feel welcome in her home. She moved around the room, speaking with each guest, making sure they were comfortable, asking if they needed anything, sharing a moment of laughter or a word of encouragement. Being a gracious hostess was second nature to Guinevere Arlington McKinley, and Daphne couldn't help but envy her that.

Daphne had been trained in the social graces, of course. One wasn't raised the daughter of Alastair and Danielle McKinley without knowing how to entertain a vast array of people. Still, she'd never taken to hostess duties with the ease that was true of her sister-in-law.

At least Daphne was acquainted with everyone present. In addition to the family—Morgan and Gwen, Woody and Cleo, and Griff—the guests included Fagan Doyle, Morgan's business manager and close friend, who had recently returned to Bethlehem Springs after overseeing a McKinley building project in Southern California; Christina Patterson, on her own for her first Thanksgiving since her husband's death; Crow County Sheriff Jedidiah Winston and his unmarried daughter Rose; Ashley Thurber, one of Bethlehem Springs' spinster schoolteachers; and Joshua Crawford.

A perfectly balanced company of six men and six women, and Daphne couldn't help wondering if her sister-in-law had matchmaking in mind when she'd made up her guest list. The thought took her eyes to Joshua who was now seated between Rose Winston and Christina Patterson.

Silly to be jealous of Christina. She was still mourning the death of her beloved husband. But what about Rose? Rose was close to Daphne's age, and while not especially pretty, she was handsome and had a pleasant demeanor. Daphne had heard that Rose once wanted to win Morgan's affections, back before he'd fallen in love with Gwen. Perhaps it was only idle gossip. Or perhaps it explained why the young woman had never married.

A wry smile curved the corners of her mouth. She could almost hear someone in the room thinking, *Why hasn't Daphne McKinley married? She's pretty enough and the heiress to a fortune. She's not getting any younger, you know. The first blush of youth is already gone. Twenty-seven and no man in sight.*

She felt a little catch in her chest as she glanced once more at Joshua. There *was* a man in sight. She just didn't know if he was interested. He'd taken great care of her while she was ill. He surely knew her more intimately than any other man of her acquaintance, and yet he didn't seem inclined to pursue her beyond as a columnist for the newspaper. How disappointing.

She turned to look at her reflection in the mirror on the wall. *Perhaps I'm not pretty enough.* Her complexion remained pale, and there were dark smudges beneath her eyes that didn't seem inclined to go away anytime soon.

Fagan Doyle stepped to her side. "Aye, 'tis a lovely reflection, Miss McKinley. Sure, and it is."

Daphne felt warmth rise in her cheeks, embarrassed to be caught assessing herself in the looking glass. "Don't tease me, Mr. Doyle."

"*Mr.* Doyle?" He grinned and gave her a sly wink. "I'm thinking we're better friends than that."

She laughed. "Of course we are, Fagan." She leaned forward to kiss his cheek. "And I'm glad you're back. Morgan won't be sending you off to another project anytime soon, will he?"

"I'm thinkin' not until spring."

"Good. We'll have time for plenty of games of chess, and I shall give you a proper drubbing."

"We shall see about that."

Fagan Doyle was a wiry sort, of average height with not an ounce of fat on him. He looked to be in his early thirties, although Joshua wasn't a great judge of a person's age. When Gwen had introduced the two men, she'd told Joshua that Fagan was Morgan's friend and that he worked for McKinley Enterprises. That could explain why Fagan and Daphne looked so chummy as they stood talking across the room from where he sat.

The two of them laughed, and Joshua felt like grinding his teeth as he watched them. Was she smitten with the Irishman?

He might have risen from the sofa, excused himself from the others, and gone to speak with her. He might have done his best to steal her away from the other fellow's company. But he was saved from the inclination by a summons to dinner.

The dining room was ablaze with light reflected off the gold-rimmed china, crystal, and silver service. Place cards marked the seating arrangements, and Joshua felt a rush of relief when he found himself on Daphne's left with Griff Arlington on her right. So much for Fagan Doyle.

He held out Daphne's chair for her. "Miss McKinley."

"Thank you, Mr. Crawford."

He scooted her chair in, then sat in his assigned place. "You're feeling stronger, I trust."

"Much stronger. Thank you." She smiled as she added, "And I have my column ready for you. If you wish, you can take it with you when you leave today."

"Of course. I'd be delighted to take it with me. May I ask the title?"

"I haven't a title for it. Perhaps you can help with that. I wrote about what we don't know about the people we know."

Joshua cocked an eyebrow.

She lowered her voice to a whisper. "Don't worry. It's inspired by you and your grandfather, but I don't say so. The piece is philosophical rather than factual."

"You're good at keeping secrets, aren't you, Miss McKinley?" He leaned closer. "I like that in a woman."

He saw her eyes widen, watched as the tip of her tongue moistened her lips. The temptation to kiss her was almost more than he could resist—even knowing it would be a disaster to do so here, surrounded by these people. Fortunately, Griff chose that moment to address her, and she turned away before Joshua could act on the reckless impulse.

But those few moments had taught him something—she was attracted to him too. She would have *let* him kiss her. He was convinced of it. And it wasn't because she was a columnist and he her editor. It wasn't because she'd written dime novels about his grandfather.

What we don't know about the people we know. Wasn't that what she'd said her column's topic was? Well, there was a great deal more about Daphne McKinley that he wanted to know. Far, far more. He was determined to learn it all, and soon.

November 2, 1872

The St. Louis Men's Association opened its doors today. Although it has no affiliation with the YMCA, Kevin and I share that organization's desire to provide safe housing and healthy activities as well as spiritual development to young men who come to the city to find work in the factories.

St. Louis is now the nation's fourth largest city, and with growth has come problems as well as prosperity. The hope of the SLMA is to serve men who would otherwise find themselves sleeping in the open and indulging in less than desirable activities (the same kind I provided to men for too many years—alcohol and women).

Kevin will manage the daily operations of the SLMA along with the fine staff we have employed, and I pray that God will use me as a volunteer wherever He sees fit.

NINETEEN

Daphne waved to her brother as he pulled away from the curb, then quickly closed the door against the encroaching cold. She went into the kitchen and stood near the stove, where the fire had taken hold after some coaxing by Morgan. Once she was warm again, she walked to the back door and looked out at the shed near the alley. Through the shed's partially open door, she saw the red hood of the McLaughlin-Buick. Sometime during her recovery, Morgan and his friends had managed to retrieve Mack from its snowy grave and bring it back to Bethlehem Springs. Bless them all. Her brother had told her the motorcar was none the worse for wear. She hoped he was right, but she wasn't interested enough to see for herself right now.

She turned and leaned her back against the door, her gaze taking in the kitchen with its stove and icebox, table and chairs. Beyond the kitchen was her cozy parlor with its upright piano and chintz-covered sofa and chairs. The rooms seemed compact and crowded after two weeks in the McKinley home, but they also felt just right. Perfect. It would be nice to do as she pleased without someone looking over her shoulder, warning her not to do too much or asking if it wasn't time for her to lie down and take a nap. As much as she loved her brother and sister-in-law, they could make her feel as if she were still a child.

She pushed off the door and walked to her office. Not a speck of dust anywhere. Someone had been in to clean her house in expectation of her return. She wondered who. Perhaps Gwen had sent Mrs. Cheevers. Or it might have been one of her neighbors. She would have to find out and thank them properly.

The Royal Typewriter sat in the center of her desk, reminding her how long it had been since she'd used it. Would she remember what she'd learned, or had her progress been lost already? She took paper from a drawer in the desk and rolled it into the platen. Then she sank onto the chair. What should she type? Another column? The next scene in her book?

Her fingers struck the keys slowly: J o s h u a C r a w f o r d

She stared at the black letters on the white sheet of paper. What on earth had possessed her to type *his* name? She hadn't even been thinking of him.

Liar!

She'd thought of little other than Joshua since they'd visited over Gwen's delicious Thanksgiving meal yesterday. There'd been moments when the look in his eyes had made it impossible for her to breathe normally. She'd scarcely heard a word anyone else at the table had said, although she'd pretended otherwise. If someone laughed, she'd laughed with them. When someone addressed her, she'd nodded as if in understanding. No matter what her outward response, her thoughts were on Joshua, Joshua, Joshua.

"Oh, my," she whispered on a sigh.

Daphne had enjoyed more than one flirtation through the years. She'd had her male callers and had received proposals of marriage. Not once had she been tempted to give up the freedom she enjoyed for matrimony. Besides, she'd never been too sure she wasn't being courted for her fortune rather than her charms. When she married—*if* she married—she wanted it to be a love match, as her parents' marriage had been.

Joshua wasn't wealthy. In fact, she suspected he had few worldly possessions beyond the clothes he'd brought with him from St. Louis and the salary Christina paid him. He might only be interested in her money too. For that matter, he might not be interested in her at all. And yet—

A knock sounded at her door, and she jumped guiltily, as if whoever was there could read her thoughts from the front porch.

"Coming."

She pulled the sheet of paper from the typewriter, wadded it, and tossed it into the small trash receptacle at the side of the desk. Another knock convinced her to hurry to the front door.

Joshua stood on the other side of the screen. "Good morning, Miss McKinley." He swept off his hat.

"Mr. Crawford."

"I hope you don't mind me dropping by. I . . . I wanted to discuss your column."

"Not at all." She pushed open the screen door. "Do come in out of the cold."

He stepped inside.

"You're lucky you found me at home. Morgan only dropped me off a short while ago."

"I know. I saw him driving up Main Street and assumed he'd brought you home."

A frisson of pleasure rolled around in her stomach. He'd come to see her as soon as he'd thought she was home.

Drawing a slow breath, she held out a hand. "May I take your hat and coat?"

"Yes. Thank you."

She hung them on the rack. "Is there a problem with my column?" she asked as she faced him again.

A hint of a smile curved the corners of his mouth. "On the contrary. I think it's wonderful work."

"You do?"

"You have a distinctive voice, Daphne."

She loved the sound of her given name on his lips and was glad he felt comfortable enough to use it again.

"I believe you're a naturally gifted storyteller. You shouldn't waste that gift. Your latest column is superior work."

"That's kind of you to say." Feeling a blush rise in her cheeks—delighted by the compliment—she motioned to the sofa. "Please, won't you sit down?" She settled onto the chair opposite him. "I hope, now that I'm feeling myself, to get back to writing every day, the way I used to do. My book publisher is growing impatient."

An odd expression crossed his face. Disappointment? Disapproval? And she realized it didn't matter that he thought her gifted. He would never like, praise, or appreciate The McFarland Chronicles. Not as long as her novels painted Richard Terrell as a scoundrel.

"Speaking of your latest book, I'm going down to the capital city this afternoon to see if I can learn more about my grandfather, about his activities while he was in Idaho."

May I come with you? She managed to stifle the question before it could burst forth. It would have been inappropriate to ask and even more so to go. There were already some in Bethlehem Springs who thought ill of the two of them. No need to add fuel to the fire.

She cleared her throat. "I hope you find what you're looking for."

She meant it. With all her heart, she meant it. She would write a hundred retractions if they would bring him peace of mind, peace of heart.

Retractions? Really? But if what she'd written was the true story—as it seemed to be, as even Joshua had to believe it to be by now—how could she do that?

"I hope to find the full story of Grandfather's time in Idaho," he said.

Do you, Joshua? What if you've heard the whole story already and just don't like it. Will you leave Idaho once it's confirmed? Will you go back to St. Louis and leave me here, missing you?

The blue of his eyes seemed to darken as he looked at her. What was he thinking? She wished she could read his thoughts. She so desperately would like to understand him, to know him better, perhaps even to love him.

The silence between them grew long and awkward.

Joshua cleared his throat. "I'd best get back to the paper. There are a number of things I must wrap up before I catch the afternoon train." He rose from the sofa.

Disappointment sluiced through Daphne as she stood too. "Will you be gone long?"

"I hope not."

He walked toward the door, Daphne following right behind. But before he reached it, he stopped and turned—so abruptly, she nearly ran into him. As she swayed forward, he caught hold of her upper arms with his hands. Surprised, she looked up into his eyes—and saw something there that stopped her in her tracks.

Time ceased its forward motion as they stood there, his gaze holding hers as she waited for something, anything, to happen. Vaguely she noticed she held her breath.

He studied her for a long moment. Then, finally, his brows drew together in a thoughtful frown. And, ever so slowly, his head lowered toward hers. She rose on tiptoe, impatient for their lips to meet ...

The kiss sent a shock wave through her. Her knees weakened and her stomach tumbled. Heat flowed through her, as did a strange longing to get closer to him.

Closer.

Closer.

Closer.

Joshua stepped back, breaking the connection far too soon. "I'm sorry, Miss McKinley." His voice sounded gruff and gravelly. "I shouldn't have done that. Please forgive me."

"There's nothing to forgive," she answered softly.

"Yes, there is." After another long look, he turned and opened the door. "Good day, Miss McKinley."

Long after he left the house, Daphne remained in the same spot, longing for the feel of his hands gripping her arms, for the feel of his mouth upon hers. She ached to feel the warmth of his breath upon her skin, to hear the beating of his heart in time with her own.

Now that he'd kissed her, she would never be the same. She was changed forever. If only he'd stayed a little longer. If only he'd kept on kissing her.

"I shouldn't have done that. Please forgive me."

Forgive him? For what? For kissing her as she'd never been kissed before? For making her feel more alive than she'd felt in all her twenty-seven years? For making her world a brighter, more exciting place?

He was wrong to seek forgiveness, and the next time she saw him, she would tell him so.

❦

Joshua thought of little besides that kiss as he finished his tasks at the newspaper and as he packed a few belongings in a satchel and as he sat in the passenger car as the train made its way to Boise.

Thoughts of the kiss lingered as he made his way from the depot in the capital city to the Idanha Hotel and checked into his room. The memories of the kiss followed him to the hotel's dining room and were ever present as he ate his evening meal. And they were with him as he lay in his bed and tried to find sleep.

Daphne had tasted sweet and innocent and passionate. She'd felt right in his arms, as if she'd been made for that very purpose, that very place. Desire had swept over him as he'd embraced her, and it had taken all of his strength to move away, to let go of her arms, to forsake the warm feel of her lips upon his.

He didn't have a right to kiss her. No matter what he felt for Daphne, he didn't have the right to kiss her until he'd spoken to Mary Theresa. They weren't engaged, but there'd always been the understanding that they would one day marry. An understanding between the families. An understanding between the two of them. He needed to tell Mary Theresa it wasn't going to happen. He wasn't going to marry her. She would be hurt but it couldn't be helped. He couldn't marry her when he cared for another woman. It wouldn't be fair to either of them.

Breaking off that understanding wasn't something he could do by letter. He knew that was true. He'd made several attempts to put his feelings on paper the previous night, but it hadn't worked. No, this was a conversation that should take place face to face. Since that wasn't possible—he couldn't wait until he returned to St. Louis for good and he couldn't afford to take the long trip back to Missouri just for that purpose—he would have to call her on the telephone. He would do it in the morning.

Then, once his business in Boise was done, he could return to Bethlehem Springs with a clear conscience and finish what that kiss had begun.

TWENTY

"I'm sorry, Joshua." Kevin Donahue's words were hard to understand over the static on the line. "Mary Theresa isn't at home. She ... she's with her cousin Blanche."

Joshua held the earpiece to his left ear, pressed his index finger against his right ear, and raised his voice as he spoke into the mouthpiece of the telephone. "When can I call back, Mr. Donahue? I'm hoping to return to Bethlehem Springs in the morning, and I'd like to talk to her before then if at all possible."

"She won't be back today. She and Blanche took a trip together. I'm not sure when she'll return, but I'm certain it won't be before the end of next week."

Mary Theresa hadn't mentioned the possibility of going on a holiday in her letters. Had she spent Thanksgiving away from her grandfather?

"Joshua, is there something the matter? Is it urgent you speak with her soon?"

"No. No. Nothing like that." But despite his words, it *felt* urgent. He wanted to speak to her. He wanted the matter settled. He wanted his conscience clear the next time he was with Daphne.

"Then perhaps you should put it in a letter, my boy. It would be much cheaper than a telephone call."

Joshua couldn't help smiling at that. Kevin Donahue was

known for his ability to pinch pennies until they screamed for mercy.

"I know, but I would like to talk with her. Sometimes the immediate is better than a letter."

"Yes, I suppose it is at your age. Is there somewhere I can have her—" He cleared his throat. "Can I have her call you?"

"No." He *could* have told Kevin to have her call him at the newspaper, but this wasn't a conversation he wanted to have within hearing of other folks in Bethlehem Springs. "No, I'll just call again when I have the use of another telephone."

"Very well. And how is your search going? Your last letter said you were told Richard really was a judge when he was in Idaho?"

"Yes, it seems that part could be true."

"Never pictured him in that sort of role, but it makes sense. Your grandfather was a good and fair-minded man."

"Yes, he was." *But apparently not when he served on the bench.*

The static over the wire grew worse.

"I'm going to ring off now, Mr. Donahue. Tell Mary Theresa I called and that I'll try again soon."

"Of course. I'll tell her. Good-bye, Joshua."

"Good-bye, Mr. Donahue." He dropped the earpiece into its cradle.

Feeling frustrated, he raked the fingers of one hand through his hair as he turned around. The small office was cramped and airless, just about every surface covered with papers of one kind or another. But it had given him some measure of privacy. He walked to the door and opened it.

Kit Shepherd, the young fellow who'd been helping Joshua search through old newspaper records, spun his chair around and smiled. "Able to make your call?"

"Yes, thank you."

"Great!" He turned back to his desk and grabbed a folder. "While you were in there, I found something. I think it's what you've been looking for." He held out the folder toward Joshua. "A couple of articles about the Honorable Judge Richard Terrell of Bethlehem Springs. Seems he earned quite the reputation during the three years he sat on the bench. Right about the time you were looking for too. Lots of trouble with law enforcement back then. All kinds of riffraff flowing into the territory. Crooked sheriffs. Plenty of thieves and ne'er-do-wells. Country still trying to heal the wounds from the Civil War. Lots of bad blood between supporters of the Union and supporters of the Confederacy. I heard tell the vigilante movement got its start right up in our mountains during the height of the gold rush."

Joshua took the folder and opened it to read the clippings inside.

March 1868 to February 1871. That's what the first article said were the years Richard Terrell had been a judge in the bawdy mining town of Bethlehem Springs, Idaho. His grandfather had returned to St. Louis in the early months of '71. The timing was right, and with this information added to what the Coughlin brothers had told him, he was running out of reasons not to believe the less-than-flattering stories about Richard Terrell. The stories that had made their way into Daphne's novels.

"There's times I'd give my eye teeth to have been alive back then. Bet I would've been a gunslinger." Kit pretended to draw a gun from his hip, then laughed as he blew on the tip of his index finger.

Joshua moved away from the younger man, trying to block out his incessant chatter so he could concentrate on the words he was reading. Could the man in these articles really have been his grandfather?

Yes, it was him.

The last of his resistance dissolved. It was all true. The man portrayed in D. B. Morgan's McFarland Chronicles was the same man portrayed in these newspaper clippings. No wonder his grandfather had never wanted to talk about his old life. In his mind, he heard again the reply he'd been given when he'd ask the old man about the years he'd lived out West.

"There I was, closing in on fifty years old, and God made me a new man. The old me, the old sinner, was gone and forgotten ... Nothing before my life in Christ matters one whit to me. Everything good came after that."

Much of the meaning behind those remembered words had changed, now that Joshua knew a little of what his grandfather's life had been like before he became a Christian. No wonder Richard Terrell left Idaho. God might forget the sins of a man's past, but people rarely did.

⤐

Daphne spun her desk chair toward the window. The wintery scene beyond the glass was picture perfect. A thin blanket of new snow lay upon tree branches, shrubs, and lawn. The clouds had long since moved on, and sunshine caused the icy crystals to sparkle and dance before her eyes.

Had snow fallen in Boise as well? Was Joshua walking along a sidewalk on his way to the newspaper, his nose red with the cold? Had he learned anything new about his grandfather?

"Who were you really, Mr. Terrell?" she wondered aloud.

In The McFarland Chronicles, Rawhide Rick was a villain, pure and simple. A man without a single redeeming quality. How unrealistic. As a writer, she should have known better. Weren't all

186

people a combination of good and bad, saint and sinner? A mixture of black and white, true and false, better and worse.

> *Brethren, I count not myself to have apprehended: but this one thing I do, forgetting those things which are behind, and reaching forth unto those things which are before, I press toward the mark for the prize of the high calling of God in Christ Jesus.*

It seemed to Daphne that Richard Terrell had followed Paul's words to the Philippians to the letter. He'd been a man with a past he'd wanted to forget, a man with secrets he'd wanted to put behind him, and that's exactly what he'd done. He'd pressed on toward the higher calling in Jesus.

Wouldn't I have done the same, were my past as shady?

She leaned forward and plucked her last book off the shelf, allowing it to fall open on her lap.

> "Monster!" Miss Claremont exclaimed. "Have you no shame? You know my father is not guilty of such a thing."
>
> Rawhide Rick laughed. "But I'll prove he did the very thing you claim he did not."
>
> "You cannot prove what is not true."
>
> His composure was exasperating to the extreme. "You might be surprised to discover how easy it is to prove as true that which is not."

How very close Miss Claremont's father had come to the hanging tree. In the end, Bill McFarland had rescued him, but Rawhide Rick had escaped justice once again — in order to appear in the next installment of the chronicles, of course.

She closed the book and set it onto her desk next to the typewriter, feeling oddly disquieted.

Joshua's voice echoed in her memory. *"I believe you're a naturally gifted storyteller. You shouldn't waste that gift. Your latest column is superior work."*

He thought her gifted, but he didn't think much of her published books. He'd made that perfectly clear. Was it only because of how she'd portrayed his grandfather in her stories or was it something more than that? She suspected the latter, although the former was incriminating enough in his eyes. Now she was inclined to believe he found her novels beneath her. But was it terrible to give the public what they wanted? Was it so awful to offer stories that let readers escape into another place, another time, for a short while? That was what her books did. Naturally they were high on melodrama. That was what made them fun to read.

She rose and left her office, but doing so didn't help her restless thoughts. For it was here, in the living room, that she had last seen Joshua. It was over there, by the front door, that he had gripped her arms and kissed her. A kiss that had lasted not nearly long enough to suit her.

A sigh slipped between her lips as the memory of those wonderful-awful moments swept through her again. Never in her life had she been kissed like that. It had seemed to consume her. It had muddled her mind and left her both empty and filled at the same time.

"I'm sorry, Miss McKinley. I shouldn't have done that. Please forgive me."

Didn't he realize she'd been a willing participant? Didn't he know that she'd come to care for him? Care for him more than she'd realized before right this moment.

"I must tell him. I must tell him what he means to me." She inhaled deeply. "I must tell him I love him."

Oh, she wished he wasn't in Boise. She wished she could pull on her coat and run down to the newspaper office and declare her feelings. And she wouldn't care one bit what anyone who happened to overhear her declaration might think of her boldness.

She hugged herself as she spun in a tight circle.

So this was what it felt like, falling in love. She'd thought she knew. When she'd written about it in her books, she'd thought she knew exactly what love meant between a man and a woman. Hadn't she witnessed it first hand between her parents, between Morgan and Gwen, between Woody and Cleo? But she'd been clueless. She hadn't known the mere thought of the man she loved would leave her breathless and anxious and as giddy as a schoolgirl. How could she know until it happened to her?

Dropping onto the nearby chair, she closed her eyes and pictured Joshua in her mind. He'd cared for her so tenderly during her illness. Was that when she'd begun to fall in love with him? When she'd awakened and there'd been only the two of them, and she'd realized all the tender care he'd given her.

Her neighbor, Edna Updike, thought Daphne forever compromised — had even told another neighbor that she thought Morgan should have insisted Daphne and Joshua be married at once. Now Daphne almost wished her brother had done exactly that.

Almost but not quite.

No, she would much prefer that Joshua marry her because he loved her, not because someone forced him to. And she hoped he would realize he loved her soon.

❦

November 28, 1872

A Day of Thanksgiving.
I have lived the majority of life without being thankful to anyone for anything. I've taken what I wanted when I wanted

it and how I wanted it. I doubt I gave a second thought to those who did me any sort of kindness. And when I look back, I can see that such people existed despite my indifference to them. There were men who gave me chances to choose a better way of life, especially in my youth. There were women who fixed me a hot meal and were kind to me. I was blind to all of it, but now I see.

President Abraham Lincoln proclaimed the final Thursday in November a national Thanksgiving Day, and so it has been from that day to this. Last year was my first Thanksgiving as a follower of Christ, but this year, I truly have begun to understand all that I have to be thankful for— my wonderful wife, my beautiful daughter, my new friends, our warm and welcoming home, my legitimate business enterprises, the opening of the SLMA. But above all that, I am thankful for God's mercy and grace, for the cleansing of my sins in the blood of the Lamb.

> *Make a joyful noise unto the LORD, all ye lands.*
> *Serve the LORD with gladness: come before his presence with singing.*
> *Know ye that the LORD he is God: it is he that hath made us, and not we ourselves; we are his people, and the sheep of his pasture.*
> *Enter into his gates with thanksgiving, and into his courts with praise: be thankful unto him, and bless his name.*
> *For the LORD is good; his mercy is everlasting; and his truth endureth to all generations.*
>
> *Psalm 100*

Amen.

TWENTY-ONE

As the team of horses pulled the sleigh along the road to the Arlington ranch, Gwen repeated a sentiment that she'd already voiced twice that day. "I can't believe the difference a couple more days have made in your recovery. You look wonderful, Daphne. Positively in the pink of health."

Daphne smiled. Everything inside of her wanted to burst forth with the reason that she looked well—because she was in love. But Joshua should be the first to hear those words, and so she remained silent.

Let him return today, Lord. If I don't tell him how I feel soon, I think I'll burst.

She folded her hands inside her muff and turned to look at the passing countryside. It was unusual for the extended family not to dine at her brother's home on Sundays after church, but on Thanksgiving, Cleo had insisted that everyone come to the ranch for dinner today.

"It's my turn to play hostess," Cleo had said. "Believe it or not, I'll be preparing the meal. I've been getting lessons from Cookie."

As the sleigh crossed the bridge over the river, Andy exclaimed, "Daddy, look!" and pointed at a herd of elk near the edge of the forest. Morgan reined in, slowing the horses.

Daphne remembered the day she and Joshua had driven to

Stone Creek and how they'd stopped the motorcar to watch another small herd of elk. She remembered standing above the river's edge and marveling at the beauty of the stag with his great rack. How could she have not known even then that she was falling in love with the man who stood at her side?

Her gaze returned to her brother. His arm was around his small son's shoulders, the two of them on the front seat of the sleigh. He held the reins in his free hand as the horses finished their walk across the bridge. Father and son looked so very right together. A perfect picture.

She hoped Joshua wanted children. She did. She hadn't known how much she wanted children until she'd fallen in love. Loving Joshua made her long for things she hadn't given much thought to before now. Was it that way for all women?

When they could no longer see the elk, Morgan clucked to the horses and slapped their backsides with the reins, and the sleigh took off again. A short while later, they entered a long valley. Now they were on Arlington land, although it would take awhile before the ranch complex would come into view.

Daphne had often imagined what it must have been like when Griff and Elizabeth Arlington first lived in this valley—a two-room log cabin, cooking over an open flame, miners for their nearest neighbors, Bethlehem Springs a much rougher place than the bucolic town it was today. What a great adventure it must have been for the two of them.

Sometimes she thought she had been born a generation or two too late. But then she would have missed loving Joshua Crawford. No grand adventure would have been worth that.

She was still lost in thought when the sleigh pulled into the yard and Morgan stopped the team near the porch of the ranch house. Before they had time to throw off the lap robes that had kept them warm for the journey, the front door opened and Cleo and Woody stepped onto the veranda. Cleo had changed out of her church clothes and into her standard Levi's, boots, and shirt, but today she'd added a white apron.

"She was serious," Daphne said. "She *is* cooking our dinner."

From the porch, Cleo called, "Don't look so scared. I don't reckon I'll poison you."

⁓

Joshua went straight from the Bethlehem Springs train depot to the newspaper office. He wanted to make certain all was ready for the Monday edition of the *Herald* to go to press. Despite it being a Sunday afternoon, he wasn't surprised to find Christina Patterson there as well.

"My goodness," she said, her gaze darting to the clock, "I had no idea it was that time already. Was your trip successful, Joshua?"

"I suppose so." He shrugged out of his coat and hung it on the rack.

Christina didn't seem to notice his enigmatic response. "You had a visitor yesterday." She held out a small envelope. "She didn't leave her name but she asked that I give you this when you returned."

Daphne's image sprang to mind, causing his pulse to quicken. But would Christina have referred to Daphne as "a visitor"? He walked to his boss's desk and took the note from her hand. His name was written across the front of the envelope in a hand that looked familiar, although he couldn't place it. He turned away as he opened the envelope and withdrew the slip of paper.

Joshua dearest,

I am here in Bethlehem Springs. Imagine my disappointment upon my arrival when I learned you were

away from town for a couple of days. My cousin Blanche
Collins (you remember Blanche, don't you?) and I are staying
at the Washington Hotel. Please hasten to see me as soon as
you receive this note.

> Yours,
> Mary Theresa

Mary Theresa? In Bethlehem Springs? He couldn't believe it. She'd never said a word about coming to see him, and he'd never indicated he would want her to come either. Why hadn't Kevin Donahue told Joshua that Mary Theresa was coming to Bethlehem Springs? Or hadn't Mary Theresa told her grandfather where she was going? But that seemed unlikely. Mary Theresa wouldn't have undertaken this kind of trip, even with her widowed cousin along as a chaperone, without getting her grandfather's permission first.

So why hadn't her grandfather warned him that he would find Mary Theresa waiting for him in Bethlehem Springs?

Warned him. Strange choice of words. Only that's exactly how he felt—as if he'd needed to be warned. Yes, he needed to tell Mary Theresa that his feelings toward her had changed, that he couldn't marry her, that it would be unfair to them both. But was he ready to do so today, in person, face to face? He supposed he would have to be.

Joshua glanced over his shoulder at Christina, but she was once again reading some papers on her desk. "It seems I must go out again. Is there anything I need to attend to before I leave?"

"No." She looked up. "Is something amiss?"

"Nothing's amiss." He lifted the note in his hand. "A friend from St. Louis is here. The young woman who called yesterday."

Curiosity was clear in his employer's eyes, but he chose not to elaborate and she let it pass. He returned to the rack, grabbed his coat, and was out the door within moments. He walked swiftly down Main to Washington Street, then turned and hurried past the post office and into the lobby of the Washington Hotel.

The hotel was one of the oldest buildings in Bethlehem Springs. According to what he'd been told, it had escaped the worst of the fires that had destroyed much of the town back in its heyday. He supposed it had changed little from the years when his grandfather had been a judge here—rococo chairs with French tapestry upholstery, heavy draperies of deep reds and golds, rosewood sideboards and tables.

He went straight to the front desk and asked that Miss Mary Theresa Donahue be advised Mr. Crawford was in the lobby to see her. While he waited, he tried sitting down but found himself too restless to remain inactive. It was a good thing that she'd come for a visit, he told himself as he paced the length of the lobby. He'd wanted to explain to her about his changed feelings face to face rather than over the telephone. Her coming to Bethlehem Springs was surely an act of Providence.

"Joshua!"

He spun around to see Mary Theresa standing on the staircase. A few steps behind her, dressed in a black gown, was her cousin, Blanche. He'd only taken two steps forward before Mary Theresa flew the rest of the way down the stairs and across the lobby. She paused only a second, grinning up at him, before throwing her arms around his neck and kissing him.

For his part, he was frozen in place, taken by surprise. Such a public display of affection wasn't normal for Mary Theresa. Naturally they had kissed before, but not like this. And not in view of others. Not even when they'd said good-bye in St. Louis.

He took hold of her hands from around his neck and peeled

her away, stepping back to look into her eyes. "Mary Theresa, what are you doing here?"

"I've missed you, Joshua. You're a horrid correspondent. You've scarcely written to me at all since you left St. Louis."

He looked around to see if anyone was watching them, then took her by the arm and steered her toward the dining room, the restaurant devoid of other customers at this hour.

"Are you surprised to see me?" she asked. "I knew you would be."

"However did you convince your parents to let you take this trip?"

She sat on the chair he pulled out for her. "My cousin helped me persuade them." She looked over her shoulder and motioned for Blanche to join them. "Besides," she added as she faced him again, "I'm not a child. Even Grandfather thought it a good idea that I visit you."

"A good idea?"

She leaned forward. "Isn't it time we begin planning our wedding?"

❦

After looking inside, Daphne closed the door to the bedroom where her nephew and niece were napping. Laughter floated up the stairs from the living room where the rest of the adults—Griff, Cleo, Woody, Morgan, and Gwen—had settled after dinner. Everyone had declared the meal a complete success, and Cleo had glowed with happiness from their praise.

The conversation had drifted from that morning's sermons at the Methodist and Presbyterian churches to some improvements the Arlingtons had made around the ranch complex before the onset of winter to the physician who had recently come on staff at the New Hope Health Spa, ending with—as Daphne returned from checking on the children — the new rocking chair near the living room window.

"I ordered it from Sears Roebuck," Woody said. "It's a gift for Cleo. I thought she might like to have it this winter. And later on too."

Daphne thought it a strange gift. Cleo wasn't the sort to sit in a rocking chair and while away the time. She tended to eschew rocking chairs for bucking broncos.

Then Gwen let out a squeal and jumped up to embrace her twin. "When? When is it?"

"In June," Cleo answered, eyes sparkling.

A heartbeat later, Morgan was out of his chair and slapping Woody on the back. "That's grand, Woody."

It was only then that Daphne realized what had gone unsaid. Cleo was pregnant. She hurried to join the other two women. They hugged and laughed and cried, then did it all over again until Woody pressed his way into their midst and claimed his wife for himself. He kissed her cheek and called her beautiful.

Tears filled Daphne's eyes as she thought of Joshua, imagining a similar scene with the two of them as the central characters. She pictured herself beside Joshua before the fireplace in Morgan's house, announcing to her family that they were to be blessed with a child. She envisioned the tender look in Joshua's blue eyes and the strength of his arm as it encircled her shoulders.

She turned and walked to the window, surreptitiously glancing at her watch. It was past time for the afternoon train to have arrived in Bethlehem Springs. Was Joshua back from his visit to Boise? Had he by any chance gone to her house to see her only to be disappointed by her absence?

Let's go home. She faced the room again, her gaze moving to her brother. *Decide it's time we leave for town, Morgan. I want to see Joshua. Oh, God. Please let Joshua be home again.*

⸎

"Grandfather has reminded me several times since you left St. Louis that he isn't getting any younger." Mary Theresa rolled her eyes. "I think he'll live to be a hundred, but it does seem he's impatient to see us married." Her expression changed, a tiny frown marking her brow. "Aren't you impatient too?"

Joshua glanced at Blanche, then back at Mary Theresa. "We haven't ever talked about a wedding."

"Isn't he silly, Cousin Blanche?" Mary Theresa laughed. "Joshua, don't you know we females begin planning our weddings when we're still little girls? There hasn't been much need for you and me to talk about it. But I do need my groom to at least agree on the wedding date."

He'd never asked her to marry him. He'd never told her he loved her. Not once in all these years. Nor, for that matter, had she said she loved him. He'd thought a genuine affection would be enough between them, that love could come later. But if so, why hadn't he proposed?

Not that Mary Theresa seemed to require a proposal.

"Joshua?"

He rubbed his forehead with his fingers. "This is all rather sudden."

"Sudden? Good heavens, Joshua. How can you say such a thing?"

"I mean, I don't know for certain how long I'll be staying in Bethlehem Springs. And I ... I'm not even sure I'll be able to get my job back when I return to St. Louis. I can't marry if I'm not employed."

"But there are other newspapers, other jobs. Aren't you working now as the managing editor of the paper?"

"Yes, but—"

"Then if necessary, we shall remain in Bethlehem Springs until you have sufficient experience to move on to another paper back in Missouri."

Panic began to churn in his chest. Where was the submissive, eager-to-please Mary Theresa of his memory? Or had she existed only in his imagination?

He cleared his throat. "How long will your visit be?"

"Until the end of the week. That was all my parents would agree to. But it should be ample time for us to settle on a date for our wedding and make whatever other plans we think necessary."

Tell her. Tell her you love another.

Mary Theresa took hold of his left hand and squeezed it between both of hers. "Oh, Joshua. I've missed you terribly. You can't know how much. How shall I manage until our wedding day?"

A waiter appeared to take their order.

"Would you like something to eat?" Joshua asked, looking at the two ladies with him.

Mary Theresa shook her head. "We dined less than two hours ago. But I would enjoy a pot of tea. Cousin Blanche?"

"Tea would be lovely."

"Tea for the ladies," he said to the waiter. "Nothing for me."

The young man nodded and walked away.

Joshua racked his brain for the right words to say to Mary Theresa. Could he tell her the truth without hurting her? This wasn't her fault, after all. It was he who'd had a change of mind, a change of heart.

Voices engaged in conversation flowed into the dining room a few moments before more guests entered. For a heartbeat, Joshua thought he didn't know any of them. Then he recognized Bert and Helen Humphrey, owners of the town's mercantile. When Bert saw him, he smiled and walked straight for their table.

"Mr. Crawford. You're back already. Christina Patterson mentioned to the wife and me that she thought you would return today." Bert's gaze flicked to Mary Theresa and Blanche.

There was no way to avoid the introductions. "Mr. Humphrey, may I present Miss Donahue and, her cousin, Mrs. Collins."

"How do, ladies. Pleased to make your acquaintance. Are you new to Bethlehem Springs?"

"Thank you, Mr. Humphrey. It's a pleasure to meet you. Yes, we're new. I came to visit Mr. Crawford ... my fiancé."

The word felt like a punch in the stomach.

"Fiancé? You don't say." Bert grinned at Joshua. "Well, aren't you a lucky man?" He looked over his shoulder. "Helen, come here and meet Mr. Crawford's intended."

Joshua needed to get away from here. He needed to talk with Mary Theresa alone. He needed to stop this before it got any worse — if that was even possible.

TWENTY-TWO

Dusk had fallen over Bethlehem Springs by the time the McKinley sleigh pulled to a stop in front of Daphne's house. Lamplight spilled through windows all along Wallula Street. Only her home remained dark.

While Gwen waited in the sleigh with the children, Morgan escorted Daphne inside and stoked the fire in the wood stove for her. Then he kissed her on the cheek and bid her good night. She waited at the open door to wave as they pulled away, disappearing around the corner a moment later. With a shiver, she pushed the door closed.

Two days had passed since Joshua stood in almost this same spot and kissed her. Two days that seemed more like a lifetime ago.

"Oh, Joshua," she whispered.

Disappointment squeezed her heart. She'd hoped she would be able to see him upon their return from the ranch, but they'd left for town too late. Daphne would have to wait until tomorrow.

A knock at her back caused her to jump. Could it possibly be—

She spun around and yanked open the door. Another wave of disappointment followed when she saw Edna Updike—not her most favorite person—standing on the other side of the screen, a lantern in her hand.

"Miss McKinley, I was so glad to see your return."

Daphne realized that her neighbor was upset and felt a sting of guilt for her less than gracious thoughts. "What is it, Mrs. Updike? Is something wrong?"

"It's Gretchen. She's missing."

Gretchen. The Updikes' foul-tempered calico cat.

"We've searched everywhere. I thought perhaps she might be in your shed. Would you mind if I looked?"

"Of course not." She pushed the screen door open. "Come through the house. The walk is swept in the back and it will be easier than if you went through the alley."

"Thank you. I've been so worried. She never runs away, and she hates going out in the snow. I can't imagine what's happened to her. She must have slipped outside when Mr. Updike and I left for an early dinner with friends at the Washington Hotel."

Daphne made a sympathetic sound in her throat as she led the way to the back door.

"Mr. Updike is fond of the hotel's pork chops, and the chef always runs a special on Sundays."

"Hmm."

"He swears Gretchen was lying on the sofa when we left."

Daphne grabbed her coat and put it on before opening the door and leading the way to the shed. Light from the lantern soon showed that the door to the shed — once used to house Gwen's buggy horse and now used to shelter Daphne's motorcar — was slightly ajar.

"Good news, Mrs. Updike. It looks like your cat could have gone in there if she wanted to."

"Oh, I hope so. Gretchen. Here, kitty, kitty."

Snow had drifted into the covered area outside the shed, but not so much that Daphne couldn't open the door wide and allow Edna entrance.

"Gretchen. Here, kitty, kitty."

There was a moment of silence, followed by a distinctly unhappy meow. Edna pressed her free hand to her chest. "Something *is* wrong with her." The look she turned on Daphne was accusatory, as if Daphne had done something to harm the cat.

They found Gretchen underneath the workbench, nesting in a pile of rags, along with three newborn kittens.

"Merciful heavens!" Edna's eyes went wide with surprise. "I've been scolding Mr. Updike for feeding her too much."

Daphne couldn't help it. She laughed.

"I thought she was just getting old and fat."

"Not too old to become a mama." Daphne reached down and picked up one of the kittens, bringing it close to her face. "Aren't you precious?" she whispered. The kitten was white and black, teeny ears sticking out from the sides of a head that seemed too large for its rather scrawny body. It began complaining in a high-pitched yowl, so Daphne returned it at once to its nervous mother. "I'll get a basket for you to take them home in."

Edna held the lantern closer to Gretchen and her babies. "However did this happen?" she muttered.

Daphne swallowed another laugh. Wouldn't her neighbor be horrified if Daphne decided to explain how such a thing could happen. She supposed she should be ashamed for entertaining the thought, no matter how momentary.

She stepped onto a stool and pulled a wicker basket from a shelf. It was covered in a thick layer of dust, but otherwise perfect for the task at hand. "This should be large enough for the four of them."

"I'll have to find homes for them quickly. Mr. Updike tolerates Gretchen, but he won't allow me to keep those kittens once they're weaned." She gave Daphne a hopeful smile. "Perhaps you'll want one?"

"Oh, Mrs. Updike, I don't know. I've never had a pet. I'm not sure—"

"A cat is a wonderful companion for a spin—" Edna stopped suddenly, a look of consternation widening her eyes, the unfinished word hanging awkwardly between them. After a few heartbeats, she finished, "For an unmarried woman such as yourself."

A spinster? My, it was tempting to tell Edna Updike to take her cat and kittens and get out. Get out and never speak to her again. Instead Daphne forced a pleasant expression onto her face—not quite a smile but as close as she could manage—and said, "Let me help you get them into the basket." She knelt on the dirt floor.

"Thank you."

A *spinster*. At one time, the word had meant nothing more than that a woman was unmarried. Two centuries earlier, it had been an official legal term: *Daphne McKinley of Bethlehem Springs, Spinster*. No judgment. Simply fact. But somewhere along the way, it had taken on a derogatory meaning. A woman incapable of making a match. An *unwanted* woman. That's how her neighbor meant it, to be sure.

"Have you ever had pork chops at the Washington?" Edna asked, her desire to change the subject apparent. "They're quite delicious. Oh, you'll never guess who we saw there. Mr. Crawford, the new editor of the *Herald*, with his fiancée. The Humphreys were introduced to the young woman and her cousin before we sat down to eat. Helen Humphrey thought Miss Donahue quite charming. Personally, I believe her parents showed an error in judgment, allowing two young women to travel this far alone. The cousin is hardly an appropriate chaperone, even if she is a widow."

The air in the shed became thick and heavy, and the walls

seemed to press in. Somehow Daphne managed to keep moving, to put the last of the kittens into the basket, the bottom of it now lined with the rags that had made up Gretchen's birthing bed. She stood and handed the basket to Edna. "There you go." The words came out a whisper.

"Oh, my. Please say you'll take one of these kittens when they're weaned. If I can't find a home for them, I'm quite sure Mr. Updike will drown them."

Daphne motioned toward the door. "Maybe. I'll think about it. Maybe the black-and-white one."

Anything to be rid of the woman before her heart finished breaking in two.

⚯

January 1, 1873

Another new year. They seem to pass more quickly all the time.

Angelica Ruth is nearly four months old. She recognizes her mother and me and smiles and coos accordingly. She also rolls from her back to her tummy and over again. Annie and I take inordinate pleasure in these accomplishments. I cannot imagine what we shall be like when she takes her first steps.

God has poured out so many blessings on me since the day I was born again. How could I not choose to serve Him in every way that I can?

When I left off writing my story, I had arrived at the summer of 1867. Just five-and-a-half years ago. About a tenth of my life. The most important tenth, to be sure. At least that is true in light of eternity. But I am getting ahead of myself.

As detailed earlier, becoming a judge didn't change me for the better. It was business as usual. But in the fall of 1869, I hired a fellow to manage the opera house. He came highly recommended by an acquaintance of mine. His name was Samuel Kristofferson, a Southerner whose family lost everything in the War between the States. His business acumen impressed me from the start, and his long associations with people in the theatrical world were just what I needed to make my latest enterprise thrive. I wanted to bring in the very best performers. Just because Bethlehem Springs wasn't the largest city in the Northwest didn't mean I wanted to settle for less.

Samuel was about five or so years younger than me and single. A good looking sort, too, so I asked him one day why he'd never married. I assumed it was because he didn't think he had enough money or perhaps because he had moved around a lot in his work or because of the hardships that followed the war. But it wasn't any of those reasons, according to Samuel. He said he was waiting on God's timing. I almost regretted hiring him because of it. In the days that followed, I wondered why I didn't fire him whenever he started what I called his "God talk."

But the truth was I was the one who started those conversations about God, not Samuel. Not that I came right out and said so in plain English. I disguised my questions and challenges in rhetoric and legal mumbo jumbo. But Samuel wasn't fooled. He saw me as no one had seen me since my mother died. It wasn't a comforting feeling at first. To have someone see the real me and not run the other direction wasn't the way things usually happened. But then, Samuel wasn't an ordinary man either. Least not as far as I could tell.

Bethlehem Springs had two protestant churches back then.

As far as I knew, most of the men who went to services were the ones who had wives—and there weren't a lot of those yet. The town was still young and rough. It wasn't the kind of place for families. Still, there were some married men who came with wives and children in tow. Most of the family men weren't miners. They came to open the mercantile and the bakery and other businesses that catered to the needs of the men working claims throughout the mountains.

What I noticed most about Samuel was that he didn't just go to church on Sundays and live like everybody else the rest of the week. And he wasn't the pious sort either. No matter who he was talking to, he always gave them the same warm handshake and level gaze. Even the scantily clad girls who worked in my saloon didn't change him. He treated them like ladies of quality, all the time keeping his eyes on their faces, never letting himself look upon the exposed flesh above their bodices. Only man I ever knew who managed to do that. Guess that's why the girls liked him so much.

Isaiah 42:16 says: "And I will bring the blind by a way that they knew not; I will lead them in paths that they have not known: I will make darkness light before them, and crooked things straight. These things will I do unto them, and not forsake them."

I was certainly blind when it came to the things of God. My parents didn't live long enough to show me the right path to walk on. I'm sure the good Lord tried to get my attention through the years, but I couldn't see it. Not when I was a boy. Not when I came west on the wagon train. Not when I was in California making my fortune.

I can look back now and say with the certainty of my faith that God sent Samuel Kristofferson to Bethlehem Springs to reach through to me when nothing and no one else could.

As it is written in John 9, "One thing I know, that, whereas I was blind, now I see." Hallelujah!

TWENTY-THREE

Joshua awoke on Monday morning with a weight on his chest. He didn't have to analyze the feeling. He knew it was because of Mary Theresa. Try as he might, he hadn't found the words or the opportunity to say what needed to be said before the two of them parted yesterday, and his failure to speak up had haunted him throughout the night.

He sat on the side of the bed and paused to rub the back of his neck where the muscles had become as hard as bricks.

Mary Theresa, I can't marry you ... I don't love you ... I love another woman ... You need to go home to St. Louis and find someone else to marry ... Someone who loves you and deserves you.

The words sounded cold and harsh in his head. Maybe he shouldn't mention loving another woman. Maybe he should simply tell Mary Theresa they were wrong for each other. That might be a kinder and gentler rejection.

As he rose and went through his morning routine — washing, brushing his teeth, getting dressed — he thought about his and Mary Theresa's grandfathers, about their hopes that the two families would be united in marriage. Would Joshua's grandfather still have wished for it if he were alive today? Perhaps not. The man Joshua remembered had loved his wife intensely. Even as a boy, Joshua had understood that. Surely he wouldn't have wanted his grandson to marry for any reason other than love. Not even to please him.

But Mary Theresa *would* be hurt, and Joshua had no one to blame but himself for it. He was an adult. He should have realized long before this that he'd put off marriage because he didn't love her. Not as a man should love his wife. What did it say about him that he'd allowed her and both of their families to believe he intended to marry her all this time? At the very least it showed a lack of judgment—and, even worse, it revealed a serious flaw in his character.

He checked his watch. Mary Theresa and Blanche should be eating breakfast in the hotel dining room right about now. Mary Theresa had invited him to join them, but he'd made no promise to do so. Better to wait until they could meet privately. Besides, he had little appetite this morning.

He slipped on his suit coat and went downstairs to the newspaper office. The first to arrive, he set about turning on the electrical lights before stoking the fire in the woodstove. Next he prepared the coffeepot and put it on the stove. By the time the water began to boil, Christina Patterson had come in the back door.

"Good morning, Joshua," she greeted him. "I hear congratulations are in order."

He winced as he swiveled his chair to face her. He shouldn't be surprised that his employer had heard the news already, yet he was.

"Why didn't you tell us you were getting married next spring?" She hung her coat on the rack, followed by her hat.

Because I didn't know myself. He wondered who else had heard the news. Daphne? Yes, very likely she had. His stomach plummeted.

"Helen Humphrey says your young lady is very pretty."

"Yes, she is." He swallowed the urge to say that Mary Theresa wasn't his young lady. He hadn't the right to deny the engagement until he'd spoken to her. Like it or not, by his silence yesterday he had turned the engagement from supposition into fact.

Christina came to stand near the stove. "Tell me about her. How did the two of you meet?"

"Our grandfathers were the best of friends. I've known Mary Theresa since she was born."

"Childhood sweethearts. How romantic."

Joshua felt like a fraud. A cad. A teller of lies.

"Nathan and I met when we were children too." Christina lowered her gaze to the door of the stove where firelight danced behind the glass. "I believe being friends first gave us a strong foundation for our marriage. We almost never quarreled. Not in all the years we were married."

"How long was that?" he asked, glad to turn the conversation away from himself.

"It would have been eighteen years in February."

"You must have been very young when you married."

"I turned eighteen on our wedding day. Nathan was twenty." She glanced toward him, and he could see tears glittering in her eyes. "I regret every day that we weren't together when we could have been. But then I never expected he would die so young." She forced a quavery smile. "Don't waste a moment with your young woman, Joshua. Love is too important, and none of us know how much time we have on this earth."

Christina meant Mary Theresa, but it was Daphne who came to his mind as she spoke. No, he didn't want to waste time. He wanted to be with her. Somehow, some way, he had to straighten out this mess.

❧

The promise of dawn had begun to lighten Daphne's bedroom by the time she opened her eyes after a long night filled with feelings of anger, betrayal, and heartbreak. She'd told herself a thousand times that she needn't feel any of those things. Yes, he'd kissed her. But he shouldn't have kissed her, and he'd apologized for doing so. She'd wondered why at the time. She didn't have to wonder any longer. She knew.

Joshua was engaged.

Pain cut into her chest again.

It was foolish to think she'd loved him, even for a day. She hardly knew him. How could she love him?

She wiped tears from her eyes with the backs of her hands.

She didn't love him, hadn't loved him, wouldn't love him. Whatever she'd felt for Joshua Crawford—which was friendship at most and perhaps some gratitude for the care he'd shown her when she was ill—was over now. Gone. Finished. Done with.

She drew in a long breath and let it out. It was time she pushed all thoughts of Joshua out of her mind. She would honor her commitment to writing her column, a job given to her by Christina Patterson, but that would be the only reason she would need to see or talk to him.

She reached for her dressing gown as she sat up and lowered her legs over the side of the bed. "I'll work on my book today," she whispered. Perhaps she would kill Rawhide Rick after all. Or better yet, she could torture one of his relatives. A younger relative with pale blue eyes.

When she walked into the kitchen a short while later, she heard the wind whistling under the eaves of the house. Would they see more snow today? It seemed as if they'd already had more than usual for this early in the season. Christmas was still more than three weeks away.

Listening to the wail of the wind caused a sadness to well up in her chest. Lonely. She was lonely. Not a familiar feeling. Daphne appreciated her solitude. She'd spent a great deal of time alone without feeling lonely. But something told her that this morning she could be in a huge crowd and she would still feel lonely.

Because of Joshua.

More tears threatened, but she fought them back. She refused to give into a crying jag. She refused to feel sorry for herself. Good heavens! She had an abundance of things to be thankful for. And besides, she had survived quite nicely without a man in her life for twenty-seven years. She would continue to do so hereafter.

She swept aside the curtains at the window over the sink. It was light enough to show that it wasn't snowing. At least not yet. Unless her eyes deceived her, the sky was a ceiling of dark clouds from horizon to horizon. She let the curtains fall closed.

A snowy day was the perfect inducement to stay indoors and write.

❦

Joshua called Mary Theresa at the Washington Hotel a little before eleven that morning, but Blanche answered instead.

"She's on her way to the newspaper right now. She wanted to see where you live and work. I told her it was too cold to go out, but she wouldn't listen to me."

Joshua thanked Blanche and said good-bye before hanging up the telephone. Perhaps he should take Mary Theresa upstairs to his apartment as soon as she arrived. That would give them the necessary privacy for the discussion that needed to take place, the sooner the better.

He heard the door open and turned, expecting to see Mary Theresa.

He saw Daphne instead.

She looked stunning in an orchid-colored coat with a silver fur collar. Her dark hair was hidden beneath a matching fur hat. When their gazes met, she stopped and stared back at him. Whatever she was thinking, it wasn't good.

"Is Mrs. Patterson here?" she asked at last.

"Not at the moment." He walked toward the front counter. "She should return soon. Would you like to wait?"

Her face was like stone. Her expression didn't change an iota. "No, I'll come back later." She turned.

"Daphne, wait."

She flinched as if he'd struck her.

"There's something I need to—"

The front door opened again. Joshua hoped it was Christina returning. It wasn't.

Mary Theresa entered the office. When Daphne glanced her way, Mary Theresa smiled and said, "Hello." Then she looked at him. "Good morning, Joshua." Her smile broadened even more as she walked to the counter.

His gaze flicked from Mary Theresa to Daphne and back again. Part of him wished that Daphne would leave before he had to make the introductions. Part of him was glad when she didn't.

"Is it all right that I dropped in like this?" Mary Theresa set her purse on the counter. "I hoped we could have lunch together. I declare, there is little else to do in this town but eat. What beastly weather. I know you said in your very first letter that you missed the bustle of St. Louis, but I had no idea it would be so quiet here. However have you stood it?"

Again his gaze slipped to Daphne, lingering a moment longer this time.

Mary Theresa must have noticed the direction of his eyes for she turned around to face Daphne. "Joshua, aren't you going to introduce me?"

"Of course." What else could he do? He moved around the counter. "Miss McKinley, may I present Miss Mary Theresa Donahue from St. Louis? Miss Donahue, this is Miss Daphne McKinley. She writes—" He stopped himself before he mentioned D. B. Morgan and The McFarland Chronicles. "Miss McKinley writes a weekly column for the newspaper."

The two women acknowledged the introductions with nods of their heads and polite smiles that didn't reach their eyes. Joshua felt as if he were drowning in quicksand.

Finally, Daphne broke the silence. "I hope you enjoy your stay in Bethlehem Springs, Miss Donahue." She glanced at Joshua. "Please ask Mrs. Patterson to call me."

"I will." He wanted to take hold of her arm, stop her from leaving, try to explain. But he couldn't. Not until he'd spoken with Mary Theresa. And so he watched her leave, a cold wind swirling into the office before the door closed behind her.

"She's quite pretty, isn't she?" Mary Theresa said softly.

He turned toward her. "We need to talk."

"I know. There's ever so much to decide." Her eyes brightened and her cheeks grew rosy. "First we must choose a date for the wedding. Mother thinks early spring would be the best. Surely you'll be able to return home by then."

To be honest, except for his job at the newspaper, there might no longer be any reason for him to remain in Idaho. It seemed there wasn't much more he could learn about his grandfather's past. And if the look on Daphne's face and in her eyes had told him anything, it was that she would prefer never to see or speak to him again. If that were true, he might as well go back to St. Louis and marry Mary Theresa.

Might as well ... but he wouldn't.

TWENTY-FOUR

For two more days, Joshua tried to find a time and place where he could speak with Mary Theresa privately. But each time he thought he'd found his chance, she seemed to slip away from him, the opportunity past. In the meanwhile, people kept dropping by the newspaper or stopping him in the street to congratulate him on the impending nuptials. All he could do was respond with a smile and a "thank you," hating himself a little more by the minute.

On Wednesday, with only two days remaining before Mary Theresa and Blanche were scheduled to leave on the morning train, he made up his mind that he would tell her what he thought when they met for lunch at the hotel, even if he had to do it in the dining room with her cousin at the same table and townsfolk and other guests seated around them.

After leaving the newspaper office, he walked along Main and was nearly to the corner at Washington Street when he caught a glimpse of an orchid-colored coat disappearing into the hat shop. Daphne. How many other coats of that unusual color could there be in this town? Had she seen him? Had she gone into the small shop to buy a hat or to avoid meeting him on the street?

Without a plan in mind, he opened the shop's door and entered. Daphne stood at a display, holding a black fur hat in her hands.

A clerk came out of the back room. "May I help you, Miss McKinley?"

"No, thank you, Miss Overgard. I'm just looking."

"And you, sir?"

"Thank you, but I'll wait." His words drew Daphne around. "Miss McKinley." He tipped his head.

"Mr. Crawford." Her expression revealed nothing to him.

"I like the silver one you're wearing better."

She waited a heartbeat, then held out the hat to the clerk. "I'll take this one. Please put it in a box for me."

Ah, that revealed plenty. She was putting him in his place. She didn't care what he thought.

As the clerk returned to the back room, Joshua lowered his voice. "Daphne—"

"How is your fiancée? I hope she has changed her mind about Bethlehem Springs now that she's been here a few more days." Although she smiled a little as she spoke, the look in her eyes was as cold as the wintery day outside.

"Mary Theresa is fine. But I'd like to explain about—"

"There's no need for explanations, Mr. Crawford."

"But there is."

Several quick steps took Daphne to the doorway to the back room. She swept aside the curtain. "Miss Overgard, I have some other errands I must see to. Would you please have my purchase delivered to my home?"

"Of course," came the answer from the other room.

Daphne faced him again. "Good day, Mr. Crawford."

He stepped aside and allowed her room to pass. The door closed behind her with hard finality.

She was angry. Very angry. He took a measure of hope from

that discovery. Surely it meant she still cared for him, at least a little.

He left the hat shop and hurried on his way to the hotel. God willing, this lunch with Mary Theresa would be the first step he took toward setting things right.

⚶

I won't cry ... I won't cry ... I won't cry.

Daphne repeated the words in her mind all the way home and was grateful that she succeeded in holding back the tears. Tears of anger, not heartbreak. Heartbreak might follow but now all she felt was fury and indignation.

How dare he follow her into that shop and speak to her? He'd used her most despicably. Kissing her the way he had when he was engaged to marry another woman. It mattered not to her that he'd apologized. All these weeks in Bethlehem Springs and not a word to anyone that he was promised in marriage to a woman in St. Louis.

She pictured Mary Theresa Donahue in her mind. The lovely red hair peeking out from beneath an emerald-green hat. The rich flecks of gold in her hazel eyes. The warmth in her voice when she'd said Joshua's name. The possessive way she'd touched his arm.

Daphne dropped onto the sofa. How could he have done this to her? She'd thought—

Oh, it didn't matter what she'd thought. Besides, it could have been so much worse. Joshua Crawford could be a charlatan for all she knew. What if he'd been after her money, as others had been before him? Or perhaps he had fiancées in several towns, never intending to marry any of them. How did anyone in Bethlehem Springs know who he really was?

Good heavens! He could be an exact replica of Rawhide Rick.

She got off the couch, hurried into her office, and began writing as fast as she could.

⚘

Joshua requested a table for two in the corner of the restaurant near the windows. Thankfully, cousin Blanche had not thought it necessary to join them for lunch. He hoped that would make it easier to say what he must to Mary Theresa.

She looked particularly fetching in a reddish-brown dress that complimented her hair and eyes. His mother—a painter of landscapes and still lifes—would have called the color burnt umber.

More than one man in the restaurant watched Mary Theresa as she and Joshua were taken to their table. He couldn't help wondering when she had blossomed into a true beauty. Years ago, no doubt. Why hadn't he noticed before? The answer was easy: because his mind had been filled with memories of her as a chubby toddler, as a schoolgirl in red pigtails, and as a skinny teenager with a figure as straight as a pencil.

After they were seated and the waiter took their orders, Mary Theresa leaned toward Joshua and said, "I spoke with Mama this morning on the telephone, and she reminded me that we really must settle on a date."

He drew in a breath and blew it out through his nose. "Mary Theresa, do you love me?"

"What?" Her brows arched and her eyes widened.

"Do you love me? It's a simple enough question."

"And a silly one. Of course I do."

Despite the correctness of her words and the speed with which she answered, Joshua wasn't convinced. "Do you find the idea of sharing my bed and having children with me an inviting one?"

"Joshua!" His name escaped on a whisper as her face turned scarlet. "That isn't the sort of thing one speaks of in a public place."

"Perhaps not, but we must talk about it anyway. You know that I'm fond of you, Mary Theresa, and I know our families have wanted us to marry since the day you were born. But is marriage to me what *you* want? Truly?"

"Joshua, what are you saying? Are you breaking our engagement?" The flush drained from her cheeks.

He wanted to remind her that he'd never proposed, that everyone had assumed he had when he hadn't, that *she'd* assumed he had when he hadn't. But he swallowed the words. They would only serve to hurt her and that wasn't what he wanted. Besides, as much as he would like to place the blame elsewhere, he bore responsibility for the situation.

"Grandfather will be disappointed if we don't marry," she said softly.

"I know. My grandfather would feel the same."

"Mother's counted on a spring wedding."

"Mmm."

She shook her head. "I never expected *this* to happen when I decided to visit you in Idaho. I thought it was all settled between us."

"I ... I'm not asking the question in order to hurt you, Mary Theresa. That's the last thing I want to do. But I need to know how you feel. Do you feel any ... passion when you think of me?"

She was silent for a long while as she stared at him. Different emotions flickered across her face. Hurt. Disappointment. Confusion. And finally a look of discovery. "No, I don't suppose I do."

"Don't you think you should?"

"I thought I would learn to love you that way. That's what everyone always says. That a couple grows to love each other as they live together." She turned her gaze out the window while worrying her lower lip. When she looked at him again, she said, "And you don't love me that way either. Do you?"

"No." He shook his head. "I don't love you the way I should, Mary Theresa. Not as a husband should love the woman he marries."

"Then I guess it would be for the best that we call off the engagement."

Surprise and relief mingled together as Joshua leaned against the back of his chair. He'd braced himself for a scene, for tears, for fury, and he wasn't sure what to do now, what to say next, when none of those things happened.

The corners of her mouth curved slightly upward. "Grandfather may throttle you when you return to St. Louis."

"Probably." He returned the smile, his body relaxing. "But I'm not sure I will return to St. Louis."

"Not return? Joshua, how can you say that?" Mary Theresa reached across the table and took hold of his hand. "Even if we don't marry, you belong in St. Louis. Grandfather won't throttle you. I was joking. What about your mother and stepfather? They would miss you. And what about your friends? You can't possibly think of staying in this little burg longer than necessary."

He squeezed her fingers. "I might stay. I like it here more than I thought I would." He pictured Daphne as he spoke. Unfortunately, he also pictured the coolness in her eyes the last time they'd met. But perhaps he could change her mind about him. He at least had to try.

⚜

Rawhide Rick had a new sidekick, a character as wicked as Richard Terrell ever hoped to be. Daphne named the character Josias

Crenshaw. She wasn't at all surprised to discover he looked a lot like Joshua Crawford—light brown hair, striking blue eyes, a dimple in his chin. Handsome enough and charming enough to fool unsuspecting, honest folks.

Daphne wrote as fast as her fingers could strike the keys of her Royal typewriter. She cared little about accuracy at this point. She merely wanted to get the story down on paper as it came to her.

A vile ruffian, Josias didn't hesitate at any terrible deed. Not if it would further his purpose. And this day he saw no reason to give a mayor's daughter a go-by. There wasn't a man in town who would stand up to him, no matter how ill he used the fair maiden.

Oh, the scoundrel. As his creator, Daphne would make certain he received his just desserts before the story ended. She would punish him until he begged for mercy—and she would take great pleasure in his suffering. Perhaps Miss Danforth would stab him. Several times. No, shooting him might be better. In the thigh, so he couldn't run away. Hadn't Griff told her about a bank robber who was shot in the leg and bled to death before anyone could bring the doctor?

Yes, a slow and painful death was in order for Josias Crenshaw. She was enjoying writing more today than she had in ages.

⸎

January 4, 1873

Samuel and I became good friends over the next year. And those "God talk" conversations I mentioned before, they often turned into spirited debates. Samuel wasn't afraid to challenge me, my ideas, or my actions. He spoke the truth. Hard truth, plenty of the times. Yet I can't say that I felt judged by him. I think more often than not he pitied me. Me, the wealthiest, most influential man in Bethlehem Springs, pitied. Made no sense to my way of thinking.

And yet it did make sense. Somewhere along the way, I began to see myself the way Samuel saw me. The way God saw me. My heart was black as pitch. My mind had been the devil's playground for four decades.

Seeing the real me, I began to change, although I didn't realize it at first. I'm sure others must have noticed. The judgments I passed down from the bench became more fair and honest. I was kinder to folks too. Not that I couldn't still be bribed or didn't think of myself first more often than not. An unregenerate heart still beat in my chest. But God was working on me, little by little by little.

Christmas of 1870 (a Sunday) arrived, and I was invited to dine with Samuel and some friends of his (mere acquaintances of mine), as well as his parents, who were visiting from Chicago. I'd paid no attention to the Christian calendar in my adult life. Christmas and Easter and such were just other days in the week to me. I don't recall buying gifts for anyone. Maybe as a young boy I made something for my parents for Christmas, but if so, the memory is too distant.

I believe it was curiosity that caused me to accept the invitation to spend Christmas Day with the Kristofferson family and friends. Mostly I wanted to meet the folks who'd raised a man like Samuel. Of course, I didn't choose to join them for the service at church. I waited until after that.

I'm not sure I can put into words what happened to me that Christmas afternoon as I sat around the table with those people who seemed unusually happy and contented. Certainly

I couldn't explain it as it happened. It was as if the heavens opened up and poured love over me, and the power of it broke me somewhere deep on the inside. I always prided myself on being a strong man, but I wasn't strong enough to withstand the all-powerful love of Jesus Christ.

Two weeks later, on the eighth of January 1871, I accepted another invitation from Samuel. I went with him to church, and it was then that I surrendered my heart to the Lord. I walked into that church the blackest of sinners. I walked out white as snow.

Only the Grace of God could work such a miracle.

TWENTY-FIVE

Big flakes of snow drifted lazily toward earth as passengers boarded the train on that Thursday afternoon.

"Is there anything you'd like me to tell your mother when I see her?" Mary Theresa looked up at Joshua from beneath a wide-brimmed hat, her left hand gripping his right.

"Only that I send her my love."

"You aren't going to change your mind as soon as I'm gone, are you? About marrying me, I mean." Her smile was teasing and without a trace of regret.

"No, Mary Theresa." He returned her smile. "We know this is the right decision for both of us."

She nodded, then released his hand, took hold of his shoulders, and rose on tiptoe to kiss him on the lips. When she stepped back, she said, "I hope we shall always be the best of friends. You're like a brother to me ... only you've never been the pest Harry and Kenneth are."

Joshua chuckled, remembering some of the many ways her older brothers used to torture her when she was a child.

"Mary Theresa, come along," Blanche called from the steps of the passenger car. "It's time to board."

The two women were leaving Bethlehem Springs earlier than originally planned. There were no reasons for them to stay, Mary

Theresa had told him yesterday, once the decision not to marry had been made.

"I'm coming." Mary Theresa grabbed Joshua's right hand one more time and squeezed it. "Please do write to me. Even if we aren't engaged, I'll still want to know what you're doing and if you're happy."

"All aboard!" the conductor shouted.

She rose on tiptoes again, but this time she didn't kiss him when he leaned toward her. Instead she said near his ear, "I hope she loves you in return. The way you want to be loved. The way you deserve to be loved."

He straightened, surprised by her words. He hadn't told her about Daphne. He'd never even hinted that he'd given his heart to another.

Speaking louder, Mary Theresa continued, "I'm going back to St. Louis to find the man who'll love me that way too. Who knows? Someone may already love me that way, and I've simply never noticed."

"Who?" Joshua asked.

But Mary Theresa only grinned, a mischievous twinkle in her eyes, as she released his hand and followed her cousin into the passenger car.

Joshua watched as the two women found seats on the platform side of the train. He continued to wait, ignoring the snow collecting on his coat shoulders and hat brim, until the whistle blew and the train jerked into motion. Mary Theresa waved and he waved back. Only then did he turn and stride away from the railroad station.

⊷

Ravenous, Daphne sat down at the table with her cold meatloaf sandwich and a glass of milk. She'd been up and at her desk hours before dawn, and the writing had gone so well that she'd forgotten to stop to eat. Thank goodness she'd had leftovers in the icebox.

She shoved her unruly hair away from her face, then held her sandwich with both hands and took a big bite.

"Mmmm."

Another day or two, and the first draft of her novel should be done. Finally! It seemed all she'd needed to bring the story together was to introduce a new villain into the series.

A strong dose of self-righteous anger hadn't hurt either.

She took several long sips of milk and began mulling over what she should do with Rawhide Rick. She would need a villain in future books, and if she killed Josias before the end of *The Dilemma of Marjorie Danforth*, she'd best keep Judge Terrell around. But she was having a hard time making him as disreputable as he'd been in previous books. She kept imagining the transformation she could take him through were he to surrender to Christ. After all, the real Richard Terrell had been the worst kind of rogue, but God had converted him into a stellar citizen and a wonderful father and grandfather. At least that's what Joshua had told her.

Joshua . . .

Her heart fluttered.

Oh, no. She wasn't going to let the mere thought of his name make her feel anything other than anger, indignation, or irritation. Better yet, all three. No sympathy. None. Not now. Not ever. She was done with tears, done with wondering what might have been between them if he weren't engaged to another woman. Her life without him had been and still was full and satisfying. She didn't need a man—and certainly not one such as Joshua Crawford—to make her feel complete.

She finished eating her sandwich, drank the rest of her milk, and then carried her plate and glass to the sink, where she washed and dried them and put them away. A glance out the window revealed a wintery scene. What had been large lazy snowflakes drifting to earth as she prepared her sandwich had become a thick curtain of white. There must be another two inches of snow on the ground since the last time she'd looked outside.

"Maybe I need a holiday."

Yes, that was a good idea. A trip someplace warm and sunny with a crystal-blue ocean and sandy gold beaches. As soon as this book was finished and mailed to Elwood Shriver at Shriver & Sons, she would make plans to leave. She would go after Christmas, though. She couldn't be away for the holidays. Her young nephew was old enough this year to take great delight in wrapped packages and a big Christmas tree, and she didn't want to miss that. But right after Christmas, she would go away. Perhaps she could get together some of her old friends from her college days —

No. She shook her head. Her friends were all married. She was the only one without a husband, and most of them had a child or two already. Who *could* she ask to go with her?

A knock on her front door interrupted her as she mentally ran through a list of people she knew.

If that was Edna Updike with the black-and-white kitten again — her neighbor had been over twice this week, trying to convince Daphne to give it a home when weaned — she feared she would shut the door in her face. She wasn't in the mood to —

The open door revealed Joshua on the other side of the screen.

He removed his hat, sending a flurry of snow onto her front porch. "Daphne, may I speak with you?"

"You'll have my column tomorrow." She started to close the door.

"No. Wait. Please."

Close the door ... Close the door ... Close the door ...

"I need to explain."

"No explanations are necessary."

"You're wrong. Hear me out, Daphne."

Close the door ... Close the door ... Close the door ...

"Please. Give me five minutes." He held up his right hand, his thumb and fingers extended. "Just five minutes."

Against her better judgment, she stepped back from the door and allowed him to enter. Memories of the last time she'd stood in this spot—in his arms, kissing him, him kissing her—flooded her thoughts as she turned and walked into the kitchen, putting plenty of distance between them.

Turning to face him once again, Daphne grasped the back of one of the kitchen chairs. "Say whatever it is you need to say and then leave. I'm busy."

"I came here from the train station. Miss Donahue and her cousin have returned to St. Louis."

"That's of no concern to me."

"We're not engaged, Mary Theresa and I."

Her heart leapt with hope. An unwelcome sensation.

"I could give you a long explanation about my relationship with Miss Donahue, but I won't. I'm not sure you'd believe me, even if I did."

She steeled herself against listening to him, against forgiving him. "I'm *quite* sure I wouldn't believe you."

"Daphne—"

"*Mr.* Crawford, if you have nothing else to say, I believe you should go."

He set his hat on his head. "I have plenty more to say to you, but I'll go, as you wish." He turned and opened the door, then glanced over his shoulder. "I'm not a bad man, Daphne. Just a flawed one. I shouldn't have kissed you when I did, and I'm asking for your forgiveness." A hint of a smile curved the corners of his mouth. "And I'll kiss you again, but only when the time is right."

The door had closed behind him before she could form a retort.

Oh, that insufferable man! As if she would allow him to get close enough to kiss her. *That* would never happen. Not a bad man? Ha! Scoundrel. Cad. Villain. Liar.

The urge to skewer him with words propelled her to her office and another writing session.

∾

Joshua walked briskly toward the office of the *Triweekly Herald*, head bent into the blowing snowstorm, hand gripping his coat collar close at the throat.

For some inexplicable reason, he felt in far better spirits after seeing Daphne. Maybe it was because of the momentary lowering of her guard when he'd said he and Mary Theresa weren't engaged. The cool look in her eyes had altered slightly. Only for a second, but he was certain he'd seen it. A look of optimism or anticipation or something similar. A look that said she might still care for him.

Yes, he *would* kiss her again, and next time, neither one of them would have cause to regret it.

TWENTY-SIX

Daphne set a cup of tea in front of her sister-in-law.

"Morgan and I were as surprised as anyone when we learned Mr. Crawford was engaged." Gwen shook her head, a frown knitting her brow. "I do feel as if he betrayed us, not mentioning he had a fiancée in St. Louis."

Now seated opposite Gwen, Daphne took a sip from her cup before answering. "He was under no obligation to do so. It was his private business. We were strangers to him. Why should he tell us?"

"But I thought . . . I thought you were forming an attachment to him."

So did I. "Well, you were wrong." *We were all wrong. But I'm fine. Right as rain. He matters not at all to me.* Still, she would rather talk of something else. "Did I mention that I'm nearly finished with my next book?"

Gwen laughed softly. "All right. I'll change the subject. No, you didn't mention anything about your book when I called this morning. I'm delighted to see you looking and acting more yourself. Will you allow me to read your manuscript before you send it to your publisher, now that you aren't keeping it a secret from the family?"

"Absolutely not. You'll have to wait until the book's published, like everyone else."

"And do you plan to ever let others know you're D. B. Morgan?"

Maybe getting the third degree about her writing wasn't preferable to talking about Joshua. "I haven't decided. I think not. At least not yet."

"Can you imagine Mrs. Updike's outrage were she to learn you write those scandalous dime novels?"

The two of them laughed. Not that they meant to be unkind toward Edna Updike, but both of them had experienced her censure over the years. They knew it took very little to earn her disapproval.

Daphne wiped tears from her eyes. "Gretchen gave birth in my shed last Sunday. Mrs. Updike was positively beside herself when she came over to ask if I'd seen the cat. Now she's trying to convince me to take one of the kittens when they're weaned. She's even told me her husband will drown them if she can't find homes for the little ones."

"Oh, dear." All trace of amusement vanished from Gwen's face. "That will never do."

Daphne sobered as well. "No, it won't do. I suppose I shall have to take one of them." As she said the words aloud, she realized she wasn't as opposed to the idea as she'd thought. It might be nice to have a companion in the house while she worked. Then another idea popped into her head, causing her to grin. "And I can give the other two to Andy and Ellie for belated Christmas presents."

"Oh, Daphne. I'm not sure your brother would approve of that."

"Leave him to me. I'll help Morgan see that kittens will be the perfect gift from his children's aunt."

❧

The South Fork had only a few customers when Joshua entered the restaurant that evening. Before walking to the table against the far wall, he said polite "hellos" to Mark Thurber and his sister, Ashley, then to Roscoe and Mabel Finch.

"Please tell Miss McKinley that I was delighted by her column in Monday's paper," Ashley Thurber said. "I had one of my students read it aloud to the rest of the class."

"Thanks. I'll tell her."

Joshua draped his coat over the back of the second chair at the table and placed his hat on the seat. Then he sat in the other chair and perused the menu. He'd planned to cook something simple in the kitchen of his apartment, but when the time rolled around, his feet had brought him to the South Fork instead. Maybe because his apartment seemed too quiet, too empty.

The waitress, Sara Henley, arrived at his table with order pad in hand. "What can I get for you, Mr. Crawford?"

Over the past two months, Joshua had dined at the South Fork often enough that he knew Sara moderately well. He'd learned that she was a landscape artist, like his mother, and that she was bound for art school in the spring. His knowledge of oil paints, canvasses, lighting, and such was modest but good enough for Sara to delight in talking with him about them whenever he was in.

"I'll have the beef stew tonight, Sara. Thanks."

"It's a good day for it. Colder than all git out."

"Yes, it is." He glanced toward the window, but all he could see beyond the glass was the blue-black of early nightfall.

"Anything to drink with your dinner?" Sara asked.

"Coffee, please."

"I'll have it out to you in a jiffy."

Joshua leaned against the back of the chair, his thoughts turning immediately to Daphne. He had hoped to see her today when she brought in her column, but she'd come when he was out of the office. He didn't think that had been by chance. She'd purposed it that way.

How was he to overcome her resistance, her anger, if she wouldn't see him in passing, let alone give him a moment to apologize again, maybe even give him an opportunity to explain? Didn't she realize there were always two sides to a story?

He wondered if God was amused by his plight. After all, it was his own hair-trigger temper that had played a part in bringing him to Bethlehem Springs. And even when he heard the truth about his grandfather, he hadn't accepted it because it didn't match what he believed. Those who disagreed with him could be hanged.

Now he wanted Daphne to listen to his side of the story, and she wouldn't. It seemed he was getting his comeuppance.

⚘

Daphne looked at the two words near the bottom of the white sheet of paper: THE END.

She couldn't believe how quickly she'd finished writing the book. The words had poured out of her at a record pace over the past few days. Perhaps because she'd needed to know how Josias Crenshaw would meet his demise. Rawhide Rick, now Judge Terrell in the fictional town of Beulah Springs, had sentenced Josias to be hanged by the neck until dead.

The plot was solid, and the resolution worked. *The Dilemma of Marjorie Danforth* might very well be the best novel she'd written. Funny, though. She wasn't as pleased as she should be. Perhaps because she'd taken mental revenge on a real person with each stroke of the keys that punished Josias.

Vengeance belongeth unto me, I will recompense, saith the Lord.

She rolled the paper from the typewriter and set it, face down, on top of the rest of the manuscript. Tomorrow she would begin reading the story for errors. Right now all she wanted was a bite to eat and a good night's sleep.

As she rose from the chair, she reached over and turned off the desk lamp, plunging the room into darkness. Was it really that late? Nightfall came early in December, but she hadn't thought she'd been writing so long. No wonder she felt stiff. Massaging the small of her back with the fingers of her right hand, she left her office and walked to the kitchen.

When Gwen had come for a visit earlier in the day, she'd brought with her some fried chicken, leftovers from the previous evening's meal. As far as Daphne was concerned, no one made better fried chicken than Opal Nelson, the McKinley cook. Now she took two pieces from the icebox and set them on a plate beside a biscuit smothered with honey. She didn't bother warming anything on the stove. A cold meal was fine with her.

Seated at the table, she thanked the Lord for the food before her, adding another word of thanks for the completion of the book.

Vengeance belongeth unto me ...

She tried to push the thought from her head. It was silly to let that verse plague her. God didn't care what happened to a character in one of her novels. The content, as long as it wasn't blasphemous, would be of little notice to the Maker of all creation.

Only that wasn't true, and she knew it. Everything about her — all that she did, all that she wrote, all that she felt — mattered to her Father in heaven. He cared what went on in her heart and mind, and it was there, in her heart and mind, that she'd taken vengeance against Joshua.

And yet, hadn't she the right to be angry with him? He'd kissed her when he was promised to another. That was wrong, any way a person looked at it.

Closing her eyes, she remembered the way she'd followed him

to the door, almost upon his heels. She remembered the way he'd steadied her with his hands on her arms as she'd swayed toward him, the way their eyes had met, the way her breath had caught in her chest. When she'd known he was going to kiss her, she'd risen to meet him.

"I'm sorry, Miss McKinley," he'd said when he pulled back.

Remembering stirred unwelcome emotions in her chest.

"I shouldn't have done that. Please forgive me."

No, he shouldn't have kissed her when he was engaged to Miss Donahue. It had been wrong of him. But he'd apologized. He'd asked her to forgive him.

Could she?

Should she?

⁓

January 10, 1873

I have learned something about myself since I began writing this account of my life. I am poor at it. What should have taken me no more than two weeks has taken me thirteen months. But there is still a little more to tell, and so I will try to do so now. At least I can write about it without feeling the heaviness of heart over my disreputable past.

After I received the Lord's forgiveness and became a Christian (I like to think my parents are rejoicing in heaven over the news, right along with the angels), I knew that I could not stay in the town where I had made my living selling alcohol to miners, misusing the girls who worked in my saloon, and doling out justice to the highest bidder. I wanted a new start. Samuel tried to dissuade me from leaving. He insisted that I was a testimony to the power of God to change a life.

But I felt certain the Lord was calling me back to the place of my youth.

And so I sold my properties and business holdings. I made restitution wherever possible to those I'd harmed. Then I bid farewell to Samuel, my brother in the faith, and to the West where I had spent all of my adult life. Instead of returning to Missouri on horseback as part of a wagon train, the way I crossed the prairies and the mountains so long ago, I rode in the comfort of a railroad passenger car. I was twenty-four when I left Missouri. I was now fifty years old, my hair turning gray, my body not so lean and hard as it once was. I left Missouri an impoverished, uneducated lad. I returned a man of wealth with a great deal of book-learning and life experiences, if not formal education. Most importantly, I was going back as a man with a new heart and a desire to serve God wherever He might want that to be.

I had no idea what work the Lord would have for me in St. Louis, but it was there He ultimately took me. I admit I sometimes grew impatient when doors for ministry didn't open instantly before me. I realize now that God was seasoning me, that He had a great deal to teach me before I would be ready to be used of Him. Patience wasn't my long suit, and I still needed to learn not to react when I became angry. "Be ye angry and sin not," the Good Book says. I had a ways to go in that regard.

Looking back, I now believe that God also had two important people to bring into my life—Annie Lincoln and Kevin Donahue. Annie came first. She will always come first in my heart, right after Christ Himself.

I remember the first Sunday I saw her in church. It was the spring of 1871. She had the sweetest face and the bluest eyes I ever saw. When she chanced to look my way, I almost stopped breathing. And after I learned that she was an unmarried woman, I made it my business to make her acquaintance.

I have known many women in my life, but with the exception of my mother, Annie was the first true lady to enter my world. That she wanted to befriend me, too, was one of God's miracles. That she learned to love me, even after I told her of my sinful past, was another.

We became engaged that summer, but Annie insisted that we wait until December to wed. I believe she wanted to give me time to change my mind—or for God to change it for me. But I knew in my heart of hearts that the Lord had arranged for us to be together. There would be no changing of my mind when it came to my beloved wife.

And so my story ends. At least the story of my old life. I have not written it down to share with others. It is for me alone. Perhaps I will read it every year on the anniversary of the day I was born again, just to remind myself of the amazing work God has done and to keep me headed in the right direction, lest I lose sight of the power of the Lord's grace and mercy.

TWENTY-SEVEN

A frigid wind whistled down Main Street on Sunday morning. The snow on the ground, close to two feet deep, had turned icy, making travel difficult, even dangerous. Even many of the most faithful of churchgoers stayed home that morning rather than risk a fall.

Daphne wasn't one of them. She was in need of divine guidance and hoped she would hear God more clearly in church.

But as she made her way along Wallula Street toward All Saints Presbyterian, she did wish the weather could have been less brutal. Even with her fur collar pulled up close around her neck, she couldn't stop her teeth from chattering as she leaned into the wind from the north. She kept her gaze lowered, watching for patches of ice or uneven ground that might cause her to slip. Thus it came as a surprise when a firm hand grasped her arm above the elbow.

"Let me help you."

Her heartbeat quickened at the sound of Joshua's voice. She couldn't help her reaction to him any more than the involuntary shivering from the cold.

"I wasn't sure I'd see anyone at church this morning," he shouted above the wind.

She forced herself not to look at him, not to reply. She might do or say something she would later regret.

It seemed to take forever to reach the steps of the church.

Joshua held onto her arm as they climbed them, not letting go until they reached the door. He held it open for her, and the wind at her back seemed to blow her into the narthex.

Walter Rawlings stood near the doorway to the sanctuary, and he smiled when he saw them. "Miss McKinley, Mr. Crawford. Welcome. It's good to see you both on such a blustery day."

"Good morning, Reverend Rawlings." Daphne loosened her grip on her coat collar and adjusted her fur hat with both hands. "That wind is dreadful."

"Indeed." The minister held out his hand toward Joshua, who stood at Daphne's side. "At least you don't have far to come, Mr. Crawford."

"It seemed farther than usual this morning."

Reverend Rawlings chuckled. "I agree. The parsonage seemed a good distance farther too."

The front door opened again, letting in another blast of cold air and a few more members of the congregation. Daphne took that opportunity to move into the sanctuary and walk toward her usual pew. Morgan and his family weren't there before her, and she wondered if they'd chosen to remain at home. She supposed that would be for the best. The road up the hill to their home could be treacherous in this kind of weather.

"May I join you, Miss McKinley?"

She glanced up, expecting to feel the anger and indignation that had been her companion ever since learning about Miss Donahue. She didn't feel it, and it unnerved her. Better to be vexed with him than to feel anything that put her heart at risk. Wasn't it?

"Please," he added.

To refuse seemed wrong, especially in this sanctuary, and so she nodded before moving into the pew and sitting down, grateful that the congregation was smaller than normal today. Fewer people to see her sitting with Joshua Crawford. Fewer people to gossip about it later.

⤙

That Sunday morning, Joshua's mind was rarely on the hymns, the reading of the Scriptures, or the good reverend's sermon. Throughout the hour, possible scenarios played in his imagination. Things he might say to Daphne. Things she might say to him in response. Ways he might act. Anything that might overcome her resistance. If he could get her to listen, just for a short while, he might be able to change her mind.

At the end of the service, Joshua followed Daphne out of the sanctuary, leaving enough space between them so she couldn't complain or tell him to leave her be but close enough she couldn't slip away. From the set of her shoulders, he guessed she realized what he was doing.

It wasn't until he followed her out the front door that he addressed her. "Might I have a word with you, Daphne?" He grabbed his hat before the icy wind could carry it off.

She turned toward him but didn't reply.

"Please. Allow me to walk you home."

"That isn't a good idea, *Mr.* Crawford." Wisps of curly black hair whipped against her neck and cheeks as she shook her head.

"Please," he repeated. "All I ask for is ten minutes of your time. Surely you can spare me that much." The look in her eyes told him she was wavering. He took advantage of it. "If you don't want me to come to your home, then come with me across the street." He motioned toward the office of the *Herald*. "We can talk in there, in clear view of any hardy souls who venture out in this weather."

There was a long moment of silence before she answered, "All right, Mr. Crawford. Ten minutes. And then I'm going home. *Alone.*"

Joshua made certain he didn't smile, even though he felt like it. Getting her to agree to spend ten minutes with him was a huge victory at this point. He reached to take her arm, but she pulled away and shook her head.

"I can manage perfectly fine on my own."

He nodded. "Of course. Whatever you wish."

She frowned, as if he'd said something objectionable.

They walked side by side across the street to the newspaper office. Once there, Joshua took the key from his pocket and opened the door, then motioned Daphne in ahead of him. A pale light fell through the windows, casting everything in a gray hue. The cool temperature of the front office would require them to keep their coats on. Joshua wished it otherwise, fearing Daphne would be able to leave without giving any advance warning.

In silence, she looked around the office, turning slowly. When she faced him again, she said, "You asked for ten minutes."

God, help her to hear my heart and not just my words.

She crossed her arms over her chest.

Joshua removed his hat and held it in his left hand. "Daphne, the only things you knew about my grandfather before I arrived were what you'd heard from Griff Arlington. But Richard Terrell was more than a dishonest judge or a saloon owner or a miner. The man I knew loved God fiercely and, because of His faith, was a servant to others. He gave of himself constantly. He helped raise money to feed and clothe the poor. He visited the sick in hospitals, both people he knew and total strangers. Whenever he saw something in this world that breaks the heart of God, his heart was broken too. He did everything in his power to alleviate suffering where he found it."

The expression on her face hadn't changed, despite his impassioned words, and he suspected she was counting down the seconds until his ten minutes were up.

"I wish you could have known him. Whatever he was before Christ, he was vastly different afterward."

She opened her mouth as if to speak, then closed it again.

"Grandfather's best friend for the last thirty years of his life was a man named Kevin Donahue. A successful businessman in St. Louis. They were exceptionally close and thought so much alike that they hoped their families would be joined one day in marriage. But my grandfather's daughter and Kevin Donahue's son fell in love elsewhere. So the two old men put their hopes in their grandchildren to fulfill the dream. They talked about it all the time."

Daphne's gaze altered slightly. "You and Miss Donahue."

"Yes."

"You became engaged to honor your grandfather's wishes?"

This part was a bit tricky to explain. "Sort of."

"Sort of?" Her eyebrows arched.

"The thing is, we don't love each other like a couple who wants to spend a life together in marriage. We care about each other like a brother and sister or first cousins. We grew up together. We spent birthdays and Christmases and Thanksgivings and Easters together. Everyone—our grandfathers, my mother, her parents— talked as if our getting married was a foregone conclusion, and we accepted it the same way."

He saw the coolness return to her eyes. He was losing her again.

"I never asked Mary Theresa to marry me, Daphne. I always thought I would, but I never did. But she didn't take notice of that fine point, and that was my fault. I'm to blame for any misunderstanding on her part and on our families' part." He raked the fingers of his right hand through his hair. "When I realized I was falling in love with you, I knew I needed to tell Mary Theresa as soon as possible. I didn't want to do it in a letter. That seemed too cold. But I couldn't wait until I could return to St. Louis in person, so I called her on the telephone while I was in Boise. Only she and her cousin were already on their way to Bethlehem Springs to see me."

❦

When I realized I was falling in love with you . . .

A shiver ran up Daphne's spine. He'd fallen in love with her.

But did that matter? A man who would woo and kiss one woman while engaged to another wasn't to be trusted. Only he claimed he hadn't been engaged. Not really and truly. But why then had he asked for Daphne's forgiveness after kissing her?

"I came to Bethlehem Springs to find D. B. Morgan. I did that." He smiled briefly as he motioned toward her, palm up. "I came to discover the truth about my grandfather, and like what I learned or not, I did that too." He took a step forward. "What I didn't come to do was fall in love with you, but that's what happened. I never planned to stay in Bethlehem Springs longer than it took to finish my business. And if you don't want me, if you can't believe me or trust me, if you think there's no chance you could ever love me in return, then I guess it's time to give Mrs. Patterson my notice and go back to St. Louis."

The Book of Jeremiah said the heart was deceitful above all things. How could she trust her heart when it came to Joshua? Her heart wanted to believe everything he'd told her. But how could she? Honesty, being truthful in all things, was a matter of character, of integrity, and Joshua hadn't been completely honest with her until Mary Theresa came to see him. The man who would win her love had to be honest above all else.

"I must go," she whispered, turning toward the door.

Tears blurred her vision, but somehow she made her way out of the office and down the snowy street toward home. Somehow she managed not to let them fall until she was safely inside her cozy cottage.

Only then did she let herself weep for what she thought could never be hers.

TWENTY-EIGHT

Lying in bed that night, Joshua counted once again the many good reasons he had to return to St. Louis. His mother and stepfather were there. The Donahue family was there. His church family was there. There might even be opportunities for him to work for a large newspaper once again.

The sole reason to stay in Bethlehem Springs was Daphne McKinley. And if she couldn't forgive him, if she couldn't trust him, if she couldn't love him, he might as well do what he'd told her: give his notice and leave.

But as he pondered his options, he discovered all the good reasons in the world weren't enough to make him want to return to St. Louis. There were more reasons to stay than he'd thought at first. He didn't want to quit his job at the *Triweekly Herald*. He didn't want to say good-bye to the new friends he'd made in Bethlehem Springs. And no matter how many times Daphne whispered, "I must go," and turned away from him, he didn't want to give up on winning her love.

If he left, there was no hope of that happening.

If he stayed, some hope might exist.

Some hope was better than none.

He would stay.

As early as possible on Monday, he would place a call to his mother and tell her he wasn't going back to St. Louis. He would ask her to ship his personal possessions—his clothes, his books, some items that had been his grandfather's—to Bethlehem Springs at her earliest convenience. Maybe if he invited her and Charlie to visit him over Christmas she wouldn't protest his decision too much.

❧

Daphne couldn't sleep. The mournful wind kept her awake throughout the night. It sounded like she felt. Lonely. Abandoned. Heartbroken. In her mind she kept replaying Joshua's words as he'd shared about his grandfather, as he'd explained about his relationship with Mary Theresa, and most of all, what he'd said about his feelings for her.

"What I didn't come to do was fall in love with you, but that's what happened. I never planned to stay in Bethlehem Springs longer than it took to finish my business. And if you don't want me, if you can't believe me or trust me, if you think there's no chance you could ever love me in return, then I guess it's time to give Mrs. Patterson my notice and go back to St. Louis."

Tears threatened again. Rather than let them fall, she got out of bed, slipped her arms into the sleeves of her robe and her feet into her house slippers, and left her bedroom. In the parlor, she added wood to the stove before going into her office. There, she sat at her desk and pulled the finished manuscript toward her.

Dissatisfaction twisted in her belly. She'd thought this could be her best novel. It had everything it should. A little romance. Danger. Intrigue. Excitement. Two villains. Suspense. A hero who saves the day. Her publisher would love it. He would ask when the next volume would be ready. She should be happy.

She wasn't.

Again she heard Joshua's voice, telling her about the man her grandfather had become. She had based the fictional Rawhide Rick on the Richard Terrell who others had known and talked about, but she had manipulated his exploits to suit her stories.

"I wasn't completely honest either."

The character in her stories was a wicked man, someone she hadn't planned to change in future books. But wasn't the true story even more exciting—a villain, a dishonest man, redeemed by the love of Christ? Wouldn't it be wonderful to write *that* story? If she tried, could she do it justice?

"I believe you're a naturally gifted storyteller. You shouldn't waste that gift."

She moved the palm of her hand across the top page of the manuscript, reading the words:

The Dilemma of Marjorie Danforth
Volume 11, The McFarland Chronicles
by D. B. Morgan

Taking a deep breath, she pushed the stack of papers to the far side of her desk. Then she pulled a clean sheet of paper from the drawer, rolled it into the typewriter, and typed:

The True Story of Rawhide Rick
by Daphne Bernadette McKinley

A slow smile curved her lips. It gave her pleasure, seeing her real name typed beneath the title. But there was more to the joy than just wanting to write a book using her real name and not a pseudonym. It was more than because she wanted to write a story about a man changed by the power of God.

Perhaps the joy she felt was because she wanted to write it for the man she loved.

For Joshua.

"I love him," she whispered as she rose from the chair. "And I believe him."

She hurried out of the office and into her bedroom. She had to get dressed. She had to see Joshua as soon as the newspaper office was open for business. She had to tell him all that he meant to her.

❧

Joshua placed the call to his mother in St. Louis before either Christina Patterson or Grant Henley arrived at the office. It turned out that she wasn't surprised by his news.

"Mary Theresa called her grandfather before leaving Bethlehem Springs, and Mr. Donahue brought us the word."

"I hope you aren't disappointed, Mother."

"Darling, I wasn't surprised. You are a man who feels passionate about many things—your work, the truth, your faith—but I never thought you were passionate about your feelings for Mary Theresa. You care for her, of course, but I wanted more for your marriage than friendship alone. I wanted you to find someone who will feel as passionate about the things you care about as you are."

Joshua wished she'd been this frank with him years ago.

"Is there a young woman in Idaho who might be the one?"

"As a matter of fact, yes."

"I thought as much. And does she love you too?"

He sighed before answering, "Not yet."

"I'll pray for you both."

"Thanks, Mother. Listen, I can't afford to talk for long. I called to ask you to send my things you've been storing for me."

She laughed. "I already did. Right after I heard from Mr. Donahue. I had a feeling you would remain in Idaho, at least until spring. Your trunk should arrive soon. Perhaps today."

Joshua laughed with her. His mother, in his opinion, was an amazing woman.

"Joshua, I found something in the attic while I was organizing your things to send to you. It was in an old trunk of your grandfather's. I don't know why I've never run across it before now. I'm certain I went through everything after he passed on."

"That sounds mysterious. What is it?"

"It's a journal. He began writing it before he married my mother." She was silent a moment. "Darling, everything you've wanted to know about your grandfather is in that journal. It's the story of his life from the time he was a boy."

Joshua wasn't sure what to feel. Everything he'd wanted to know? The answers to all his questions, in his grandfather's own handwriting.

"I sent it to you, dear. I put it in with the rest of your things."

If his mother had found the journal years ago or even a few months ago, Joshua might still have his position as a reporter for the St. Louis paper, he would never have made this trip to Idaho, and he would never have met Daphne McKinley.

Thank God the journal hadn't been found too soon.

❧

The light was still gray, the sun not yet topping the mountains in the east, when Daphne left her house and hurried down the street toward the office of the *Triweekly Herald*. Her heart pumped fast, and she couldn't quite settle upon whether she wanted to laugh or cry. Either one would have been for joy.

The windows of the apartment over the newspaper office were dark. She was certain she would find Joshua at his desk. But when she entered through the front door a short while later, she was disappointed. He wasn't at his desk. No one was in sight.

"Hello?"

"Just a moment," Christina called from the room in the back.

Daphne clasped her hands in front of her chest and controlled the urge to run on through the office to find Joshua.

Christina looked out the doorway. "Oh, Daphne. It's you. What are you doing here so early? Was there a problem with your column?"

"No. No problem. But I need to talk to Mr. Crawford." A tiny thrill ran through her as she amended her words. "To Joshua."

If Christina noticed, she didn't let on. "I'm sorry. You just missed him. He's on his way to the depot to meet the morning train."

"The train?" She was too late. He was leaving, just as he'd told her he would.

"Yes. He told me he—"

Daphne didn't wait to hear whatever Christina had to say. She whirled around and raced out into the frosty morning. She ran as best she could through the snow. As she reached the rise in the road, she saw the train was already at the station.

Please don't go. Please don't leave.

She slipped on an icy patch and fell to her knees. A cry escaped her lips as she struggled back to her feet and kept going. She saw him then, climbing the steps to the platform.

"Joshua!"

He didn't stop, didn't turn. She was too far away to be heard over the hissing of the train.

"Joshua!"

Breathing hard, she ran on.

"Joshua!"

Now walking on the platform, he hesitated, then looked over his shoulder.

She waved her arm over her head. "Wait!"

He returned to the top of the stairs.

Daphne dragged in a deep breath and pressed on, hoping not to slip and fall again. She had to reach him. She had to stop him from leaving. It seemed an eternity before she reached the steps to the station platform. She paused to catch her breath again but kept her eyes locked on Joshua.

He came down two steps and stopped again.

"Please don't go, Joshua."

"I wasn't—"

"I was wrong. Terribly wrong."

"Wrong about what?"

"I shouldn't have walked out yesterday the way I did. It was rude. I should have stayed and listened to everything you had to say. I should have given you a chance to explain."

"You did. I'd said it all."

"Don't go back to St. Louis. Please stay."

The hint of a smile curved his mouth. "Why?" He came down one more step. Close enough that she could almost drown in the blue of his eyes.

"Because I shouldn't have judged you the way I did. I haven't always told the whole truth either. About my writing. About lots of things. If you're guilty of wrong doing, then so am I."

"I'm not sure that's reason enough for me to stay."

"Not reason enough?" Panic ignited in her chest. "But I love you, Joshua."

In a flash, he was off the last step and his arms were around her. "That's the only reason I need." He lifted her feet off the ground and kissed her, right there for anyone and everyone to see. Kissed her until she was more winded than the race to the station had left her. Kissed her thoroughly, completely, and until there was no doubt left in her mind that he loved her still.

When her feet touched the ground again, she opened her eyes to gaze into his. "You'll stay?" she asked softly.

"Actually, I came to see if my trunk has arrived." He gave a small shrug and grinned. "Mother shipped my things to me since it appeared I would be staying longer than first planned."

"You weren't leaving?" She drew back.

He shook his head, the grin fading away. "Not without you, Daphne. I'm not going anywhere without you. Not ever. Looks like you're stuck with me, for better or worse."

⁂

September 1, 1904

I am taking up this record of my life one last time. Much has happened since I made the last entry more than thirty years ago. Many good things. Some hard things. There has been great happiness and great sorrow.

Now I am dying. Although the physician doesn't say so, I know it is true. Perhaps I will live another month or two. Perhaps I will die before tomorrow comes. I don't mind. I am eighty-three years old. I've outlived many others. My eyesight is no longer good, and my aged body aches in many ways. It is time. My only regret is that I must say good-bye to those I love.

This journal has been a private thing, but now I wonder if it should be shared. I have never told Angelica Ruth about the man I was before I met her mother. Perhaps that is well and good. But there is Joshua to consider. Perhaps the boy should be told. Mine would be a cautionary tale, lessons that might keep him from making similar mistakes as he grows up without a father or a grandfather. I know too well what that is like.

As I look back over my years in St. Louis, these are the strongest memories:

My Annie died in the night, February 13, 1885, her body ravished by the disease that tortured her for five months. I did not know if I could bear the pain of my loss. Nor could I understand why God took her when I needed her as I did. The years we had together were too few, but the Lord sustained me.

Angelica Ruth married William James Crawford on November 2, 1888. She was only sixteen, more than half the age of her mother when Annie married me. She was a beautiful young woman, loving and devoted and all of the things her mother and I wished her to be. But how difficult it was to give my little girl into the care of another man, even a good man such as Bill Crawford.

One of the best days of my life was on August 8, 1889, the day I became a grandfather. Joshua Richard Crawford was born early in the morning. Even as a newborn, I could tell he had his grandmother Annie's blue eyes. He still has them today.

Sadly, Joshua never got to know his father. At least not long enough to keep him in his memories. Bill Crawford was thrown from a horse on the Fourth of July while racing in the Independence Day celebration. He died the next morning of his injuries. Angelica Ruth and little Joshua came to live with me soon after the funeral. While I was glad to have them, I was heartbroken because of the reason. I prayed that God would enable me to be a good influence on the boy, that his faith would be strong from his youth, and that he would not make the kind of mistakes I made.

Joshua is fourteen now—tall, good looking, and smart. He excels in his schooling. His worst character flaw is his temper, so much like mine in my earlier years. Still, I have high hopes for my grandson.

There has been a downturn of my fortunes in recent years, and I will not leave him or his mother as well off financially as I would have wished. But they will be comfortable and what they will have has been honestly earned. I am glad of that. Perhaps my true legacy for the boy will be that he saw me use what I had to make a difference in the lives of others. I hope that will be so. I hope he will do the same.

Joshua, if you are reading this, then I was right. My time has come. I'm sorry I wasn't able to live long enough to see you grow into manhood, graduate from college, perhaps even marry and start a family of your own.

Know this, my dear boy: that I loved you and that I was as proud of you as any man could be.

Put God first, Joshua, and He will guide your steps throughout your life. Listen to His voice, heed His corrections, and you will avoid the many traps and snares of this world. I hope reading this record of my past did not discourage you or make you feel less of me. I hope you will see in it the power of the Almighty to change a life, to turn all things to good to them that love God, to them who are the called according to His purpose.

And now, may the Lord bless thee, and keep thee. May the Lord make His face shine upon thee, and be gracious unto thee. May He lift up His countenance upon thee, and give thee peace. Amen.

Until we meet again in Heaven, I remain
Your loving Grandfather

EPILOGUE

June 1919

As dusk settled over Bethlehem Springs on an unusually warm evening toward the end of June, Daphne Crawford parked her motorcar at the curb on Wallula Street and dashed into the house.

"You missed it!" she proclaimed as she dropped her straw hat onto the entry table.

Joshua rose from the chair at the kitchen table. "What do you mean, I missed it?"

"It's over. Cleo had her baby already. It's a boy. Healthy and beautiful and perfect in every way."

He looked at his pocket watch. "But you said I didn't need to rush over to the McKinley's. You said—"

"Cleo didn't waste any time." As she spoke, she went to him and slipped into the circle of his arms. "Don't worry. She didn't mind that you weren't downstairs with Woody and Morgan, and she wasn't in labor long enough for her husband to even start to worry. Griff didn't get there either."

"I bought cigars for everyone."

Daphne wrinkled her nose. "You can pass them out tomorrow. Just don't smoke them around me. Nasty things."

"I promise we won't." He drew her closer.

She smiled as she tipped back her head to receive his kiss. There was no place on earth she would rather be than right there in Joshua's arms, his lips warm upon her lips, his heart beating in unison with hers. Although others might disagree, she knew she was the happiest woman to ever live.

When the kiss ended, she pressed her cheek against his chest. "I never imagined seeing a child born could be so amazing. It's a miracle. It really is." She pulled back to look him in the eyes. "And Cleo was wonderful. She said childbirth wasn't any harder than breaking a wild mustang."

Joshua laughed. "Only Cleo would make such a comparison."

"That's exactly what I said to her." Daphne slipped out of his embrace and went to put the kettle on the stove. "Would you like some tea?"

"No, thanks."

She busied herself at the counter. "Woody and Cleo still haven't agreed on a name. She doesn't want anything too lah-di-dah." As she said the word, she heard Cleo's voice in her head, and it brought back her smile.

"I can't blame her for that." Joshua's hands alighted on her shoulders. "But I'm wondering, do you care to know why I was delayed in coming to the McKinley house?"

Something in his voice caused her to turn around. Yes, there was a definite twinkle in his eyes, a sparkle that told her he had a secret he was dying to reveal. "What?"

"You had a telephone call."

"From whom?"

The corners of his mouth tipped upward. "From a Mr. Elwood Shriver of New York."

"Mr. Shriver? He called here?"

"Yes."

Her heart skipped a beat. "What did he want?"

"He wants to publish your book about Grandfather. He loves it."

"He does?" The words were barely audible.

Joshua chuckled. "Did you really doubt he would want it? Didn't I tell you it was wonderful before you sent it to him?"

She shook her head, nodded, shook her head, nodded.

"The book is wonderful." He kissed her forehead. "I'm so proud of you." He kissed the tip of her nose. "Grandfather would be proud of you too."

Daphne's throat tightened and tears flooded her eyes. She and Joshua had gone to St. Louis for their honeymoon just so she could spend time with those who had known Richard Terrell best—his daughter, his closest friend, the people who ran the orphanage and the men's shelter. Now, several months later, it felt to Daphne as if she had personally known Joshua's grandfather, and she wanted others to come to love and admire him the way she did. Now, with the publication of this book, perhaps they would.

As Joshua drew her close and kissed her on the mouth once again, inexpressible joy blossomed in her heart. Who could have imagined a year ago where she would be today? Who could have guessed that she would fall in love with an editor from St. Louis and go on to write a book about his grandfather? Who could have foreseen the happiness that embodied her days and nights?

No one. Not even she had imagined it. Not in her wildest dreams. If she'd plotted her life as carefully as she plotted her novels, she still couldn't have imagined a more perfect ending than this one.

Nor a more perfect beginning.

A NOTE FROM
THE AUTHOR

Who says a woman can't be a dime novelist?

Dear Friends:

I hope you enjoyed getting to know Daphne and Joshua and that you were rooting for their Happily Ever After as much as I was.

Long before Daphne McKinley put fountain pen to paper, women had entered the publishing world using male pseudonyms. However, it wasn't unheard of in the late nineteenth and early twentieth centuries for women to write dime novels under their own names. Most often, these women writers wrote romantic fiction for women readers. Sounds similar to today.

Another similarity that arose while I was writing, revising, and editing this book in 2009–2010 was the nasty flu season. For us it was the Swine Flu. For the people in Daphne's time (1918–1919) it was the Spanish Flu. That earlier pandemic is estimated to have killed between fifty million to one hundred million people around the globe—between three and seven times the casualties as from the First World War.

And now it's time to bid farewell to the Sisters of Bethlehem

Springs and the men who won their hearts. I'm going to miss Gwen and Morgan, Cleo and Woody, and Daphne and Joshua. Yet I have complete confidence that these three couples will do well, that they will march into their futures with confidence, that they won't be afraid to open new doors and try new things, all the while honoring God and family.

What's next? you ask. First up is *Bounty of Silver*, a stand-alone historical romance set in the late 1800s, followed by a new historical romance trilogy (as yet unnamed).

For the latest information about my past and future releases, please visit my website or drop by my fan page on Facebook.

In the grip of His grace,

Robin Lee Hatcher

www.robinleehatcher.com

A Vote of Confidence

Robin Lee Hatcher,
Bestselling Author of
When Love Blooms

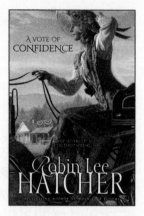

In *A Vote of Confidence*, the stage is set for some intriguing insight into what it was like during 1915 to be a woman in a "man's world."

Guinevere Arlington is a beautiful young woman determined to remain in charge of her own life. For seven years, Gwen has carved out a full life in the bustling town of Bethlehem Springs, Idaho, where she teaches piano and writes for the local newspaper. Her passion for the town, its people, and the surrounding land prompt Gwen to run for mayor. After all, who says a woman can't do a man's job?

But stepping outside the boundaries of convention can get messy. A shady lawyer backs Gwen, believing he can control her once she's in office. A wealthy newcomer throws his hat into the ring in an effort to overcome opposition to the health resort he's building north of town. When the opponents fall in love, everything changes, forcing Gwen to face what she may have to lose in order to win.

Available in stores and online!

ZONDERVAN®
.com

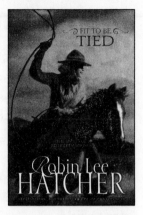

When Love Blooms

Robin Lee Hatcher,
Author of Wagered Heart

From the moment Gavin Blake set eyes on Emily Harris he knew she would never make it in the rugged high country where backbreaking work and constant hardship were commonplace. She would wilt there like a rose without water. He'd be sending her back to Boise before the first snows. He'd be willing to bet on it.

She could say what she wanted. Emily Harris didn't belong in the hard life of the Blakes. Beautiful and refined, she was accustomed to the best life had to offer. Heaven only knew why she wanted to leave Boise to teach two young girls on a ranch miles from nowhere. He'd wager it had to do with a man. It always did when a beautiful woman was involved.

Emily wanted to make some sort of mark on the world before marriage. She wanted to be more than just a society wife. Though she had plenty of opportunities back East, she had come to the Idaho high country looking to make a difference. Gavin's resistance to her presence made her even more determined to prove herself. Perhaps changing the heart of one man might make the greatest difference of all.

Wagered Heart

Robin Lee Hatcher,
Author of Return to Me

When Bethany Silverton left the gen-
teel life of Miss Henderson's School for
Young Ladies back in Philadelphia for
the raw frontier town of Sweetwater,
Montana, she had no idea how much
she would enjoy the freedom and danger of this wild country.

A conservative preacher's daughter, Bethany can't resist the
challenge of charming the most attractive cowboy in town into
attending her father's new church. She never dreamed that the
cowboy would charm the lady.

But Hawk Chandler isn't the only man vying for Bethany's
affections. Ruthlessly ambitious Vince Richards thinks Bethany
is perfect for him: attractive, gracious, just the woman to help
him become governor. And he is determined to get what he
wants at any cost.

Drawn to one man, an obsession of another, Bethany's quiet
life is thrown into turmoil. She wagered her heart on love. Now
she has gotten more than she bargained for — and the stakes
are about to become life and death.

Available in stores and online!

Return to Me

*Robin Lee Hatcher,
Bestselling Author of
A Carol for Christmas*

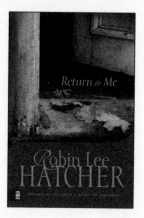

When Roxy Burke left home for Nashville, she swore she wouldn't come back until she was a star. But it's desperation that drives this prodigal back to her family, and no one is prepared for what happens next.

Roxy has crashed and burned. She's squandered an inheritance, lived a wild life, and wasted her talent. Desperate and ashamed, she now must return to her father and sister, neither of whom she's talked to in seven years.

Roxy's father welcomes his daughter with love and tenderness. But his easy acceptance is hard on Roxy's sister. After years of being the dutiful daughter, Elena feels resentment and anger toward her wayward sister.

Even more problematic is the reaction of Roxy's former boyfriend. Once a rebel, Wyatt has given his life to Christ and plans to enter the ministry. He and Elena are engaged, but Roxy's return raises questions that could mean the end of Elena's perfect future.

The Burke family faces the return of the prodigal and must reach out for healing. Will they each be able to accept God's grace?

Available in stores and online!

Loving Libby

Robin Lee Hatcher,
Bestselling Author of
Catching Katie

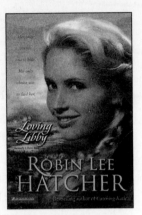

Be not forgetful to entertain strangers, for thereby some have entertained angels unawares.

Yes, well, Remington Walker was no angel …

He posed a more serious danger to Libby than she'd ever faced.

Libby Blue had found a refuge from her past in the Idaho wilderness. Leaving her ruthless father and a privileged Eastern girlhood behind, she finally found freedom in the wild West. Libby could run a ranch, make her own choices, and never have to answer to any man.

But then Remington Walker rode into her life. Despite herself, Libby found Remington breaking through all her defenses. Threatening the fragile safety of her western refuge. But what she doesn't know is that Remington has a reason for being there. A reason that could well destroy them both.

Available in stores and online!

In His Arms

Robin Lee Hatcher,
Best-Selling Author of Firstborn

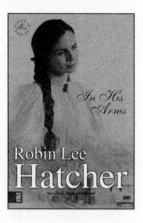

Dear Inga,

I'm thinking it is not good for my baby and me to stay much longer in Whistle Creek, Idaho. The sheriff is showing altogether too much interest. I suppose I should feel flattered, for Carson Barclay is not only strikingly handsome, but a man of character and faith who has shown Keary and me considerable kindness. But I'm afraid his affections are ones I cannot return. The secret I bear makes a future with him impossible.

Yet Inga, when Sheriff Barclay is near, it's everything in my Irish heart that wishes otherwise.

Your friend,
Mary Emeline Malone

Idaho: mountainous, rugged. Men go there to find their fortunes in the silver mines — and lose their pasts. But as Mary Malone discovers, sometimes the past is not so easily shaken. It will take a good man's strong, persistent love to penetrate the young immigrant's defenses and disarm the secret that makes a hostage of her heart.

In His Arms is Book Three in the Coming to America series about women who come to America to start new lives. Set in the late 1800s and early 1900s, these novels by best-selling author Robin Lee Hatcher craft intense chemistry and conflict between the characters, lit by a glowing faith and humanity that will win your heart. Look for other books in the series at your favorite Christian bookstore.

Dear Lady

Robin Lee Hatcher,
Best-Selling Author of Firstborn

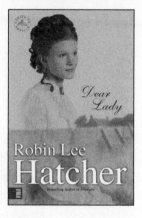

Dear Mary,

New Prospects, Montana, is nothing like England — so terrifying and beautiful at the same time, and much larger than I dared imagine when you and I first embarked on our adventures in the New World.

I have had the good fortune of becoming the town's schoolmistress. Young Janie Steele is as precious as I imagined from her letters. As for her father, Garret Steele . . .

Oh, I feel like such a fool! I've run halfway around the world to escape a man I loathed, only to discover I'm losing my heart to a man still in love with the wife he buried.

The mayor, kind man, has been most attentive. But I wish he were someone else. I wish he were Garret.

With affection,
Your friend Beth Wellington

In the big-sky country of Montana, the past doesn't always stay buried. Circumstances have a way of forcing secrets into the open, sometimes bringing hearts together in unlikely ways, and sometimes tearing them apart.

Dear Lady is Book One in the Coming to America series about women who come to America to start new lives. Set in the late 1800s and early 1900s, these novels by best-selling author Robin Lee Hatcher craft intense chemistry and conflict between the characters, lit by a glowing faith and humanity that will win your heart. Look for other books in the series at your favorite Christian bookstore.

Share Your Thoughts

With the Author: Your comments will be forwarded to the author when you send them to *zauthor@zondervan.com*.

With Zondervan: Submit your review of this book by writing to *zreview@zondervan.com*.

Free Online Resources at

www.zondervan.com

Zondervan AuthorTracker: Be notified whenever your favorite authors publish new books, go on tour, or post an update about what's happening in their lives at www.zondervan.com/authortracker.

Daily Bible Verses and Devotions: Enrich your life with daily Bible verses or devotions that help you start every morning focused on God. Visit www.zondervan.com/newsletters.

Free Email Publications: Sign up for newsletters on Christian living, academic resources, church ministry, fiction, children's resources, and more. Visit www.zondervan.com/newsletters.

Zondervan Bible Search: Find and compare Bible passages in a variety of translations at www.zondervanbiblesearch.com.

Other Benefits: Register yourself to receive online benefits like coupons and special offers, or to participate in research.